THE NATURE OF ENTANGLED HEARTS

EMMA HARTLEY

This book is dedicated to my dear father.
You are always in my heart.

PROLOGUE

Insecurity nestled in my breast like a needy child. I grew restless as it sucked something essential from me, thriving on my offering just as I, in turn, withdrew. I didn't wish anymore, it seemed so pointless. I didn't wait for some great epiphany. I existed, and that was enough, I told myself, for in contrast with the suffering of the rest of the world, it seemed only right to be thankful for the quietude of Maine.

I created relative to this insecurity, allowing it to flow into my work like water moistening clay. Without water, clay is dust. I thought that without my flaws—insecurity the reigning tyrant of lesser beasts—that my work would crumble under the weight of its own mediocrity. So, I let it govern my forms, my choices, my superficial acceptance of appreciative art collectors. Insecurity was the excuse that allowed me to embrace inferiority. With hope all but lost of finding any true meaning besides beauty in the world about me, I crept catatonic through my life, eyes barely open, heart nearly closed.

I'd spent most of my adult life in the great state of Maine. Portland drew me in after grad school and never let me go. There was always some new allure: The skeletal remains of an ancient pier ascending bleached from the ravages of low tide, exposed like the ribcage of a long extinct behemoth; verdigris copper edging along a crumbling slate roof, tattered like the lace on an old prom dress; the punishing crash of waves against the ferry's bough, speeding undaunted through winter waters, as I enjoyed my own private cruise. This place had almost everything I needed to thrive. Almost.

Might not love play a part, I wondered in weak moments, in this deceptive spring landscape? Like a lupine seed blown from afar, rooting along the roadside, might it flourish? Then, how could this fragile shoot grow strong enough, fast enough, to outpace the onslaught of winter, or can love thaw the very air around it, creating a protective shield against the elements? Would time then corrupt it? Erode it like tiny drops of water on stone, wearing away elasticity and alacrity, making barren what would have borne fruit?

I had felt winter's claws dig in, pinning me down like prey, waiting to crush my spirit. I had felt the rebirth of sunshine and growth, spilling into crevices nearly abandoned, a resurgence of breath to revive the long dead. The lost, the lonely, the artistically bereft, we have found ourselves drawn to Maine for an age, it's the mercurial edge between civilization and wilderness. We flock here yearning to flourish, as a tree may cling to a forbidding cliff, rooting desperate between chinks in granite, gaining purchase against elemental odds: we grow despite ourselves, our rugged forms belying the improbable tenacity of our hidden will to thrive, of our frozen desire for love.

CHAPTER ONE

"Listen again. One evening at the Close
    Of Ramazan, ere the better Moon arose,
    In that old Potter's Shop I stood alone
    With the clay Population round in Rows.

And, strange to tell, among that Earthen Lot
    Some could articulate, while others not:
    And suddenly one more impatient cried-
    Who *is* the Potter, pray, and who the Pot?

Then said another with a long-drawn Sigh,
    "My Clay with long oblivion is gone dry:
    But, fill me with the old familiar juice,
    Methinks I might recover by-and-by!"

THE RUBAIYAT OF OMAR KHAYYAM
TRANSLATED BY EDWARD FITZGERALD

I couldn't get out of my own way. It was embarrassing, really, to be this inept at regular stuff: getting dressed, putting up my hair, walking to work. I struggled with ordinary tasks, gracelessly, allowing time to fold in on itself, over and over, like an unruly piece of origami, swallowing up the meaningful moments with the mundane. Wash, rinse, repeat.

Morning ablutions complete, first coffee of the day in hand, I finally got to work. I nodded to the security guard and wished I had more to offer in exchange for his wide smile. He always greeted me the same way, "G' morning, Professor D.!" He was cheer itself and I was thankful for it. I hoped that showed.

"Hi, Jerry," I said, with the most enthusiasm I could muster. "Have a good one, OK?"

"Can do, you too." He seemed content with doing his crosswords all day, greeting the college kids that were in constant flow through the doors. Jerry was kind and funny, a good man. I never asked him a personal question and he never seemed to mind.

My office was an enlightened disaster area. The casual visitor may not have been able to see past the clutter or the closetesque size of the space, barely adequate to contain the contents within. For me, however, it was a resource, a haven, an inspiration. Art books were piled in corners, overflowing from antique bookcases and spilled across the dowdy old armchair I rescued from beside the dumpster out back a few years ago. Its gold velvet upholstery was sporadically gilded in the slim rays of sunshine that crept through the office on sunny mornings. My walls were plastered with images of sculpture, pages from magazines, old photographs, famous paintings, sketches and any other bit of ephemera I felt the need to see regularly. I checked my email and sat in a sliver of sun for a moment before my day began in earnest.

I relished the solitude of my little sanctuary; it perched, fortress-like, amidst the chaos of the art school drama continuously unfolding outside its door. Year after year I appreciated it more, as the students

4

foamed like the tide outside, while within, time stood relatively still. New faces, new year, same stories.

Maybe it's just an art school thing, but it seemed that students' lives were inherently more dramatic here. Artists take everything more personally than the rest of humanity. Or maybe that's just me.

First class of the day was Advanced Topics in Ceramics—an independent study for seniors whose concentration was clay. They tended to be a little more serious than the average student, and some of them even went on to careers as artists. I liked this crop—they were interesting and funny, personable too. I didn't get too involved in their lives, and they didn't get too interested in mine, but we had great and compelling conversations about our work nevertheless.

The kids filtered into the studio, in various states of exhaustion or elation, as was average. May is crunch time in ceramics, where drying times vary depending on the thickness of each piece. In order to bisque and glaze fire everything by end of term, the students need to be seriously involved because there's so little time left. The seniors were particularly sensitive to this fact, as it was their final opportunity to work with clay in such an unrestricted way, unless, of course, they went on to get their MFA.

Claire, a wild-haired, willowy gal, entered the studio only minutes after me, setting up two wheels away. It was her way of being friendly.

"Good morning, Derrin," she said, in her surprisingly husky voice; her skin seemed sallow in the fluorescent light. She had clearly just awoken, as evidenced by her rumpled attire.

"Hey, Claire. Long night?"

"Yeah. I was in here until after two. I got a lot done, though."

"Great. I'd love to see it when you're ready."

"I'd like that. I need some feedback on getting more consistency. My lips are wonky."

"Anywhere else, that would sound really funny," I commented.

She smiled. I started trimming up some pieces I'd made the day before. They were leather hard and looked good. "Getting things the same is hard," I reassured her. "It took me years before I could get to the point where four mugs looked like they belonged together. It will happen, though!"

"I know—practice, practice."

"It's the only way to tame the clay!"

She rolled her eyes and got back to work. I was often purposefully cheesy with the students. It was my little private joke, one I derived a near constant stream of amusement from. More importantly, I wanted to separate myself from them just enough to help maintain the notoriously fuzzy hierarchical boundaries between art professors and their students. It worked fairly well, most of the time.

Claire's work was pretty good; it had potential. She struggled with form, though, lacking the elegance of other students I'd had. She, like most of the artists I've known, understood this limitation. It frustrated her, but it also drove her to constant improvement. As her professor, I was OK with that. Whatever it took to drive millennial students was fine by me.

A few more people filtered in, greeting me and setting up their work. The sculptors all vied for the worktables near the windows on the far side of the room, and as a light-obsessed artist myself, I totally loved watching their facial expressions when they entered. When they got their favorite spot, it was cool joy. When they didn't, it was mild fury. Hilarious.

"Ben," I called to one of the sculptors, "I'm firing Max this weekend. Will you be ready?"

Max was our biggest gas-fired reduction kiln. Prime Max space was coveted even more than the window tables, especially by the mature students.

"Yeah, Derrin. I've got a ton of small stuff going in. It's glazed and I feel pretty happy with it. I don't know when this big guy is going to be done, though. The sculpture stand wheel caught a crack on the floor a couple of nights ago while I was rolling it out and the whole piece landed on the ground, flat as a pancake."

"Whoa, I had no idea." I walked over to peruse the damage. It didn't look so bad.

"I learned a lot, I guess. I've been coil building all my big stuff and this sort of taught me that it's a waste of time for something this big. I'm slab building now, and as long as the slabs are thick enough, it's saving me a ton of time."

"Great. Just watch out for fissures in the slabs, you don't want weak walls. Are you making a support structure inside as you go?"

"Yeah. Struts, just like we talked about a while back."

"Good. Keep it strong. It looks like you've gotten the form back on track. Still working from the sketches or are you getting free-form on me?"

He took out his battered, clay-spattered sketchbook and flipped through to the page that resembled the form on the sculpture stand. We both appraised the work. "What do you think of this curve?" I asked him, pointing to the sketch.

"It's the one part I can't get right. It keeps folding over, I can't seem to get it to support the weight of the clay."

"Are you being patient with it?" I chided.

"Yes, mom, I'm being patient with it." He laughed and rolled his eyes.

"Use the heat gun, but sparingly, and it should hold. Have you thought about flying buttresses?"

"Uh, no."

"What if you used an outside structure that would hold it while you build and then trim it off later. Temporary support. It's worth a try. I think the rest looks good. Get it into the final Max firing or you're going to have a sticky situation with your final thesis. You hanging around this weekend?"

"Yep."

"Good man. Carry on."

The class was over before I knew it. "Work is Play" was our motto, written in big letters over the door. I knew that of all my classes, the kids in this one took it the most to heart. They didn't clean up when the class was over—they wanted their time to matter. I covered my wet work, cleaned my wheel and bid them farewell, thankful for such serious students.

Four years in college is an eternity. A lot of growing happens in that space and the students I graduated were not the children who walked in the door four years before, once so uncertain about their places in the art world. These kids had metamorphosed into unique creatures, all their essential qualities distilled into adult form. For better or worse.

I wandered outside for a walk, feeling pensive. Coffee and the possibility of lunch drove me subconsciously to the Public Market. The spring air was a tonic, the sunlight refreshing after being in the studio for four solid hours, not to mention having been stymied by winter for six months. I walked slowly, stretching my back, deliberately not looking in the store windows or at my dreaded reflection in them, focusing instead on the architectural details of the buildings I passed, familiar as brothers.

Why are there mirrors everywhere? I asked myself. Reflections chased me like shades, apparitions in mid-air, shimmering with milky eyes and auric penumbra. I didn't like to complain, but even inside the market, perusing cheeses, I was confronted with my own visage floating above the offerings, staring back, challenging my selection. "Really? The camembert?" she seemed to ask, disapprovingly. I shook my pale face, my wide brown eyes lonely, as I turned away from myself, again and again.

The market was quiet. Fewer people than usual awaited their freshly made sandwiches and skinny lattes. I glanced back at the cheese case, only to be reproached once more by my ghostly doppelgänger. "Not the camembert," she reminded me. We shook our heads at each other and I turned away once more. I scanned the market's offerings again, and that's when I noticed a man staring at me. I was startled by this rare display of boldness. Who does that? I asked myself.

The stranger was my polar opposite; he was the embodiment of grace and effortless elegance, beauty and refinement. Fair hair, skin like porcelain, deep blue eyes that followed me with azure intensity, seeing through me like I was a reflection in a window overlooking the sea, rather than flesh—a memory, a ghost. *What can he be seeing in me?* I really wondered. All I could see was brown hair that used to curl and could no longer commit to the effort; bad skin, marked with years of struggle against my body's own defenses; posture tainted by too many hours hunched over my potter's wheel. Clay-spattered clothes. Insecurity gripped me harder and I folded my hands over my chest, a subconsciously protective habit. It's just me, I thought, nothing to see here. Yet he stared.

Our eyes locked and he looked away, coy, for just a moment, perhaps so I could steal a better look at him, and I did. We were antitheses. Where I was dark, he was light. Where I was oppressive movement and a long lost wish for beauty, he was air and music. Lithe body, muscles taut beneath lavender oxford, statuesque features Michelangelo's David would have envied, all enveloped in that effortless grace. He caught my gaze again, this time his expression more carnal, yearning. My breath hitched, my stomach clenched. Embarrassed, I glanced away, back to the cheese counter and to my own disapproving reflection. *I have no idea how to deal with this.*

He isn't looking at you, I told myself. He must have been looking at someone else. I glanced furtively behind me: no one.

My heartbeat raced as he began to walk towards me. Closer and closer he came. He was quite tall, especially from this proximity. Unable to prevent myself, I looked up from beneath my dark lashes, as though in prayer, and his eyes held me frozen, in fear, in elation, in confusion, but I maintained his gaze. He really *was* looking at me.

Suddenly, I burned with anger as understanding bloomed: he was just toying with me. It must be a sick game he played with homely women—making them feel desirable and then leaving them to wonder how this beautiful man might have any interest whatsoever. I frowned involuntarily, fiercely, and it broke whatever spell he had woven. His expression hardened almost imperceptibly; looking slightly pained, he continued on.

He moved with his companion, a plain, rounded man who had been eclipsed entirely from my notice, towards the door. I watched them leave, my anger ebbing as suddenly as it had appeared, replaced by the desperate, familiar ache of lonely loss and dejection.

He glanced back momentarily, met my eyes once more, this time a melancholy farewell. I couldn't even muster a slight smile, not that it would have mattered on a face like mine.

I was left bereft of my appetite, the cheese counter now a desolate landscape, only my apparition lingering to scold me about another opportunity lost. I fled the market moments later, unexpected tears welling in my eyes, threatening to spill onto the sidewalk and flood the city before me. The May sunshine, so welcome twenty minutes ago, felt harsh on my flushed skin. I took a deep breath, full of diesel fumes from the bus that had just left, and wished for something, anything to distract me from the absurd sense of loss that had filled every crevice within me. A rebel tear streaked down my cheek and I laughed once, mirthlessly, at its audacity. *Why should I mourn the loss of something so childish, a case of mistaken identity or some cruel game of hearts?* But I could not shake the feeling that I had lost something deeply important. It was haunting.

I took another steadying breath, ready to forgo lunch, coffee somehow forgotten. I turned to walk back to the studio, and there before me, standing not eight feet away and blocking my path, staring—this time unabashedly—his expression inscrutable, was the stranger. I was struck dumb, eyes wide, horrified that he could have observed my private moment of despair, and gratified at the same time that he wanted to.

The street scene before us blurred, leaving him in stark focus, a connection I could not explain pulling me towards him. Something within me yearned, tore at ancient restraints, begged with the fervor of a dying inmate to be set free, and I felt the snap within me as years of carefully constructed barriers crumbled to dust at my feet. I was naked; I was exposed to my core. And somehow, I didn't care.

He stalked toward me as though caught in a gravitational field, driven by forces I could not see, yet strangely felt with my entire being. He stood before me, blue eyes like exotic seas, engaging my attention. His face was in perfect proportion; I wanted to draw him. The absurdity of this urge struck me as funny, but I remained rooted to the brick sidewalk, unable or unwilling to move, even slightly, for fear of shattering this strange spell again. For the first time in an age I was less aware of my own visage than I was of his, but I imagined that my expression was a mirror of his own, a mix of fear and wonder and an intangible attraction in the depths of my being.

When he spoke, the unfamiliarity of his voice startled me, for reasons I could not fathom. I noted apology in its tenor, yet curiosity was the overwhelming note. "I saw you in the market," he said.

"Yes," I returned, my voice clearer than I would have expected, "I noticed."

He laughed a short, honest laugh. "I didn't mean to stare at you."

"Well, for not meaning to do something, you did a pretty good job of it."

He paused, not sure if I was joking. I pitied him with an infinitesimal smile and mollified, he tentatively continued.

"I know we've never met, I'd remember, but I feel like I know you anyway. Like our quantum strings are tuned to the same pitch. That must sound crazy. I'm sorry."

"What are quantum strings?"

"Physics. It's my way of looking for answers."

"Answers to what? I just assumed you were playing some game with me, making the ugly duckling feel like a swan for just a moment. Please, tell me the truth. Are you?"

I couldn't help myself. I confronted him with my suspicion and immediately regretted it. His expression deflated a bit from hopeful to confused to sad. "No," he replied softly. "I don't play games with people. Besides, you aren't ugly, you know." He paused for a moment to inhale deeply, and my heart tugged as I assumed he was about to turn away. Instead, he asked, "Can we go somewhere and talk for a minute without blocking pedestrian traffic?"

I was suddenly aware of the fact that we were in the middle of a busy sidewalk in the lunch rush, waves of people streaming past on either side, parting as though we were simply a pair of lampposts. I laughed, finally allowing a genuine smile to bubble through my skepticism. "I'm from New York," I explained. "I don't go with strangers."

His smile crinkled the corners of his eyes in relief and good humor. "Somewhere public."

We looked around, searching the bustle for a private corner. "Longfellow Garden?" I offered. He smiled again, nodding slightly, and together we walked in silence towards the courtyard behind the museum across the street.

We passed through the open black iron gate; this minuscule, forgotten oasis in the city greeting us with an instant hush and emerald calm. The benches were all occupied on the upper level, so we descended well-manicured garden steps into the lower courtyard. We were engulfed by the scent of plants awakening from winter, protected from the cool breezes beyond the high brick walls. Leaves and flowers bent towards the sun as we found the last unoccupied bench. It was my favorite spot, at the rear of the garden, nestled in dappled sun, framed by an ivy-covered trellis.

He motioned gracefully for me to sit first, gallantly waiting for me to situate myself before he sat next to me. I angled toward him, my bent leg resting on the seat of the bench, marking my space, my ankle tucked under my other leg, which dangled just above the stone pavers. I noticed the bustle of the ants busy at their work, crawling inconspicuously along the mossy seams between rocks. I noticed the hum of bees searching for spring nectar. Everything was so intense, colors brighter than normal, sounds crisp, the sun bathing the scene in a Maxfield Parish sort of light—surreal, sensual and golden.

My companion breathed in, drawing my wayward attention back to him. I wanted to freeze the moment in time, to galvanize it in my memory so that I may return to it later, at will: his face was tense with unspoken thoughts, his sandy blonde hair refracting the sunlight, a thousand infinitesimal prisms casting rainbows into the uninspired atmosphere. Alas, my mind has never been so compliant; memories always pale in comparison to the true moments of beauty. I held on tightly, nevertheless.

"I don't know where to begin," he began.

"That's a good beginning," I quipped, quietly, just in case he was sensitive to sarcasm.

Smiling, he continued, "When I saw you today, I was trying to muster the courage to talk with you. I've seen you before, here and there. The bookstore, a coffee shop, but today I decided I needed to do more than watch you like some common stalker."

He said this last word in jest, thankfully. The corner of my lip curled up involuntarily, urging him on.

"When you caught me staring at you, and you looked so hurt and angry, I lost my nerve. I left and regretted it immediately, so I waited outside. Watching your expression change from surprise to embarrassment to anger to sadness, I realize I caused you distress. I'm sorry."

"It's ok. I'm sensitive." I smiled sardonically and rolled my eyes, my tone acidic.

"You are though, aren't you?" he mused. "You use sarcasm to protect yourself. I get it."

I blushed at the truth of this, knowing that my usual veil of acerbity wouldn't hold with him. He looked towards the sky, his eyes reflecting the light and clouds and magnified by the duality of tones, they blazed with intensity. Rayleigh scattering, I thought distractedly. *It's why the sky is blue. Maybe that's what makes his eyes seem so bright.* The thought reminded me of his physics reference.

"What were you talking about when you said we were like strings?"

He chuckled a little and replied, "String theory. It's the idea that everything is comprised of vibrating strings of energy at the quantum level. It felt like ours were vibrating at the same frequency. I am kind of into physics, I guess."

"That's cool," I said, unable to add anything to the subject, now wondering why I had bothered to ask. I shifted on the bench, fidgeting my hands restlessly, unsure what to say next.

"Since I was a kid," he mused, "I've had a recurring dream. It has stayed with me, haunting me, even into adulthood. It always leaves me with a feeling of such intense loss, because someone I loved left me alone. When I saw you for the first time, I felt like a moth drawn toward the light, like I had known you in that dream. I debated whether I'd ever even tell you any of this if we finally met; it sounds so crazy. I thought maybe I wouldn't need to explain it—that we could just start from the unknown, like everybody else. Everything changed today. Somehow, it seemed wrong to start out with a lie. I don't want to lie to you."

"OK." I sounded so dumb, my voice like a clubfoot, limping along, ungainly and slow. Dumb, however, is exactly how I felt. I was mystified. *What is he talking about? Is he sane? He looks sane... Is he fucking with me? Is there a camera somewhere recording my reactions?* I scanned the environment. Longfellow Garden was my idea, so it wasn't that. *Is he serious? He looks serious.* I looked into his eyes and was drawn in. Before I could stop myself, I started speaking, like a tap left on a drip for so long that it finally overwhelms its gaskets and gushes forth, a torrent of words I didn't recognize as my own, yet as I heard them spoken in my own voice, I knew that they were my truth.

"For a second, just now, I felt like I had no clue what you're talking about. I thought maybe you were a little off balance or something. But... I don't know. My life has always felt like fitting together lost puzzle pieces, wind-scattered to the ends of the globe. I keep searching inside and out. It's overwhelming and pointless and feels desperate. I've settled into melancholy, I guess, a lament for my fruitless search for impossible pieces of the puzzle. I wish I could explain it better, but maybe I don't need to. Is that sort of what you mean?" My eyes had been focused on his as I spoke. Now, I grew shy in the silence, overwhelmed with my own words, wondering at their inherent and poignant truth.

He was so engaged; he leaned forward, his eyes had softened when our gaze met again. He reached for my hand, an involuntary reflex, then he pulled back, unsure. I was thankful, for it all seemed too much to bear. I stirred as though ready to bolt back to the chaos of the street outside our garden, to leave behind this private, strange moment, like being thrust from a dream, but I couldn't. I was held there by primal forces, well beyond my scope of understanding.

He sensed my uncertainty and eased back, leaning against the sun-warmed brick wall. We both breathed in the spring air again, restoring ourselves with its honest chill.

"Puzzle pieces. That's such a good way to describe it. I am missing some integral pieces of my own puzzle. I think you might be one of them. An important one."

His voice was so hushed. He waited for me to react.

"I hate mirrors," I said too loudly. He laughed uncertainly at the non-sequitur. "No, really," I continued. "I always assumed it was simply about my looks, but maybe it's because every time I see myself, I only see what's missing and not what's actually there, a shattered image of self. I can't see the whole picture because of all the missing pieces."

"Maybe I can see all the things that you don't see," he replied softly.

"This is very weird," I said finally, shaking my head slightly. I smiled, and I didn't need to look at his face to know that he was smiling too.

"May I ask your name?" His voice was as arresting as his eyes, a liquid melody, perfectly in tune, resonating deep within me. "I mean, we should formally introduce ourselves, right?"

I could have said anything. I mean, what is a name, after all, but something someone saddled us with before they even knew who we would become? I stopped that foolishness as soon as the thought formed in my mind, and I told him my name. "Elwyn Beatrice Derringer, believe it or not. I thought for a moment I could change my mind about that and start fresh as Jenny or Penny, but despite it's being my name, it's not mine to change. I really don't know what my parents were thinking."

"Elwyn. Do people call you Elwyn or do you go by Winne?" If his smile hadn't been so disarming, I'd probably have hit him. Instead, I just groaned.

"Ugh. No, people call me Derrin. I've always sort of struggled with this whole name thing, like a skin that didn't fit quite right. Same as the mirror, I guess."

"I get it."

"And you are?"

"James Finnian Dunbar, III, at your service." He tilted his head in a mock bow, and I giggled as I reached to shake his outstretched hand.

Our skin came into contact for the first time and it was a lightning strike. As our grasp grew stronger, our hands became a bridge into places I could not fathom. I was sucked backwards out of time and place and self, images rushing past me like ribbons stretching into space, my stomach was wrenched and twisted and my head felt like it would implode. I caught glimpses of the rushing montage, images of life that cut into my flesh, incising me with the intensely personal physicality of their persistence. I was drowning in a raging torrent of memories, a turbulent river sucking me down, deeper, and as my last breath was raggedly exhaled I finally alighted on a stone bridge, the scene around me snapping into clarity and sudden stillness. I was prone, staring up at a star encrusted dome, my head cradled gently as a baby's, a raindrop hit my cheek. It can't be a raindrop, I told myself viscerally, for there was not a cloud in that peerless sky. Only infinity stretched on before me. It was then that I realized it was a teardrop, then another, warm and gentle, falling from a face poised above me, just out of my line of sight. I tilted back to see him, anguished, possessed with grief, dying as I died in his arms. Though the face was unfamiliar, I knew the eyes. They were James' eyes.

Pain found me suddenly, intensely, searing through my flesh, tearing my soul from my body. I writhed and gasped as the schism overtook my being. Then, as I could bear no more, I was hurled back into Longfellow Garden, crouched on stone pavers, the ants still going on about their business, heedless of my distress. I was heaving and panting and viscerally so thankful that I hadn't bought the camembert earlier, because I would have been revisiting it unpleasantly now.

James was kneeling on the ground next to me, holding me up with one arm across my heaving chest, the other on my back.

"Holy shit, I'm so sorry, Elwyn! Are you OK? Elwyn!" His

words of comfort streamed forth, reassuring, apologizing, begging me to forgive him. Forgive what, I wondered, what is he talking about? Then, suddenly, I understood. It was his dream I fell into, as I died in his arms. But how could that be?

I scrambled to my feet, as ungainly as a newborn foal, grasping for a foothold in a reality I couldn't be sure of anymore. I backed away, looking around wildly and found that the courtyard was deserted. We were alone and I needed to run. I barely heard his pleas for me to stay, to let him explain, begging me to tell him what I saw. His voice was a lonely echo in a mountain valley. I just needed to be as far away as possible, to mend this break with reality and proceed with my mundane life. Tears streamed down my face; I couldn't catch my breath; I needed to run.

I looked at this beautiful man before me, the terrible aching sadness in his eyes, their azure depths liquid with unshed tears. I was so torn, as the adrenaline rampaged through my veins. I held his gaze, knowing viscerally that my expression was that of a fox in a forest fire. His voice filtered back to me through fathoms deep water, icy dark depths, I was sinking, still dying in the dream, unsure where the line between reality and that other world lay.

"Elwyn. It's OK. I'm so sorry. It's OK."

The tears spilled like molten metal down my cheeks, searing my skin as they carved their path in my soul. "What was that?" I demanded, my voice finally surfacing from the deep. "What the hell was that?"

My voice was shaky and low, a mirror of the panic in my heart. My eyes searched his warily, no longer playful as they had been only minutes—or lifetimes—ago.

"Sit down, please, Elwyn. Please. Give me a chance. I didn't mean to scare you. I didn't know that would happen. I'm so sorry! God, I should have left you alone today. I should have let you live your life without the burden of these memories. I'm so sorry." The grief in his eyes was a mirror of the man from the hallucination. *It really was him.* I knew it. It was *us.* But, that can't be, I told myself.

That's insane. I shook my head to straighten my thoughts out, as though that would help.

"Tell me," I said slowly. "Tell me what the hell just happened."

"I don't know for sure, but I think you got sucked into my dream, somehow."

"Tell me what your dream is." I needed to know.

He hesitated, as though merely voicing the words carved fresh wounds into ancient scars. "I am on a bridge, London, I think, the sky is full of stars and," he hesitated, his voice unsteady. "My wife, the love of my life, lies bleeding, dying in my arms. I cradle her, our eyes meet and the life slips out of her. My soul is torn in two and I awake."

I shook my head, squeezing my eyes closed, expecting the corroboration, yet rejecting it at the same time. I buried my head in my hands. "How did you make me see it? Is it a trick? Tell me the truth." I was deadly serious. I straightened up and turned accusingly toward him. My tone left no room for lies.

"I didn't make you see anything. It's not a trick. It's..." He paused. "Oh, my God. How do I explain this without sounding insane? It's our shared memory. From our past lives, I think. You died in my arms that night, Elwyn. I still don't know how I've carried that memory with me for a hundred years or more. I don't have any explanations. When I saw you again today, though, the sense of familiarity, of deep connection, overwhelmed me. I had to be near you again. I think it was love, Elwyn. Our love lasted through life-times of searching. And now we're here. Together. Finally, together."

"No. How can that be? It's fucking crazy. It's crazy and you know it. I've got to go. Now. Don't." I swatted his hand away as he reached for me, his eyes pleading. "This is insane and I need to... to..." I broke off as the tears started again. I looked at his heartbroken expression, his eyes bereft, and although I knew in the depths of my being that we were connected, I backed away. I knew that if I didn't leave now, my break with reality would be irreparable. My expression mirrored his torture and all I could say was, "I'm sorry."

I turned and ran up the stairs of the great poet's garden,

wondering viscerally what he would have written about this craziness, my heart ready to split apart at the seams. I ran like a wild
animal, fighting for my own survival. I flew back through the doors
of the college, not seeing anything before me, faces blurred. I locked
myself in my office, I sat down against the oak door and I sobbed
until my tears had traced all the rivers of the earth and back again to
James. *What have I done?*

His face was before me, his eyes haunting me. The James from
the dream was there with me, melding with his current form. I inter-
nalized his agony, as I left him in the garden, as I left him on the
bridge. I longed to undo what I had done, but my rational mind
raged against these impossible demands. *How can it be? How is it
possible?*

I replayed the moment in the garden with James over and over,
trying to make sense of the irrational. Then, as I visualized him, I
realized something else about the scene. My bag was still on the
bench. Everything was in that bag. My license with my address. My
credit cards. My phone. My keys. My notebooks. My stomach
lurched. I asked myself again, What have I done?

I finally got myself up off the floor, not daring to assess the
damage to my visage in the mirror on my wall. I couldn't imagine
what a horror-show it would be, but nothing could be done about it. I
stilled myself, breathed in. I stilled myself, breathed out. I stilled
myself, I found my center, as flawed and fucked up as it was, and I
focused my energy inwards, as the adrenaline rush began to ebb.
What will I do now?

I glanced at the clock. I had class in fifteen minutes. I needed to
be downstairs, in some semblance of sanity, ready to deal with my
responsibilities. I headed to the lady's room, splashed water on my
flushed face, forced a smile to my features and walked back down to
the front desk.

"Professor D.!" It was Jerry. His kind eyes looked concerned.
"You OK?"

"Yes. I had a little scare earlier. I'm fine now."

"Oh, is it because you lost your bag? Nice guy brought it in a minute ago." Jerry lifted my bag out from behind the counter. I felt like he'd just handed me a winning lottery ticket.

I laughed and tears threatened again, despite my best effort to hide my emotion. I was so relieved. "Thank you," I said shakily, taking the bag from Jerry's outstretched hand. "Thank you so much."

"All part of the job, Professor D., all part of the job."

He smiled, knowing he had made me so happy. I headed to class, thankful that James had done the right thing. He hadn't asked to see me, he hadn't held my bag hostage. He just brought it back, expecting nothing in return. My heart clenched painfully at the knowledge that he had himself convinced that he cared about me. Maybe he actually did. Maybe he believed everything that we'd seen in our minds. Maybe I did too, but I just couldn't face it. I stilled myself, I breathed in. With each step forward, my life began again, unrecognizable, un-chartable: a tiny fire within me had finally kindled, ready to burn bright as a supernova and consume everything in its path. I felt the ashes of my old life scatter in the wind.

CHAPTER TWO

"How long, how long, in infinite Pursuit
    Of This and That endeavour and dispute?
    Better be merry with the fruitful Grape
    Than sadden after none, or bitter, Fruit."

THE RUBAIYAT OF OMAR KHAYYAM
TRANSLATED BY EDWARD FITZGERALD

My afternoon class was Ceramics 1. Newbies. They were enthusiastic and inexperienced students, which I found enjoyable. They readily absorbed information, they asked me to do demonstrations of techniques they'd learned about in their homework, and they had noticed my unfortunate addiction to coffee and brought me weekly offerings, despite my protest.

I walked into the studio, just in time to interrupt a fierce discussion on clay bodies. Here we go, I thought, and smiled, lying to myself: I am OK. Releasing all the tension my body had stored up since meeting James, I moved into the fray.

"Porcelain is so outdated," argued a thickly muscled student named Josh. "I mean, with so many clay bodies to choose from, why would you pick the wimpiest, most temperamental kid on the block? It can't even hold up its own weight!"

Josh's sparring partner today was a slightly built African-American girl named Elaina. She simply shook her head, hair beads clacking gently, and retorted, "Just because you don't have the skill required to work with porcelain, doesn't mean it's not worth the time to use. It's the difference between velvet and burlap. I'll take velvet, thanks!"

"Hi, everybody," I interrupted. "Great discussion. I think artists have been debating this for centuries. Historically, we see great work in both media, and just as the artist defines his or her own style, so the medium defines the boundaries of the work. How can we push those boundaries? How can we work within them to create work that is compelling?"

I let the kids continue their discussion, and having redirected them to a more constructive and respectful path, I put on my apron. I wedged up some porcelain, just for kicks, as well as some stoneware. Their conversation continued, but without the gusto it had had before my intervention. When I was ready, I called them over to see the demo.

"Ok. Porcelain versus stoneware. You have been working with clay for a couple of months now, long enough, evidently, to formulate some strong opinions." They smiled. "Why do some artists continue to work with egg tempera, a favorite medium of artists hundreds of years ago?"

"Because they want to," Elaina said.

"Sure, they want to," I agreed, "but why?"

"Because they see something beautiful in the medium that compels them to create." This answer was proffered by a reticent, very talented young man. At twenty-five, he was older than the others, and his penetrating gaze always unsettled me. I didn't know what it was that made me so nervous around him, but his answer was dead on.

"Right, Brent," I returned. "So even a medium that might be considered outdated can provide the right artist with some inspiration. It might be just the perfect thing to express a form or an idea."

I centered while I talked, gently bending the buttery porcelain to my will. Centering is what had hooked me on clay in the first place—that magic moment when chaos could either spin the clay out of control or when strength and skill could tame it, center it, manipulate it. As the mound spun, I squeezed water from a sponge onto the crown, a baptismal ritual, an ancient way of beginning. Looking down at the mesmerizing rotation, I suddenly saw James' face in my memory, as clearly as if he were before me. The tangible pang it caused must have shown on my face, for I noticed that a couple of students shot each other glances. "Sorry," I covered for myself. "I pulled a muscle earlier. It's fine."

"Did you fall again?" asked Josh, unsympathetically.

Elaina elbowed him surreptitiously, and I smiled.

"Something like that," I replied. I stretched my back dramatically and concentrated on my form, bringing the clay up and pushing it down a few times.

I settled on a closed, domed form, twelve or so inches high. I plunged my thumb into the soft mound, allowing the porcelain to swirl sensually around on the wheel. I widened out the bottom, rounded it with my fingers and re-centered the work. As I pulled up the sides, I started to talk again.

"The clay whispers, sometimes, about what it wants to be when it grows up. Don't forget, this is a second life for this material, having been dug out of the ground, pulverized, mixed and aged. Once you create, you commit. Once the piece is fired, it is irreparably changed on a molecular level into something entirely new. It can't go back to its origins, so to bring clay to the point of firing is to end its existence as clay and to transform it into something immutable. It's a great responsibility."

The students were silent, staring at me as though a chimera had appeared before them. It was not like me to wax philosophical. I smiled to myself for a moment. I examined my form. It was tall, tapered in the middle and belled out at the ends, like an hourglass. I was ready to close the top. "OK. Closed forms. What do we need to remember about closed forms?"

A few students raised tentative hands. "If you keep them closed, you need a hole somewhere for the air to escape during firing or it will explode." It was Josh's answer.

"Precisely. If you're going to close the top, it needs an air hole somewhere else. Anything else?"

No answers. I explained the process of closing off the top. I pulled the clay over with my rib tool, keeping equal and opposite pressure with my fingers on the inside of the form until my fingers no longer fit inside. I swept the rib gently over the top, applying just the right amount of pressure at just the right angle until the form closed.

"Cool," said Andrea, another of my promising students. She seemed genuinely impressed.

"Can someone grab me the heat gun?" I asked. "Ordinarily, I would just let nature take its course, but we don't have all day. Thanks," I said to Brent, as I took the heat gun he offered me. His dark eyes searched mine for a moment, his thumb purposefully brushing against my fingers. "Thanks," I repeated trying not to sound annoyed as a little thrill of adrenaline lurched uncomfortably through my belly. I wish he wouldn't act like that, I thought, reproachfully. This was not the first time Brent had done something to make me uncomfortable. I frowned, involuntarily.

"OK. I'm going to dry this out a little so I can show you another step." When the work was solid enough, I reiterated, "You shouldn't take shortcuts like this—like I said, it can weaken and stress the clay. This is just for the purposes of demonstration."

I cleaned up the bottom of the piece, incising against the base until a strip of clay loosened and disengaged, spinning outwards into the slurry bowl. Then, taking my needle tool, I pressed into the porcelain gently, three inches from the top. Slowly the wheel revolved, the needle tool staying stone still, until the entire top popped off into my hand. "And there you have it," I said with a smile. "Now I can make a box or lidded container out of this without having to throw a separate lid. I did a whole series of little yurt shaped boxes once. It's pretty fun."

"What's a yurt?" I heard someone murmur at the back. I decided not to answer, again smiling to myself.

I set the top aside, reworked the raw rim so that it would be of a smaller circumference than the lid, which would then fit nicely, as though the pieces of clay had never been separated. I double checked with my calipers and set the work aside on its bat.

I repeated the demo with the stoneware, this time leaving the closed form intact, thinking I'd create a sculpture with it later. The students got to work, their ideas buzzing in the atmosphere, charging it with creative energy.

Over the course of the next two and a half hours, I saw a lot of good work, as well as some very cranky people whose forms had collapsed. I encouraged them accordingly.

Brent's form intrigued me the most. It was so figural, so feminine. I examined it for a moment while he washed his tools. He came up close behind me and said in a hushed voice so only I could hear, "It's called Persephone. I wanted something of the woman and something of the goddess in it. A little ode to springtime."

I was startled by how near his voice was behind me. His close proximity gave me the chills. Brent was pushing the boundaries of propriety with me as no student had before. It was a danger I desperately wanted to steer clear of. I moved subtly towards the side and he walked around me. "It's incredibly nuanced for a first year potter. But, then again, you're not a first year, are you." It was a statement of fact; I looked at him candidly when I spoke. "Why didn't you tell me you had some experience?"

"I'm a man of mystery," he said, turning uncharacteristically playful for a brief moment. Then, "I studied at a rather well-known school in Rhode Island for a few years. I left, wandered around a bit, and now I'm working on completing my education. This was the only ceramics class that had an opening, so I took it. I hope that's OK."

"I thought as much. I probably know some of your former teachers. Why'd you leave?"

"It's personal," he said, his expression closing off as though he realized he had said too much, the darkness in his eyes growing more prominent than it had been before.

"OK," I replied lightly, knowing there must be a story here. "It's still lovely work."

"Thanks," he muttered, thereby ending the conversation.

It was rare for a student's work to intrigue me the way that Brent's had. For months, I had been watching him work. He couldn't pretend to be a beginning potter; he was just too talented. His work, when he wasn't pretending to be a beginner, had that rare edge that made it kind of genius. It was a blend of skill and aesthetics that most teachers go decades without encountering. Yet here he was, in the flesh, an artist who could easily command New York City level gallery attention, in my beginner level pottery class. But Brent was also broody, dark and obsessive, which was hardly unusual for an artist, but his eyes always unnerved me. Sometimes, I caught a glimpse of deep pain in his expression. Other times, I was sure he was looking at me with longing or romantic interest. He rarely smiled. When he did, it was either sardonic or melancholy, depending on the moment. I shook my head, knowing that Brent had some serious inner battles raging.

All of these things intrigued and repelled me simultaneously. I felt unnerved by his attention, sorry for his sadness, bewildered by his talent and all around unsure what to do about him. It was barely worth thinking about, however. Brent was a student and the boundary between professors and students was Hadrian's Wall.

Brent, however, had other ideas.

I completed my rounds, thinking that it was audacious of Brent to name a sculpture before it was finished. Persephone, I thought. *Brent is a piece of work.* I reminded the class to clean and then clean again, as I was not interested in acquiring silicosis, and as they filtered out, my nervousness returned. When the last student left, I looked around, thankful for the few hours of focused respite from the tumult of the day, and I took a deep breath. I went back to my stoneware form, decided that it wasn't as graceful as Brent's and scrapped it, taking my own advice to not immortalize an inferior object.

It was after six when I left the studio. I was afraid to leave, thinking that James might be outside, and I wasn't ready to see him again. I returned to my loft, which was only a short walk away, I washed up, avoiding the mirrors again, and basked for a moment in the last of the sun with my philodendron. As hard as I tried, I could not help but think of James. His eyes, his form, his graceful gate, how sculptural his arms were beneath his shirt, the Barbados blue of his eyes. I thought maybe if I could draw him, it would help alleviate some of the pain and guilt I felt at leaving him. I fished in my bag and found my sketchbook. I flipped to the next blank page, pencil in hand, and instead found a page of unfamiliar writing. It was from him. My heart froze.

Dear Elwyn,

I am so sorry about today. I never meant to hurt you. I hope that, with time, you can forgive me. I want you to know I don't blame you for running away. I might have done the same in your position. If you ever decide that you want to talk, I am here.

Yours,
James

I was heartbroken. Already, I regretted leaving him, and this galvanized my feeling that I had made a terrible mistake. I read the letter again. *No number, no address, just comforting words.* I laid my head down on the table and wondered what to do. I felt awful. I hadn't eaten since breakfast, I realized. Thinking that a full stomach might help me clear my head, I started making some dinner. I had been planning to make tom kha gai, Thai coconut chicken soup, anyway. I mixed all the spices and chilies with the coconut milk and set them to simmer while I cut up the chicken, mushrooms and limes.

Somehow, cooking always made me feel better. The tasks, the aromas, the wonderful outcome, knowing that even when you can't change anything else, you can still cook a meal. It was comforting. I poured myself a glass of scotch. I downed it and then poured another. This one, a double.

As the chicken cooked and the soup's flavors came together, I broke out my laptop. If James actually had a company of his own, he shouldn't be that hard to find, I told myself. I was aware of the irony that I was Googleing a man that I had bolted away from just a few hours ago. I shook my head at myself, and continued the search, sipping my drink.

One click later and I was on his company's website, staring at his picture. I was suddenly in the throes of a mild coronary, just to see him again. He was so beautiful and aloof in this picture. None of the haunted sadness or epic loss I had witnessed in him showed through in this expression. Before me was the very epitome of a collected, intelligent, put-together businessman. It was not the James I met that I saw before me, rather some pale simulacrum of him. A mask. I stared and stared, and I didn't know what to do. Now who's the stalker, I asked myself, mildly embarrassed.

I closed the computer and walked to my bedroom. I put my clothes in the laundry and brushed my teeth. When I turned off the lights, I felt terrible loneliness flood through my veins, replacing the detached coolness induced by the scotch. When I finally fell asleep, my dreams were incredibly vivid.

I snapped into a garden world, warm and soft and lush, the lullaby of the breeze through leaves was my soundtrack. It was infinitely peaceful. My head rested on someone else's arm. I turned my head to see his face, and it was James. I smiled widely, he turned his face towards me and kissed me on the forehead. We were enthralled with each other, dizzied and giddy as we lay beneath a canopy of pure green. I awoke with the feeling of deep peace still enveloping me. I analyzed the dream, searching for answers that would make some sense, but all I could discern was that James' face had been the Victorian one from the dream in the garden, not the modern one of the man I had met.

My inner peace slipped away, replaced by frustration. I shook my head. Now James had infected my dream-life with his fantastic ideas about our past together. He had no right to get into my head. It was crowded enough with just me in there and I resented the intrusion. I didn't dare let myself entertain the possibility that it might have been a real memory. I wasn't ready for another break with reality. After all, I hadn't had any coffee yet.

All day, through classes and clay, through studio cleaning and a sudden spring thunderstorm, I willed myself not to think about James. The farther I put the experience in Longfellow Garden from my mind, the easier it was to just chalk the whole experience up to an anomaly. That doesn't explain your dream last night, I scolded myself, the romantic in me vying with the realist for supremacy. *It's uncanny that you could have a dream of the Victorian era James in a garden with you. It's not random!* I redirected my wayward inner Danielle Steele and worked just that much harder. My forms belied the emotional turmoil I felt; they were off kilter, sort of explosive, full of tension.

I had another night of vivid dreams and restless sleep. This time, I was being haunted by a dark shadow, someone was following me and it was very disquieting. The sensation was extremely uncomfortable and I awoke gripped by fear. Was it James following me? Who else would have the audacity to enter my crazy time-travel dreams after all! That assessment didn't seem right, though, as James really didn't seem like a dark force. In fact, when I let the Fort Knox-style guard surrounding my heart down for just a moment, all I felt was a pull towards him.

The following day, I had advanced ceramics in the morning and then the newbies again in the afternoon. I had been uncharacteristically snappy all day, even when the students didn't actually deserve it. I was not very good at recovering from sleep deprivation, even with massive amounts of caffeine.

When Brent came in, I just held my breath and sarcastically thought, *Great. Now this.* I don't know why. Disquietude had settled into my heart the night before and his presence seemed to exacerbate it. His work may have intrigued me, but more and more his actual presence unnerved me. His eyes were on me from the minute he entered the studio. He usually set up his work on a wheel across the room, but this time he chose the wheel right next to mine. It was an obvious move. He wanted to talk. I swallowed hard and greeted him. I was the teacher, after all.

"Hey, Brent. How's everything?"

"Do you really want to know?" He fixed his intense eyes on mine. I looked away.

"Of course. Are you not feeling well?"

"I feel well enough, I guess. Just have a lot on my mind. You don't mind if I sit here, do you?" His voice was quiet; his tone was intense.

"Not a problem. All the wheels are for student use. How's Persephone?"

He turned and stared me right in the eyes again and answered, "She's dead."

I was confused. Two days ago, he had named his sculpture Persephone. Did he not remember?

"The sculpture you made during last class. You told me it was called Persephone. An ode to spring?"

His expression darkened. "Yeah. I shouldn't have named it. I jinxed it."

"That's too bad, it was really beautiful."

"It's just clay, Derrin. You know that."

"True," I answered, feeling a little annoyed that Brent would say those words to me—the same words I used all the time in class to ease the disappointment of a failed piece.

After Brent had gotten his clay wedged, he came back over to start throwing. The first mound was off center from the start. He looked frustrated. I certainly hadn't seen him struggle to bring up a form before and I wondered what was going on.

"Really," I asked him. "What's going on?"

"Haven't been sleeping too well," he answered, rubbing his forehead with his sleeve. He tried again, with more success this time. "Fucked up dreams."

"Something in the air, I guess. They say solar flares can have an effect on dreams—maybe it was that."

"I don't think that's it," he replied, distantly.

"So, RISD?" I asked him, referring to his last school. "You didn't like it there?"

"I don't want to talk about that place. I have some bad memories." He looked away, back to his struggling form.

"Sorry. It's a great school, though. I'd have loved to go there. It was like the holy grail art school when I was in college."

"Which was not that long ago," he added. "You're not more than 30, right?"

"Right. Feels like an eon, though."

"I know what you mean."

"I loved college. We were such goofballs," I shared, not sure what had gotten into me. I never told the students about myself. "We were like overgrown children."

"Look around," he replied, sounding miffed. "This place is full of overgrown children. That's what college is. A fucking playground."

"Maybe that's why I came back to teach. I guess I have a soft spot for that silliness."

"I don't. I can't imagine why people are here unless it's to work."

"To learn, to grow up. Not all of us come out of the womb fully formed."

I was trying to be playful, but I missed my mark. Brent ended the conversation, focused back on his clay and left me wondering why I felt so petulant, all of a sudden. I was not at all myself.

I cleaned up my wheel, put away the strange sculptures I had made and checked in with the other students. Their noisy banter seemed like a good distraction to my increasingly sullen mood. That was the friendliest I had been all day, and Brent had snubbed me. I had made the effort to be nice to him, even though I found his presence unsettling, and he was the one who shut me down! The next time someone asked me where the calipers were, I snapped at them. I couldn't wait for class to be over, but then what? I was still subconsciously working through my experience with James, and it finally bubbled into my conscious thought. I was angry with him. He was right, I thought uncharitably, he never should have come near me.

When everyone finally cleared out, and Brent hadn't so much as looked back at me to say goodbye, I stormed out, ready to be done with the day. My first instinct was to call my friend Carly, but I thought better of it. She was very empathetic and right now, I wanted to yell, which she did not need to hear.

Instead, I stopped by Geno's Rock Club on my way home. I ordered a beer and talked with the bartender for a while. They played punk rock all the time and sometimes the shows they had were pretty good. Sometimes. The bartender was nice enough, which I wasn't expecting, and there were no people around to start a fight with, so I went home.

The first thing I did was sit down with my favorite photo of my dad and cry. I don't know why. I didn't even lock the door behind me. I missed him so much at that moment that it felt like a physical ailment. I knew that he would have had some sage advice or at least have said something sardonic and funny to cheer me up. But I was alone. All those puzzle pieces I had told James about felt wildly disconnected, as though they really were scattered to the wind. I wanted so desperately to feel connected, to be well and truly loved, yet at the same time, I was both afraid to let myself open to the possibility and actively denying that the possibility existed. I was a mess.

I decided to continue my light stalking of James online. I went back to his website to learn what I could, and again, his cool good looks gazed back at me through the screen. What was I thinking? He was out of my league, he was gorgeous, and if he really wanted anything to do with me then he must be crazy as well.

I went to the "contact us" page on his website and found the phone number. I still don't know why I called it. Was I going to leave him an angry voice mail? Was I going to hang up after I heard his message? That velvet, sensual voice—I was sure if I heard it again I would not be able to remember why I felt so angry with him. Even now, I wasn't sure. Why was I so mad?

I thought about it and tried to be honest with myself—no easy feat. I was angry because I was vulnerable. I had let myself get sucked into his dream. I was unaccustomed to having someone else wield power over me and it was wildly uncomfortable. But like it or not, James did have some sway over my emotions. I released my guard a little bit and allowed myself to test whether there was a real connection between us. What I found was that I missed him. How I could miss a man I didn't know was beyond me, but I did. I wanted him. I recklessly dialed his office number before I could change my mind.

When he answered the phone himself, I was startled beyond reason. I wasn't prepared for this outcome. I had thought I'd just listen to his message a few times and hang up like a teenager, but instead, I was confronted with his voice on the other line.

"Dunbar Financial, James Dunbar speaking."

He sounded so formal. The man in the picture would have this voice, I thought, not my James. I couldn't speak.

"Hello?" There was a hard edge to his voice now and I didn't want to hear it. I was about to hang up when he breathed my name, softly, gently. "Elwyn."

It *is* him, I thought.

"Yes," I answered, so quietly I could barely hear my own voice. "I got your note. Thank you for returning my bag."

"It was the least I could do."

"I'm so sorry for running away from you," I continued, unsure. "I felt like reality was slipping out of my grasp and I needed time to recalibrate."

"You have nothing to explain and no reason to be sorry. I shouldn't have put you in that position and I regret it."

"Don't."

"Don't what," he pressed.

"Don't say you regret it."

"I do, though. I caused you so much pain and distress. I would never hurt you, Elwyn. Please know that. Never on purpose."

"I know. I still don't want you to regret meeting me."

"I don't regret meeting you, Elwyn. I just didn't want you to get hurt."

"I had a dream about you. About us. We were laying together on the grass in a Victorian garden. It felt very, um, real." I paused for a moment, trying to be courageous. "I want to understand what happened. I want to know why we're connected and how. And," I paused, unsure if I should say what was in my heart.

"And," he urged.

"And I, um, I want to find my missing puzzle pieces."

I felt like a cliff diver, as though my stomach remained upon the precipice as I leapt. I was suspended in midair, in terror, as I awaited the inevitable wall of water below. The silence stretched out, amplifying my heartbeat into my skull, deafening me, paralyzing me. This was a terrible mistake, I told myself. *Will he reject me now? Was it just a hoax after all?*

Finally, after I had stopped breathing and fear had wound its poisonous tendrils around my heart, he said, "Thank you, Elwyn." His voice was thick with emotion. My heart ached in agonizing relief. "Will you meet me tomorrow?"

"Tomorrow?"

"Yes. Why should we wait?"

Insecurity. Fear. My natural flight response. I commanded myself to calm the fuck down and I squeaked out, "Where?"

"Noodle House? At six?"

I hesitated again, wondering if this was really the right thing to do, terrified that it was too soon. Finally, I acquiesced, "OK."

"I will see you there, Elwyn. You are courageous. Thank you for giving me a chance."

"It's the least I can do," I replied, repeating his words.

He laughed, just a little, the oppressive weight of uncertainty still upon us both.

"James?" I asked, suddenly overwhelmed with curiosity.

"Yes?"

"Do you always answer the phones at work?"

"No," he admitted, sheepishly. "I was praying that you'd call."

"Maybe you do know me better than I know myself."

"Maybe. We'll see."

"Good night, James," I said, reluctant to end this moment.

"Good night, fair Elwyn."

We hung up and I felt like my heart had turned into an eagle, all beating wings and screeching joy, careening over mountains and lakes in freedom unparalleled by any being.

CHAPTER THREE

The next day was Friday. I woke up and rushed out the door, thinking that if I kept myself wildly busy I might not dwell on my evening plan to meet James. I didn't have classes on Friday, but I had studio time. I needed to load the kiln, and Max was so big that it could take six hours to do it right. I had some students signed up to help, and I hoped that they would keep their word. A good start on Friday would mean an easier Saturday. It was going to be a long weekend.

The students and I assessed the work and tried to organize the firing according to what needed to be in the kiln's sweet spots to get the best reduction in the glazes. Colors wouldn't develop properly in certain parts of the kiln. We spent hours configuring and stacking and assessing the arrangement. The students brought me a steady stream of coffee, knowing that it would keep me going and in good cheer. I appreciated their enthusiasm.

Brent showed up around 2:00, hoping to be involved in the process.

"Sorry I didn't get here earlier," he apologized. "I had a class."

"It's fine," I replied. By this time, I was covered in sweat and trying not to look quite so tortured. I wiped my brow with the back of my hand, knowing that I would need a shower sooner rather than later.

"It looks good," Brent commented.

"Thanks," said Elaina. She smiled at him, but he didn't really seem to notice. He was watching me intently.

"We've worked hard," I replied to the both of them. "There's a lot left to do. We've mapped it all out, so Elaina will tell you where to put things."

"I'm sure I can figure it out."

"Actually," I retorted, "I'd prefer if you didn't. We've got a plan for getting all the work in and I'm the kind of person who likes to stick to the plan."

"Got it, boss," Brent responded, pretending not to be offended. I could tell, however, that he was.

We worked for another two hours and at 4:00 p.m. I excused myself and reminded them that the highest section of shelves was the most delicate to stack. "Don't let it fall over," I warned them. They laughed. I was serious. "I mean it," I said sternly, "This kiln load of clay represents thousands of hours of work and you know how much of ourselves we put into it. Please be careful. If you want to wait for tomorrow, I don't mind finishing. I'll be in early. Lighting is at 7:00 a.m., if you want to see how it's done."

Brent followed me back toward the door as I packed up my stuff.

"Are you OK? You seem distracted today," he stated, his eyes blazing with intensity.

"I'm fine, thanks." My tone was obviously guarded.

"Let me know if you need anything," he said, reaching out to pat my arm. His about face from the day before startled me. He had been so standoffish and now here he was trying to be friendly. I couldn't keep up.

"Thanks, Brent." I was caught in a corner, literally, backed up against the wall where I had retrieved my coat. I felt like a threatened animal. I shifted my weight uncomfortably.

"Sorry if I was rude yesterday," he said. "I've had a lot on my mind."

"It's ok, and you're right. I have been distracted." At that moment, all I wanted to do was leave the studio, but Brent was not the type to open up for no reason. I was curious where he was going with this conversation and at the same time, afraid that I already knew.

"I think we understand each other, you and I," he continued, moving still closer. "I know you see my work deeply. These kids," he said derisively, gesturing behind himself towards the room at large, "They don't understand anything. They've been handed an education and they don't appreciate it at all."

"They work hard," I said defending my students.

"Not really. Not like us. We have an inherent ability they can't understand."

"Like I said, I think you're very talented."

"We should get together and talk about what drives us, Derrin."

"My office hours are posted on the door, if you need advice on your work, but I've got to head out now."

"You always have your guard up," he persisted quietly, eyes burning into me.

I scooted sideways against the wall and headed for the door. "Thanks for your concern, Brent. I really am fine. You just focus on your work and don't worry about me."

He looked crestfallen and a little broodier than usual as I turned to leave, hoping he wouldn't touch me again.

"Derrin," he called out after me. I turned to look. "I'll see you tomorrow."

I smiled, halfheartedly, knowing that my suspicions about Brent would prove true. He was interested in me and I was going to have to end it before it began. I hadn't had to do this with a student before. He was older than most of my students, which made it seem a little less unreasonable on his part, but it was uncomfortable nevertheless.

I tried to put Brent out of my mind. I walked home, breathing deeply, looking up at the rooflines of the buildings I passed. There was a rhythmic elegance to them, I thought. It calmed me. I wanted to draw the connectedness I saw, the filigreed Victorian edges against the stark blue sky, brick façades lit tangerine with late afternoon sun. Maybe pastels, I thought viscerally. I tried not to let the panicking bird fluttering in my breast burst through, as I considered my imminent meeting with James. What would we say to each other? How would it go? Would I feel awkward? Would he?

I reached my loft and climbed the three flights of stairs to my landing. I showered and dressed, and desperately tried to make my hair and face presentable. The dreaded mirror was too honest regarding this point, so I left feeling less than optimally ready to meet the statuesque James.

On my way to the Noodle House I tripped over some uneven bricks and landed on my knee, the weight of my currier bag propelling me forward. I had opted for a skirt and tights and I now realized the extent of my mistake. The tights had a nice, round, increasingly bloody hole right over the knee, which was well below the daring hemline of my black skirt. Knowing that nothing could be done about it, I brushed the grit off my hands, stood up and moved onwards, dodging my own reflection in every storefront window I passed. Ugly duckling indeed. Not too graceful, either.

Feeling very self-conscious and now surly, I entered the restaurant. It was 6:00 on the nose and there was James. His immediate look of concern incited my ferocity for a moment. I wasn't used to anyone caring for me and it was disconcerting. Plus, I knew I must look wonderful, bleeding and disheveled—to think that I had actually put some thought into my appearance was laughable. I had wanted this meeting so badly and now I was going to fuck it up.

"You're hurt," he said, standing and reaching for my bag. He placed it on the back of my empty stool.

"I'm fine. I'm not a five year old."

"You should clean out that cut. Do you need help?"

I glared at him and said, "It's fine. Really. I get hurt all the time. I fall everywhere. It's no big deal. I'm not graceful and that's that."

"I think you're graceful," he said softly, almost hurt.

I laughed a little too loud. "Well you haven't seen me in the winter. It's like what would happen if you put ice skates on a moose. Not pretty. Anyway, what are you drinking?"

"Allagash. It's their Belgian style tripel."

"Great." I hailed the waiter, ordered the same and finally settled onto my high stool. I took a deep breath. "So much for my grand entrance and new beginnings," I began.

James smiled at me and I just felt stupid.

"So," I started again. "About what happened in the garden." I started dabbing my knee with a napkin under the table, but gave up on it a second later, as James responded.

His smile disappeared. "What about it?"

The waiter came with my beer. I took a sip of the tripel and smiled involuntarily. It was my favorite, always reminding me of a trip to Bruges I had taken when I was studying in Europe years before. I steadied myself and inhaled before I continued. "We need to talk about the dream, or whatever it was."

"I know, but first I'd like to get to know you a little."

"Fine. My favorite color is cerulean, my favorite place is Paris, or the beach, and if I could be any animal, I'd be a peregrine falcon. Your turn."

James was getting annoyed. This was not what he had expected me to act like and it wasn't how I wanted to act. I was nervous, though, and insecure and angry, but I had no idea why. It was clear that I was hurting him with my cavalier attitude, my blustery over-compensation for my own shortcomings. This was my pattern, to draw people in accidentally and then push them away intentionally, before I could be hurt. I had vowed not to get hurt anymore.

In James' expression, however, I realized that now I was doing the hurting and he didn't deserve it. I didn't want to hurt him, I just wanted to protect myself, but I could see that I was failing for both of us. I felt horrible and angry with myself for getting carried away. "I'm sorry," I said quietly. "I'm being a defensive jerk. I'll try to tone it down."

"No," he replied, "It's OK. I'm expecting too much of you, we don't know each other anymore and it's not fair for me to expect anything from you. I'm sorry."

"Anymore. That sounds so weird. I just... I don't know." I paused for a moment and we both studied our beers in silence. Finally, I asked, "Well, what is your favorite color, just so I know?"

He smiled. "Mine's cerulean too. It's deep and peaceful and evocative." He paused to think and then continued, "And my favorite place is Bali, for all the same reasons, and if I could be any animal, I would be a duck."

"A duck?" I giggled a little, choking on my beer. "You must know that's really funny."

"Ducks are funny animals," he replied. "I'm not offended on their behalf. They know they're funny."

Mercifully, the waiter came, putting an end to this conversation before it could get even further derailed. We ordered our ramen and another beer. We leaned in towards the center of the table as soon as he had taken our menus, as though to fill the new void. James reached out for my hand, which lay next to my beer. I pulled away instantly, terrified of his touch and of possibly repeating the outcome of our handshake in the garden.

Before he could comment or look hurt, I said, "I'm not sure you should touch me until we know that I'm not, um, going to be sent back in time to my death. Again."

Looking pained, he pulled back his hands and uttered, "I'm so sorry. I had no idea that would happen. I would never intentionally cause you pain."

"It's not something I'm eager to repeat," I admitted. "Maybe now that I'm more prepared I can keep my mind closed, or something. The pain was horrific, I just wouldn't want to collapse and make a scene in the Noodle House, or anything. They probably think I'm weird enough."

"Should we try just a tiny point of contact?"

"Do you think it will happen again?"

"I really don't know. I mean, who could have imagined that it would happen the first time, but I don't think so."

I hesitated, holding my breath. "I'm scared." Finally, I looked in his eyes, reached out my hand and allowed him to touch me. Nothing happened. I laughed in relief.

He stroked my finger gently as a feather, running his along the edge of mine and back up. He traced the back of my hand, lightly grazing my wrist beneath my sleeve. I felt a slight tingle of electricity as his finger moved on my skin. Heat flooded my cheeks as I realized that even this slight contact with his skin set my blood to boil. I was deeply attracted to him, and I could not deny it. It must have shown in my face because James asked, "Is it OK? Does it hurt?"

"I'm fine. Just hot all of a sudden. The ramen hasn't even come yet. I have no excuse."

James smiled, and resumed his exploration of my hand. He turned it over and examined the lines of my palm, pretending to read them. He was effortlessly seductive and my heart was racing.

"Tell me the good news first," I said, my voice unsteady.

His expression darkened, almost imperceptibly, for just a moment before he said, "You will have a long and happy life."

"And the bad?" Now I was beginning to suspect that he felt more than he would tell me.

He placed his other hand on top of mine, holding it firmly. "No bad. Not for you." He brought my hand to his lips and kissed it gently. Never had a man kissed my hand before. It was deeply touching and tender. I was at sea.

He took a deep breath, leaned back, still holding my hand in one of his, and looked at the ceiling. His eyes still looked worried. "What?" I asked him.

"Nothing. I am just praying that I've made the right decision."

I wasn't sure how to respond. If I were to let my insecurity get the best of me, it could be a mess. Instead, I said, "Tell me a story," trying to lighten the mood.

"I don't have any good ones. What do you want to know?"

"Just tell me about yourself."

"Um, I was engaged a while back, it didn't work out. No kids. I'm very focused on my work and I'm pretty good at it, I guess. I run my family business now that my father has retired. I have done everything according to the path that others chose for me, and I never gave it a second thought. That is, until I saw you for the first time at the bookstore. It was crazy. At first, I thought I knew you from college. Then, I realized that wasn't it, but I was drawn toward you. Everything suddenly seemed less important than it had—all my decisions, all my goals—it hit me that those weren't *mine*. They were other people's desires for me that I had been living out. Seeing you set off a seismic shift within me and I didn't know how to process it. That was a few months ago. Since then, I guess I've started to question my own choices a little more. I'm working on some investments that I think will pay off and then I can sell the business and retire early. I'd like a yacht. Will you sail around the world with me?"

I got the feeling he was only partly joking. "Sure," I said, playing along. "But I'm terrible crew. I won't swab your poop deck."

James laughed heartily for the first time since we'd met, a clear, robust laugh. It made me so happy I felt like a little kid. "OK," he said, still smiling, "Your turn."

"Turn for what?"

"Tell me a story."

My heart skipped a beat. "I don't know where to begin."

"That's a good beginning," he quoted.

I giggled and tried hard to figure out what to say. "I can't think of anything on the spot like this."

"But you put *me* on the spot just a minute ago!"

"That's different," I argued. "I don't like talking about myself."

Our ramen arrived moments later and got me off the hook. We ate together, speaking little, marginally more comfortable with the silence.

In the middle of our meal, James paused, looking towards the counter.

"What is it?" I asked through a slurpy bit of ramen.

"Nothing. Just this guy at the bar keeps looking at us. At you, I think. You know him?"

I turned around and my heart stopped for a moment. It was Brent. Somehow, I had known it would be. Was he following me? It must have just been a coincidence. He wasn't looking at me any more so I turned back to James. My face always shows what I'm thinking. "You know him, right?" James asked.

"He's a new student of mine this semester. He's been unnerving me more and more. Like the other day, he handed me a heat gun and..."

James interrupted me, "A heat gun? What do you do?"

"Yes, a heat gun. I teach ceramics at the College of Art. He handed it to me and brushed my thumb with his fingers and I know it was on purpose. His eyes said it all. Then today..."

James interrupted, "I didn't realize you were a professor when I dropped your bag off there—I just noticed your ID badge. That's really cool."

"Thanks, I guess. It's really fun, most of the time. Plus, I get to make my own work in a really well-equipped studio and I have full control over the firings."

"Oh! You can talk about yourself! Not that hard, was it."

"Ha!" I laughed, he was right. It was easier when you weren't put on the spot.

"Sounds like the perfect job, if it weren't for assholes like this guy." James looked back at Brent and glared hard. I wouldn't want to be the recipient of that look, I thought. I wondered if it would scare Brent off and in a few moments, I had my answer. James informed me that Brent was leaving.

"He's actually incredibly talented. His work is way more mature than most of my students. He's had some experience. But he's very dark and broody and like I said, his attention can be unnerving."

"Keep your distance," James cautioned.

"Always. It's my job."

"Right, but he doesn't care."

"Thanks for your prescient advice. I've got it covered."

My tone was probably more acerbic than I had intended. I reached out to touch James' hand in apology and he readily accepted mine, intertwining our fingers. Our remaining ramen had finally gone cold. I was ready to leave anyway.

"Would you like to go for a walk?" James asked me, rather formally.

"Why, are you courting me, sir?" I asked in my best British accent.

"I believe I am, m'lady." We both giggled. In all our silliness, I forgot to pay my half of the bill, and James had taken care of it so suavely that I hadn't noticed. He got up to leave, picked my coat up from the back of my chair and helped me put it on. He hoisted my bag onto his shoulder.

"What about the bill?" I asked, bewildered.

"It's free. Your lucky night." James actually winked at me.

I rolled my eyes and said, "Thank you, but I prefer to pay my own way."

"Next time, fair Elwyn," he retorted softly.

"Thank you, that was most kind," I replied, resuming my accent.

"Tis my great and abiding pleasure, m'lady. Your wish is my command." He bowed a little and I took his arm. I felt like I was floating, and not because of the beer.

We walked hand in hand together through the city we both loved. The air was brisk, but after our hard winter, the cool May wind felt like a reprieve. The streets were crowded, for Portland, that is. We ambled past lit storefronts and architectural master-pieces, as well as the travesties of urban renewal. I pointed to the Fidelity Trust building and said, "I've always loved those faces on the façade. They've overseen the goings on in Monument Square for a hundred years. Imagine what they've seen?"

"In some cases, I'd rather not," James returned, cheekily.

We both giggled. It seemed so natural to laugh with James over banal things, to walk together as friends.

"You like architecture?" he asked after the third feature I'd pointed out on one of the buildings along Congress Street.

"You could say that. I have a thing for antiques, history, anything with a story. Buildings always tell a story. I guess most of the time, people just don't stop to listen."

"Right. So, what's this one trying to say?" James pointed to a new building full of loft-style condos. It was startlingly modern against the late Victorian landscape surrounding it, and strikingly plain.

"It's new," I answered, without much emotion. "I barely even see it. Like a mirror, I guess. I just walk by without a glance."

"You and mirrors," he mused, shaking his head. "Wanna take a field trip?"

"A field trip from our field trip?" I giggled. "Sure."

He steered us towards one of the more modern buildings and took out his wallet. Without even opening it, he waved it at a sensor to the left of the bank of glass doors. I heard a click and we pushed into the building.

"Should we be here?" I asked.

"No one will mind. I have a key card!" He waved his wallet in the air dramatically before returning it to his pocket. I never understood how men carry everything they need in pockets. If I didn't have a bag, I'd be lost.

The security guard nodded to him and said, "Good evening, sir."

James returned, "Hey, George."

"Sir?" I whispered, giggling.

"Shh!" James admonished, smiling broadly.

I followed James into the elevators, and as the doors closed, we were confronted by our images, bisected by the division between the doors. We were mirrored in sickly bronze and I reflexively averted my gaze. "Wait for it," he said, almost gleefully.

We rode up to the penthouse. The doors opened with a refined swooshing sound and we encountered more doors. A sign in bold lettering read "Dunbar Financial."

"It's your company."

"Yes. My father started it in the 60's, grew it into a pretty impressive little empire, and now it's mine. I suppose it's quite something, seeing as how he started out with nothing. He loved this place like it was his child, which, I guess, in a way, it was. Investing is second nature to me, he talked about work so much. I was expected to run it when he retired, but after college, I got my MBA just so I wouldn't have to start working here so soon. Here I am anyway. Come on."

He took me to the far corner of the office and put his finger on another keypad, this one scanned his fingerprint. "Cool," I muttered.

James looked at me like a mischievous child. "I know!"

We entered his office. It was spacious, with floor to ceiling windows overlooking the Old Port and Casco Bay beyond. It was a phenomenal view. I traversed the hardwood floors, noticing the leather settee and wide oak desk, definitely antique, as well as the lawyer's bookcase with the glass doors—a style I'd always admired—stocked with beautiful, leather-bound books. "Nice office," I remarked, stupidly, not sure what else to say. "I like the desk and bookcase. Are they family pieces or did you get them?"

"I bought them when I inherited the space. My dad liked everything to be new, maybe because new made him feel like he had succeeded. But I feel the same as you do about things. I like an object with history."

We stood at the window and looked out over the city. The lights sparkled along the streets and glinted in windows, mirroring the stars overhead. I hadn't seen Portland from this vantage point often and I was enamored. James was standing close to me, closer than I should have let him. I didn't want to stop him, though. For unlike earlier, in the studio with Brent, I felt nothing pushing me from him. It was quite the opposite; my connection to James felt natural, deep and comforting. I noticed our reflections in the glass, ghost images against the city beyond. I loved the juxtaposition; the way the city lights twinkled through us, as though lighting us from within. "Beautiful," I murmured.

James was mesmerizing. His eyes were midnight blue blended with the black night beyond. His expression was serious, intense, focused on the horizon. He must have sensed me looking at him because he shifted his gaze to meet mine in the glass. Then, he stepped behind me and held my shoulders, still looking at my reflection.

"Can I tell you what I see when I look at your lovely face mirrored in this window?" James' voice was low and quiet.

"If you must," I answered, feeling unsure.

"I see your kind, sad eyes, full of creativity and intelligence. I see your artistic nature as you absorb the beauty around you. I see your past, present and future all wrapped into one perfect package of humanity, a child of the universe. See those stars dotting your reflection? You are made of stars. I ask you, Elwyn, what's not to love about that?"

"James," I began, suddenly stymied by the lump in my throat. "I don't see it like that. I never have. But thank you."

"You will, Elwyn. You will come to see the same beauty that I see." He spoke in such a serious, intense way. It struck me that this said a lot about his personality.

"You're a very serious person," I stated, not sure if I should speak my mind.

"I'm focused, I suppose. I take my work seriously, I take life seriously, and I take people seriously. So, I guess that makes me a serious person," he mused, smiling. "I don't like bullshit. I don't have time for it." He paused, still looking at my reflection. "You're serious too, although you use humor to hide it, just in case someone looks too deep. How come?"

I turned away from his eyes and thought about it. "I guess it's just how I've always been. I don't like bullshit either and I feel like most people offer you bullshit most of the time. It's like genuine interactions are few and far between, and when I've let my guard down, I've paid for it with a broken heart. So, guards go up, jokes are made, hearts are fortified. Defense mechanisms, I guess."

James inched closer to me. He reached out and touched my hip, gently turning me towards him. I let him move me without resisting, attraction for him welling up within my body. This was wildly unfamiliar territory. He reached out with his other hand and stroked my face gently. I closed my eyes, leaning into his touch, letting the thrill of his skin against mine consume me. When I opened them again, I half expected him to kiss me. Instead, he arrested my gaze and with passion he said, "There will be no bullshit here. This is real. I haven't got any guards up with you, Elwyn. Please remember that."

It was so unexpectedly solemn, yet so forceful, that I laughed. I shouldn't have, but I did. Then I smiled wide and said, "Thank God." I leaned forward, reached my hands up to touch his face and brought him closer. I touched my lips to his, a feather-light kiss. I smiled again and slid my hand around his waist, turning sideways so he was holding me against him, our twin reflections merging to one, against the heartbeat of the city below.

We eventually sat down on the floor and he held me close against him for a long time as we gazed out the windows. Finally, I couldn't keep myself from bringing up the events in the garden again. The more I ruminated on them, the more I knew that unless I processed it with James, I could not let myself move on.

"James," I began, "I don't want to invade the silence, but I need to know something. Did you know that that crazy mind meld was going to happen?"

"Mind meld? Isn't that from Star Trek?" He sounded amused.

"Don't laugh at me! Do you have a better word for it?" I sat up and turned to face him, sitting mermaid style on the floor near the windows.

He took a deep breath and turned towards me. I was suddenly very nervous about what he might say.

"No. I told you, I had no idea," he began. "I was overwhelmed with feeling at that moment, my memory of the dream was very close to the surface. Maybe that's what did it. I don't have a satisfactory explanation, though. I'm sorry."

"It felt so real. I need to know how it happened. I trust that you're not trying to trick me, or anything. I know that. But it was insane. One minute we're just sitting there, the next minute I'm sucked into the distant past. It was like being dragged right out of my body. All of a sudden, I felt like I was drowning. I was yanked down a swirling vortex of time and experiences into that moment, staring up at the stars and then at your face, except it wasn't yours exactly. Is that what your dream has looked like your whole life? Holding a dying woman on a bridge?"

"Yes, only more vivid and there is a lot more to it. Do you really want me to tell you about it?"

"I don't know. It's like, I don't want you to tell me the story. I want to remember it for myself. But will I?"

"I have no idea."

"I want to believe it. I really do. But couldn't there be other explanations for what happened?"

"Like what? How is it that I could see you from afar, a total stranger, and know that we were linked somehow? How is it that the image you describe—the whole experience you had—was identical to the one I've had my entire life—only not from my perspective, Elwyn. From yours. You just said you were looking up at my face, at the stars. I've always experienced the memory looking down. At you. At your pale, precious face, turning cold as the life passed out of your eyes."

"Then how come I didn't know about this until that moment in the garden? How come I don't remember the past? Why is it just you?"

James paused a moment to ponder the question before answering. Finally, he said, "I think it's because you left. You died. And I had a lifetime to think about losing you. Maybe I wanted so badly just to hold you again that the memories never fully faded. Can spirits return? Are souls recycled? Who knows? But I believe that we loved each other in that past. All I ask is to please give the present a chance."

"I'm trying," I replied. "It's overwhelming, though. I want to see the whole picture. I want to know for myself that it's real."

"I don't know how to get you that certainty, Elwyn. Besides, nothing in life is certain. You know that. People fall in love all the time. They take the risk because sometimes it's worth it! What if we're supposed to be together? Don't we owe it to ourselves to be courageous and try?"

"It's just too crazy, though. I mean, this is real life, not some crazy sci-fi movie!"

"I know it's crazy, but the universe is a crazy place. Think about the fact that at the subatomic level, we're mostly empty space. Empty space! How could empty space have emotions this deep or memories this strong if it's not real? You're real, Elwyn, and you're right here, and how I feel about you is real. Sci-fi or otherwise!"

I couldn't deny his impassioned logic. He was so sexy when he talked physics that I just smiled. He was right. I needed to be courageous.

"My friend Carly's mom is friends with a soul reader. I think her name is Angela. Maybe we should go see her. It sounds nuts, but maybe it's worth a try."

"A soul reader? What is a soul reader?"

"I don't know, but Carly says she can see deeply into people's selves, their pasts, their hearts. Kind of like a psychic, I guess. I've always thought it was a little odd, but the more I think about what happened in the garden, the more I think she might be able to help."

"I will do anything to help figure this out. Elwyn, I was a little child when I started having dreams of holding a dying woman, feeling like my heart was being gnawed out of my chest. I have struggled with this pain, these memories, my whole life. I mean, can you imagine telling your mom that the dying lady was back again, every night? She thought I was crazy; she was so upset. Eventually, I stopped telling anyone about it because I didn't want to see the horrified looks on their faces. It's part of why my fiancé left. I was freaking her out with the frequency of my nightmares. I haven't slept well my entire life. You should see the battery of pills I take now just to let myself sleep without dreams. I want to understand this just as much as you do. I'd love to live a normal life, whatever that is." His tone was fervent and I knew that he couldn't be lying.

"OK. I'll get Angela's number and call her on Monday. When can you go up north with me? She lives in Belfast."

"I'm supposed to be in Boston Monday and Tuesday, but next weekend would be fine." He paused for a moment and then said, "Thank you." His voice was quiet, prayerful. "You could have stayed away. You didn't have to call me. You could have assumed I was crazy, just like everyone else has, all my life. I am so thankful you didn't."

"Don't thank me yet," I quipped. Then growing serious, I added, "I can't imagine what it must have been like, especially as a child, to have had that memory plague you. It's so violent, so intensely sad. What I do know is that what I felt inside your memory was as real as anything that has ever happened to me in this life. You aren't crazy, and neither am I."

"We will figure it out, I'm sure of it."

"In the meantime, I'm going to need sleep. I've got to work all weekend."

We exhaled our tension, letting our bodies come back together in an embrace.

James sprang lightly to his feet and pulled me up. "I'll drive you home," he said.

"You really don't have to," I answered, my inner New Yorker surfacing for a moment. "It's not too far."

"I want to." He said it firmly, and I imagined that this was how he addressed his staff. "Besides, that way, we can spend a few more minutes together."

I actually blushed. Luckily, we had never bothered turning on the lights, so it went unnoticed. "Fine," I relented.

We left the building, saying goodbye to George the guard on our way out. We held hands as we made our way towards James' car.

"Where do you live?" I asked.

"I'm in the West End," he answered. "I bought the place a few years ago when the market crashed. Pretty good investment, really, but that's my job."

We got into his car, which I was very thankful to see wasn't a Mercedes or a Saab or something fancy. It was just a normal hybrid, although it was meticulously clean inside.

"God," I gasped. "You should see my car. It's such a mess! This is scary clean."

"I don't mean to startle you with my neatness." He was clearly laughing at me.

"Well, I am a potter, I guess. I'm supposed to be messy."

"I think messy is cute," he retorted, winking at me.

"You wouldn't think so if you lived with me!"

"We'll see."

My heart was instantly in my throat at the implication of his statement. We were both quiet for a while.

"Which street?" he asked.

"Pleasant Street," I replied. "The lofts near the bakery."

"Got it," he smiled.

We drove to my place in silence, although it was not uncomfortable. I was amused when he parked and got out of the car to help me out. I was already mostly out of the car by the time he got to my side and we both laughed. "So much for chivalry," I said, smiling.

He walked me to the door and as I fished out my keys he shuffled his weight from side to side a couple of times, clearly nervous for the first time all evening. I knew an internal debate was raging and I wasn't about to make it easy for him. I stayed coy, taking my time with the lock. When I had pulled the door open and held it with my body, I turned to him. "Thank you for dinner," I said quietly. "It's been a very interesting evening."

"Interesting, huh? Not fun?"

"Fun too, I suppose, in a broadly defined sense of the word."

He moved closer to me, his eyes intense and full of desire. It hit me in the pit of my stomach to see that look. My expression held all of my feeling as clearly as his did, I was sure. He took my face in his hands, slid one hand behind my head and bent forward to kiss me.

His mouth was hot and soft on mine, his body tense under his light coat. I placed my hand lightly on his chest, just above his heart, and slid it upwards toward his neck. I moved my fingers against his skin, up into his hair, and pulled him in even closer. We kissed deeply, intensely, passionately. It felt so right, as though the long lost pieces of my self were snapping back into place, finally, after a life-time of being scattered to the universe. I wanted him to come in, but I knew it was too soon. So when the kiss finally ended, I gently caressed his face and with one last look of longing, I said, "Good night, James."

"Good night, Elwyn."

CHAPTER FOUR

"Then to the rolling Heav'n itself I cried,
   Asking, "What Lamp had Destiny to guide
   Her little Children stumbling in the Dark?"
And - "A blind Understanding!" Heav'n replied."

THE RUBAIYAT OF OMAR KHAYYAM
TRANSLATED BY EDWARD FITZGERALD

In the morning, I awoke to a radiant glow flooding my loft. It matched, with startling accuracy, the luminous feeling inside my body. It had not been my imagination—something had snapped into place within me the night before—some long-disjointed aspect of my being finally felt aligned. I pictured a psychic chiropractor and giggled a little to myself.

I made coffee, reveling in the warmth of the spring sunlight flooding my loft. I sat in my favorite oversized chair near the wide windows, basking like a cat, reading up on modern ceramics in one of my long ignored magazines. I couldn't focus on the words for long, though, as James kept invading my thoughts. It was a pleasant invasion. A big breakfast seemed unnecessary, so I had a banana and some yogurt just to keep myself in good spirits. Today was Max-firing day and I was stoked.

I took my time getting ready, paying a little closer attention to my appearance than usual. I thought of James' words the night before. I thought about what it meant to be a child of the universe, as he had put it. It was like having my own interest in myself sparked for the first time. I forced myself to look in the mirror after my shower and reflected on my skin, my eyes, my nose, my hair. I reexamined my body, which was appealing enough, considering my disdain for exercise.

I analyzed the features I had hated about my appearance for so long. I mean, it was obvious that my skin was a wreck, it was marked with acne scars and its uneven surface literally repelled makeup. It was just a part of me, though, why should I hate it? Did it matter, after all, in the grand scheme of things?

The eyes staring back at me were deep set and though they were brown, the irises were shot through with amber and gold in the right light, ringed with a deep brown edge. No one but my dad had ever said they were pretty, but he had studied them more closely than anyone else had bothered to, I guess. His words came back to me, "The most beautiful eyes have a dark ring around the iris. It draws the focus inwards." I had always thought he was just trying to make me feel better about my homely looks, but in examining them now, I saw a glimmer of what he might have seen, so many years ago. There was something exotic about them, almond shaped and fringed with dark lashes. I never would like my nose, I decided. There was just a bit too much of it. My mouth was average, nothing to speak of: full lips, but not too full. I smiled and suddenly it made sense. I hated mirrors so much that I rarely smiled into them—it was so easy to scowl. With that smile, however, there was a glimmer of something attractive, something compelling. Maybe I should smile more often, I thought.

I put on makeup, just a little, another rare occurrence. I applied subtle eye shadow and jet-black mascara and a little lip-gloss, noting the slight improvement. I was not as repelled by what I saw as I had been for so much of my life. Could I be coming to terms with myself? How, I wondered, could this happen overnight? Just because some man is interested in me, I finally see the good parts of myself? Why should I need a man's validation?

It occurred to me that it wasn't James' validation of my physical attributes that had helped me see myself. It was that he seemed able to see my essence, not the superficial aspects that everyone else, including me, had focused on, and that the inside and the outside may just complement each other. Or perhaps our supposed connection wasn't craziness after all. Maybe we really were linked by a past adoration that was filling my interminable, age-old emptiness. I smiled at myself in the mirror for the second time. It felt really, really good.

I walked up to the studio, ready for the insanity of the day. I stopped for a fill up at my favorite coffee shop, savoring the aroma and the way the sunbeams kept following me around, bouncing through the front window and off the walls and floor. It was like the bright light of eternity, I thought. If my soul really was recycled from just over a hundred years ago, might I not have been bouncing through time for all of eternity past? And what could that mean for the future? It made me feel very small and, somehow, quite content in my awe.

Still aglow, I sauntered into the deserted studio, and assessed last night's work. If it is one thing art students are generally known for it's their disdain for early mornings. I was the same at their age; I preferred to work all night, uninterrupted, in a fairly quiet studio. These kids were the same way. Good luck with that 8:00 a.m. art history class, I thought, rather wistfully.

They'd finished off the stacking and the rolling door stood open, awaiting my approval. No one broke any kiln shelves, I mused. *At least there's that.*

I adjusted a few things and patiently awaited the appointed hour. At ten of seven, a few bleary-eyed students rolled in. Claire and Ben were used to the drill, and Elaina seemed excited about watching the magic for the first time.

We slowly rolled the door closed, which was tricky and dangerous, seeing as the entire load was balanced on it. Crazy design, I thought, but in order to have a kiln this big, it's the only way.

"Easy," I said in a low, serious voice. "Easy does it."

"This is insane," said Elaina, as she pushed against the door with her slight frame. "Why would the door and the shelves be the same unit? How does this not just fall over and break every time?"

"Because we're careful," retorted Ben, smiling slyly.

We finally closed the door, and I noticed Brent lurking in the doorway to the kiln room.

"Didn't want to help?" I looked directly at him.

"Nope. You obviously had a plan."

"Thanks, dude," said Claire in her low, gravelly voice. "It only weighs a couple thousand pounds."

"Enough," I said. "It's done. Let's check everything and light the pilots. It needs to candle for a few hours before we can fire it up in earnest."

I explained the process, mostly for Elaina's benefit, and lit the pilots. She was clearly fascinated. With the smaller kilns, I let the students take responsibility for firings, but with Max I was reluctant to let them take charge. "I'll be here on and off all day. This evening I'll do the reduction, and people are welcome to join for any or all of this process. It's great experience."

The morning was a waiting game. Some of the students got out work to do. I was feeling so unfocused that I decided to go for a little walk.

My cell phone rang. It was James.

"I didn't expect to hear from you so early," I said by way of greeting.

"Nice to talk to you too." He laughed.

"What's up?"

"Nothing. Just wondering what you're up to today."

"Firing a kiln," I answered. "It's our big gas kiln and it takes 36 hours. I'll be at the studio all day and part of the evening doing the reduction."

"With that creepy guy?"

"I hadn't thought about it," I answered, honestly.

"I don't like the sound of that."

"It's not your call," I retorted. "It's my job. I wouldn't tell you how to do *your* job, you know. Your company would tank."

"Sorry. He just makes me nervous."

"I'm at school. What can happen?"

"People are insane. You never know. This is not how I wanted our conversation to go, by the way. But then again, nothing with you is how I expect it to be."

"I'm unpredictable," I answered, sardonically, letting a little of my New York accent filter through.

"I am beginning to see that." He paused for a moment. "What's reduction, by the way?"

I laughed, not expecting the question. "It's when you reduce all the oxygen out of the kiln environment, forcing the fire to consume elements from the glazes instead of the air in the kiln. It produces beautiful colors and effects."

"Sounds cool. Would you want company?"

I stopped walking as his words sank in. "You'd want to watch a kiln get fired?"

"With you? Yes."

"That is so weird."

"Thanks, Elwyn. I appreciate the compliment."

"I didn't mean that you're weird. Although now that I think about it..."

"Ha, ha," he said.

I thought about it a little longer and finally said, "OK. Sure, you're welcome to join me. It's actually really pretty. That's why I always reduce at night. The colors of the flames are kind of mesmerizing."

"I look forward to it. Shall I meet you with take out at 6:00?"

"Take out?"

"Yes. It's when you go to a restaurant and..."

"I know what take out is, dork," I interrupted, laughing. "Fine. With take out. It'll be a picnic."

"See you this evening, then."

"OK. And James?"

"Yes, Elwyn?"

"Thanks."

"For what?"

"For wanting to keep me safe."

He paused. "I promise I will do a better job of that this time around."

I didn't know how to respond to this reference of my other death, so I remained silent.

"Good bye." His voice was distant, thoughtful.

"Bye."

CHAPTER FIVE

"Another said - "Why ne'er a peevish Boy,
    Would break the Bowl from which he drank in Joy;
    Shall He that *made* the Vessel in pure Love
    And Fancy, in an after Rage destroy!"

THE RUBAIYAT OF OMAR KHAYYAM
TRANSLATED BY EDWARD FITZGERALD

I walked down to The Holy Donut and picked up a dozen for the clay denizens who would be devoting their day to the cause. It was a dangerous place, full of temptations. I exercised as much forbearance as one can in such a garden of earthly delights.

When I returned to the studio, I noticed that only Brent and Ben were working. It was Saturday, after all. They seemed pretty absorbed, but at the announcement that donuts had arrived, they swarmed the worktable like hungry tigers. I always forgot how much guys can eat. I contented myself with a single maple bacon donut while they each ate three. It was pretty amusing.

When they had finished their impromptu feast, Ben returned to his work but Brent hung back with me at the worktable. He stared through me with those dark, intense eyes. I was suddenly very nervous again. This had to stop.

He watched me for a moment before he spoke, his expression almost one of pain. "I make you uncomfortable. I don't mean to."

"It's OK. I just get a vibe from you that seems to transgress the student teacher boundary. Tell me if I'm wrong."

Brent took a deep breath and looked at me intensely. "It's true. I'm very attracted to you. You get to me somehow. Your artwork speaks to me, which is very rare. Most of what I see is total crap. But your work has a balance of power and femininity that I really appreciate."

"Thank you," I said solemnly. "You know I like your work too. I respect your drive and your skill. You've got what it takes to be competitive in the art world, which is saying a lot."

"Listen, Derrin. I've been holding this in too long and it's just too painful. I can't hold it in any more. I'm very drawn to you. I think I'm in love with you."

I hesitated, kind of blown away by this declaration. When I regained the faculty of speech, I said, "I'm flattered, Brent." I could feel my cheeks glow scarlet. I took a deep breath to still my racing heart. "Really, I am. But I'm your teacher. I'm not allowed to date students."

"We're both adults. I don't see the problem. I'm not some 18-year-old kid fresh out of high school."

"I know that, Brent, but the administration is very clear on this point. Teachers don't date students. I happen to love this job. I can't jeopardize it."

"Please, just give me a chance. I can't deny my feelings any more. I know you're drawn to me. I can feel it."

"I respect you as an artist. I really do. I barely know you as a person, though, Brent. And to be fair to you, since we're disclosing our innermost hearts here, I don't feel a romantic attraction to you, and I don't want to string you along. Like I said, it can't happen. I know I can't tell you how to feel, but this is going nowhere. There's a lot of nice gals around, find one of them to shower with affection."

"What, you think I can just turn it off? Just decide to like someone else?" Sincere anger infiltrated his voice and flickered into his expression.

"I'm suggesting that you reassess your feelings for me and redirect them elsewhere. This is a dead end."

"What the fuck, Derrin. You're not giving me a chance."

"No, Brent. I'm not. I can't. I don't want to be mean, and I certainly don't want to hurt you, but you've got to let it go."

"Derrin, please. Come upstairs with me. I want to show you something in my painting studio."

"I don't think that's a good idea, Brent."

"It won't take long. It would mean so much to me."

I looked across the studio at Ben who had been inadvertently witnessing this entire exchange. He looked beyond uncomfortable. "I will go upstairs if Ben comes too."

"What, you're afraid to be alone with me?"

"I'm not afraid of a goddamn thing in this life or the next, Brent." I spoke with more vehemence in my voice than I had thought I could muster. "I do, however, have some sense. Ben," I called, not bothering to disguise my tone, "Will you please join Brent and I on an excursion to the painting studios?"

"Sure, D."

He came straight away, his expression guarded, and we all headed upstairs.

In the studio, Brent led us past several painting spaces, each with three tall walls and one side open, each displaying a different and distinct style, some better than others. When we approached Brent's, I didn't even have to ask, it was so obviously his work. My stomach was in knots. There were three enormous canvases, one on each of the three walls. They were gigantic mandalas of various body parts, all lovingly and accurately rendered in a circular pattern of radial symmetry. They were absolutely beautiful and incredibly unnerving.

"I was hoping you would see that there's a connection between us, Derrin. I can feel it. You understand expression and impermanence, and how making great artwork bridges the divide."

"I am not suggesting that art does not connect me with my students. It's supposed to. That's my job. That connection, however, is a tool to bring out the best in people. Nothing more. As for art being the bridge between the two worlds of permanence and impermanence, I agree. There is something larger out there in the universe that we can tap into—that as artists it's our *privilege* to tap into. But that's a bridge we cross alone."

He glared at me with unabashed emotion, an epic battle between love and anger seething beneath his features. "You don't see the connection! You don't see anything," he bellowed, clearly out of control. Ben moved a little closer to me in a protective stance.

"What," Brent demanded, staring at him hard. "You think I'm going to hurt her? What am I going to do? Can't you see it? She's eviscerating me! I'm the one who is fucking bleeding here!"

"Jesus." I looked around the deserted studio. "Calm down, Brent," I urged softly. "Show me the work you wanted me to see."

His hands were shaking with anger and emotion as he rifled through the contents of his messy desk. It was piled high with sketchbooks. One fell on the floor as he rifled through. As it hit the floor, it opened to a page with a dark graphite sketch on it. The marks were forceful, bold and so deep they incised the paper. The image was a view along an arm with a gun at the end. The subject at the end of the barrel was out of focus, fragmented and mostly erased, but definitely a female form. It was a very disturbing sketch.

Brent snatched the sketchbook away before I could see any more. He thrust a smaller painting at me. It was done on stretched canvas that had been gashed and painted and had a piece of new canvas sewn to the back. It was as though I was looking through layers of skin and to organs beneath. It was shockingly accurate and beyond disturbing.

"What do you want me to say, Brent. It's technically flawless and very evocative. You know that, though. Why was it so important that I see this?"

"Because it's me. *This* is what you've done to me!"

"I've done? Brent, I haven't done anything but teach you. All of this angst is in *your* head and in *your* heart and it's *your* responsibility to deal with it. I'm as viscerally involved as a painter's model is to the final work: an object for your attentions, not a person. If I were a person to you, you wouldn't blame me for your pain. That's not how love works, Brent." I was really worked up and hadn't meant to shout, but that's exactly what I had done. "Now, I have work to do. Thank you for sharing. I really do hope you find someone worthy of your attentions and that next time, she returns the sentiment."

He turned away, clearly gripped with rage.

"You're a talented artist, Brent. Don't let this get in the way of making work."

He turned back to me for an instant, his eyes cold. "Don't worry. I won't." His tone was menacing, and I felt that his reaction was totally disproportionate to the situation.

As we left Brent's studio space, I glanced at Ben who had been a silent and unwilling participant in a very uncomfortable situation. I shook my head, my expression bewildered.

"Well that was fucked up," he commented. I had to agree. I was so relieved that he had been present and thanked him accordingly; maybe it had tempered Brent's reaction to my rejection, which was a scary thought. At any rate, I was relieved that the confrontation was over.

When we got back into the studio, I tried to put the encounter with Brent out of my mind. Every so often, I had to fight back feelings of sorrow and guilt about hurting him. Even if James had not entered the picture, I still would have had to shut Brent's feelings down. I needed to let it go and focus on my work. I had some bisque ware to glaze, so I set up a space and got to it.

Glazing wasn't my favorite part of the process of making clay works. When I could work with a self-glazing body, or in a low fire situation, or with salt firings, I was the happiest. I vowed that someday I'd move to the country and build my own salt kiln and wood ash kiln, have raku parties every weekend and say goodbye to glazing forever. Then I'd unload a gas kiln after a reduction firing and remember just how much magic happens inside a glaze. Frankly, I just loved clay in all its many wondrous forms.

I had a set of soup bowls to glaze and I wanted them to be consistent. I'd sell them in sets of four, but there were sixteen of them. That way, if someone wanted to buy two sets, they'd match. So much thought went into the decisions about color that it took me hours just to finish those bowls. I didn't like to add up how much (or little) I would make per hour based on the sale price of work like this, but luckily, I wouldn't have to. I wasn't a production potter. I was a sculptor and a professor.

I walked back to the kiln room and checked on Max. The candling was going smoothly, the temperature was rising slowly, just how I wanted it. With student work, you can never be too careful. I explain the rules over and over, but one wet glaze will create an expensive disaster. So I candled the kiln to eliminate any moisture from the glazes and then I would fire it up.

Satisfied with progress, I left the studio for some lunch. Brent had returned and was working sullenly at a far off wheel in the corner. A few more first years were scattered about. Outside, it was another perfect day, all sunshine and fresh air. I wished I could be out on the water, sailing or something. I enjoyed a leisurely sandwich outside in the Longfellow Garden, thinking largely about James, trying to examine and define my feelings. It was a losing battle.

By the time I got back to the studio it was just past 12:00. Time to turn on the main gas jets. I put on some eighties punk to get us in the mood. Elaina had returned and the other first years were there. Claire and Ben took their positions on the gas valves on either side of Max, I watched the flame colors coming out of the peep holes on the front. We adjusted the gas and air ratio, giving more fuel to the environment, bringing up the temperature a little faster now.

"So, can someone tell me why we had to go slow at the beginning of the firing? You'll probably remember from your homework."

The first years looked at each other sheepishly, and I shook my head. No one ever did the homework. Claire piped up, "We want to burn off moisture in the glazes."

"Thanks, Claire! Do your homework, people. It's important." I shook my finger at them and looked surly for a moment, only partly joking around. "The next important temperature to slow down at is 1063. Anyone remember what that's called?"

Silence. "Claire?"

"Quartz inversion."

"Thank you, Claire." I shook my head and looked at Ben. He shrugged his shoulders as if to ask what else I would expect.

We all got back to the studio to work until the next turn up. I set my phone for hour increments. The next time my alarm went off, we repeated the process. We got pretty high pretty fast, eased through quartz inversion and then blasted the gas. It was nearly 6:00 by this time.

James came into the studio looking charmingly out of place in his clean jeans and tucked in baby blue oxford. At least the top button was undone. He scanned the room, finding me, but not before Brynn, another senior clay major spotted him. "Hi there. Can I help you?" she asked in a slightly more suggestive way than I would have expected her to with a stranger. I'm pretty sure she batted her eyelashes.

James looked a little uncomfortable. "I've found what I'm looking for, thanks," he answered, nodding at me. I smiled. He really was objectively good looking. Brynn's jaw dropped as she saw that James was referring to me. My lifetime of insecurity had been fueled by moments like this: attractive girls who didn't mean to be mean, silently referring to the Ugly Duckling. I took a deep breath and vowed to remain unperturbed.

I noticed Brent glaring at James, and then at me. I realized that having James in here today was extremely bad timing. It was awkward and probably cruel after the revelatory conversation I'd had with Brent earlier. I certainly wouldn't have planned it this way, but I had failed to connect the dots. Brent slammed his toolbox closed and stalked over to the sink to wash up. James didn't register any notice, he kept his sultry eyes fixed on me as he moved across the room.

He leaned over and kissed me on the cheek.

I blushed and said, "Hi."

"Hi." He lifted the bags he was carrying and said, "Thai?"

"Perfection. Thank you. I've got one more turn up to do before we reduce. Want to see?"

"Sure!"

I got up from my wheel and crossed the room, noticing the uncertain glances from students as I passed them. I called out, "One more turn up before reduction. Come on!"

The students headed towards the kiln room while James and I brought up the rear. Brent walked past the group of students and towards me. As soon as he had seen James, he had packed up and was ready to leave. As our paths neared, I thought he was going to pass me by and give me the cold shoulder, but instead he grabbed my arm hard and said quietly, "Now it all makes sense!" His expression was wild and livid.

Brent's anger was totally disconcerting and James reacted instantly. He reached out to separate Brent from me, his face contorted into an unrecognizable mask of ferocity and anger. "Don't touch her," he said in a low, dangerous voice, his muscular body now between Brent and me.

Brent scowled at him and with one more intensely terrifying look of hatred aimed at me, he stormed out of the studio. The rest of the students had already reached the kiln room, so at least I was spared the horrified looks I would have otherwise gotten. I was shaking with anger at Brent's audacity and was having a hard time slowing down my racing heartbeat. How could he have professed his love for me one minute and been transformed into a jealous maniac the next?

James asked, "Are you OK?" His expression was one of deep concern.

"Yeah. I've got a lot to tell you. It's been an eventful day."

"Looks like it."

"Later," I said, steeling myself as best I could and not stomping off to the kiln room. I tried my best to hide my emotion. We repeated the turn-up procedure from earlier, this time letting some of the first years take over on the gas valves, under the supervision of Claire and Ben. I watched the flame color, looked for the pyrometric cones to tell me what the internal temperature was, noted that the first cone had fallen and the second was getting ready. "Reduction in 45," I stated. "See the cone? The 8 is down, the 9 is ready. Not long now."

We replaced the stoppers in the peepholes so the kiln didn't get a draft, and we returned to the studio. I could tell people were excited. Reduction is pretty fun and worth getting excited about, I thought.

James looked interested in the firing, although he couldn't hide his anxiety about the incident with Brent. I didn't want to bore him with a technical lecture on kiln environments—I gave enough of those as it was. Instead, we hit the Thai food pretty hard. I invited the students to join us, and most did. Free food was always popular among artists. I introduced them to James, who was very personable, winning people over left and right. I was thankful that Brent was long gone at this point so as not to have him glowering at us from the corner. The food was great but I was antsy. I was ready to get past the reduction and hang out with James.

"Time's up," I declared at exactly seven. The remaining students came into the kiln room with me, followed by James. I started giving directions, we turned off the lights and in the darkness, Max glowed with an otherworldly, primal beauty. I loved this process.

I asked the first years to team with the experienced students so they could learn what to do. On my command, they slowly closed the damper, starving the kiln environment of fuel. The flames lapped out of the peepholes, changing color from deep red and yellow to orange and green. They licked the kiln bricks, fanning out, begging for air. They were alive, predatory, desperate. They forced their way through every crack and crevice in the kiln, along the edges of the door and between loose bricks, desperate for any oxygen they could consume. I monitored the cones, everything looked stable. I started my timer again and we watched in silence as the process continued. Every few minutes we adjusted the gas, watched the flame colors and strength and hoped for the best reduction possible. I had a ton of work in this firing, and so did the older students. When there's so much riding on such a subjective process, there is a lot of pressure. We wouldn't know for sure that things had gone well until the kiln was cool.

When it was time, we opened the dampers again, bringing oxygen back into the kiln, saying goodbye to the wild green flames. Over the next hour, the kiln would rise in temperature to cone 10 and the firing would be complete. Then, we would shut down the gas, close all the dampers and let the kiln cool down slowly. It was important that no one open even one peephole during cool down because of the possibility of flash cooling, which would cause dunting. I reminded everyone and went so far as to put up a sign warning people against messing with our kiln environment.

Ben said, "I can do the final turn off, if you want. You don't have to stay. I'm going to be here a while anyway."

"You sure?" I asked, feeling a little jolt of joy at this unexpected gift of time.

"Yeah. I'm set."

"Don't forget to close all the dampers and peepholes."

"I won't."

"I'll check in later. Promise to answer the phone?"

"Yes, mom. I'll answer the phone."

"I love when you call me mom." I smiled at him wickedly and he laughed. "Thanks, Ben. I appreciate it. And thanks for earlier."

James and I cleaned up our Thai food, leaving the leftovers for scavengers. I put all my work away, glad to have gotten something done earlier and we walked out together.

"That was really cool," James said when we were outside.

"Thanks. I think so, but I just assume most people will think it's kind of boring."

"Not at all. When else do you get to be around something so powerful? It's kind of a primal excitement, watching fire act like that. Thanks for letting me come."

"Thanks for wanting to." I was still feeling antsy, having a hard time shaking the feeling Brent's anger had left within me.

"So. That was a pretty intense encounter earlier. Are you OK?"

"Yeah, I'm fine," I lied. Trying to infuse humor in what was the least amusing situation I could imagine, I continued, "I suppose I should have expected some kind of reaction, after having extracted Brent's heart, stomping on it and ultimately kicking it across the room earlier."

"What are you talking about?"

"He declared his love for me. He had the courage to be honest about his feelings. He even brought me to his painting studio and showed me his work—which was intensely disturbing, by the way— as though to prove a point about how deep his feelings for me were. He wanted me to see that as artists, we both have some under-standing about the universe that links us together. And I told him to take a hike."

"You wouldn't have been cruel to him, what did you actually say?"

"I told him that I was his teacher and that I cannot ethically date one of my students, nor would I even if he wasn't. I didn't tell him about you."

"Why should you? It's none of his business."

"Because a couple of hours later, you show up with food and kisses. It was like pouring salt in his wounds. I should have thought about it before you got there, I just didn't think of the repercussions. I feel really bad."

"Elwyn," James said, stopping abruptly on the sidewalk, "You didn't mean to hurt him. You know that. Besides, he overreacted. There was no call for him to grab you like that. It was very disre-spectful."

"Never the less, I shouldn't have kissed you in front of him. It was unkind."

"I'm sorry. I had no idea."

"How could you?"

He studied me with a sidelong glance as we walked. "He really makes me nervous," James said. "What's his problem?"

"Don't know," I admitted. "I think he's a little unstable. Ben heard the whole conversation, so at least there was a witness."

'So weird. Do you want to get a drink or something?"

"Yeah. That sounds good."

We headed down to a bar called The Hunt and Alpine Club and ordered some esoterically named drinks. We sat together in their little red room, crowded together on the bench in the corner. I let myself relax for the first time all day. I leaned back against the wall, my leg touching James' leg, our hands intertwined. He shifted closer to me and I breathed in his scent. I suddenly wanted so badly to kiss him, but we were surrounded by people. I breathed in deeply and exhaled, enjoying the drink I'd ordered. It had absinthe in it, which I'd never had the pleasure of tasting. I felt it flood impishly through my veins, creating a strange sense of security, driving out the dark feelings that Brent had sown. I was happy and the unfamiliarity of that feeling was disconcerting. When the waiter came by, we ordered another round of drinks and settled back against the wall, nestling into each other.

James leaned closer to me and brushed some of my hair aside, as though to whisper something in my ear. Instead, he kissed me. He trailed tender kisses down the side of my face as I sat with my eyes closed. I opened them lazily and turned my face toward him, and he kissed me again, on the lips this time. It sent warmth and energy and a divine wellbeing through my body. I was feeling euphoric and fearless and wild.

"Do you think that this is why so many people are unhappy?" I asked, after we separated a little bit.

"Because they kiss too much in public?" James was playful and I rolled my eyes.

"No, that's not what I mean. What I mean is maybe people are unhappy because they're searching for a loved one they can't find and don't know they're missing. Maybe happiness is setting those urgent desires to rest."

"Maybe," he replied quizzically. "I've had a lifetime to think about this. Do you want to know my theory?"

"I do."

"I think that we're all entangled and we don't know it because we can't quantify the force that is entangling us."

"Entangled? Like quantum entanglement?"

"Yes. Exactly!"

"You are a physics guy, aren't you?"

"Ha! I told you! Well, quantum entanglement is a force that we have just started being able to observe the effect of. But the actual force that entangles particles to begin with? It's still a mystery! Everything is connected, Elwyn. Just look—if the early protozoa had not divided in a certain way, we would never have evolved into human forms. If our star had not coalesced into the sun we love, life would never have bloomed on this planet. We are purely a piece of a thermodynamic puzzle. Time's arrow moves only forward and we're along for the ride, our lives causalities of an immutable past, yet linked for the immeasurable future. Do you want to know what else I think?"

"Go for it."

"I think the connecting force is love."

I thought for a moment, with a bemused expression. Finally, I answered, "So, love is a force so strong that it acts upon us at the quantum level?"

"Not only that, it holds the entire universe together. When we absorb love, or act with love, we strengthen something elemental. When we act with hate, we are working against that elemental force."

"Maybe hate is an elemental force as well. Maybe they're equal and opposite forces in the universe and that when you're entangled from love, you act with love. If you're entangled with hate, you act with hate."

"God, that makes so much sense."

"Does it? Really?" I was beginning to get slightly defiant. "It doesn't make sense at all!"

"You just told me that you think we're happier when we find people we're connected to through love."

"Yeah, but it's not physics. It's more, I don't know, more abstract than that!"

"Of course it's abstract. That's what physics is!" He was getting passionate now. "Abstract forces created and drive the universe. With entanglement, when a force acts upon one entangled particle, it has the same effect on the other entangled particle, regardless of distance. *Regardless* of distance! That's insane. It has to be a force that looks abstract from our point of view. Just like gravity must have looked to Isaac Newton. Why can't love be that kind of force? We can't see gravity, we can't see magnetism, we can't see love."

"We can measure gravity, James. We can see its effects pretty obviously."

"But before we understood it, it was just taken for granted and no one thought about it. That's how we view love right now. We just haven't put the pieces of the puzzle together yet."

"We have," I returned, looking at him closely. His cheeks were flushed, his eyes sparkled, his passion was inspiring. I was wildly attracted to him on such an elemental level that I thought his theory might just be right. I smiled suggestively.

"So you're happy right now?"

"I am happy right now. I want everyone to be happy," I said childishly. I finished off my second drink and seriously considered ordering another. "Three soup bowls," I mused, enigmatically, ready to change the subject.

"What?" I was really taking James on a tour of my labyrinthine mind, its twists and turns like those of a hedge maze.

"Three soup bowls are what I would need to sell to cover the cost of these drinks. It's fine, but just kind of funny to think about. I'd like another, and then you'll have to carry me home." I let my finger trail suggestively up his thigh, a move so bold I could hardly believe I'd done it.

"Maybe I should just carry you home right now?"

"Not yet. Let's be wild and daring."

"Wild and daring. What do you have in mind?"

"We could climb up a fire escape and gallivant along the rooftops. They're all connected, just like your universe."

"I don't really want to spend the remainder of the evening in a jail cell. Other thoughts?"

"How about a ride on a water taxi?"

"We don't live on an island, Elwyn."

"I know that, James. I just like being out on the water. Now that would cost two platters and a few mugs, but might be worth it to have the sea air send my hair flying into knots."

"Another night, Elwyn."

"Why do you call me Elwyn?" I suddenly demanded. "Everyone else calls me Derrin, like I told you."

"Do you mind?"

"I don't know," I replied, fuzzily. "Maybe a little. I've never really liked the name. And Derrin's what I'm used to."

"Elwyn is a graceful name. I looked up its meaning, you know."

"You did not!" I actually hit his arm like a playful schoolgirl.

"Wise friend or Elf friend."

"Well, I'm not exactly wise, but I *have* known a lot of elves."

"I'm not your first? I'm hurt!" We both laughed, acting as silly as we felt. A moment later, though, James' tone turned serious. "I think you are wiser than you give yourself credit for. You just use humor to circumvent the truth."

"Back to truth, are we?"

"Always."

"OK. Truth: I am letting myself go farther with you faster than I have ever done in my life and I'm terrified."

"I thought you wanted to be wild and daring." He ran his hand down my back and rested it on my hip.

"For me, this *is* wild and daring. We met just days ago, for Christ's sake. I'm just trying to tell the truth, James. Don't make it harder. Your turn."

"Well, let me think. OK. Truth: I'm scared too. Loss hurts and I don't want to lose you. Ever."

I let the vastness of that statement sink in for a while. "Ever. That's big. Really big." I looked at his eyes, captivating and deep, and asked, "Are we crazy?"

"Maybe, Elwyn. But I don't care. I've waited lifetimes to feel like this. Lifetimes!"

He pulled me in for another kiss, this one full of longing and desperation. I wanted to be alone with him, to explore the possibilities laden in that kiss, to feel his body against mine and to let my mind free itself of the burden of fear. I wanted to let myself love him. Then my phone rang.

It jolted us from our reverie. It was the studio number and a deep chill ran through my body. I shuddered as I answered it, apologizing to James with my expression. Fear crept back in as I imagined all the horrors lurking on the other end of the line.

"Elwyn here," I answered, realizing at once that no one at the studio would have the slightest clue who the hell 'Elwyn' is.

"Who? I'm looking for Professor…"

I cut Ben off in mid-sentence. "It's me, Ben. It's Derrin. Sorry. What's up?"

"Um," he started, sounding confused. "Max is cooling too fast. The dampers were pulled out when I checked just now. I don't know how it happened. I swear I closed them when I turned off the gas."

"Shit," I answered, the dread I had felt seeping through my body palpable in the air around me. "Did you close the dampers again? I'll be right there. We have to keep it safe through the 1100's. Shouldn't dive this early. This is bad." I hung up.

"I have to go back to the studio," I stated quietly, wistful that our romantic moment had been interrupted. "I'm so sorry. I guess I should have stayed."

"Is everything OK?" James looked genuinely concerned.

"I don't know. The dampers were wide open. I should have stayed; I don't know what is wrong with me. I need to babysit tonight." I sighed deeply and looked regretfully at James. "I'm glad I didn't have that third drink, I guess."

"Next time, Elwyn."

We gathered our coats and my bag and paid our tab. This time, I insisted on paying for myself. "Three bowls," James said, shaking his head. "I want to see more of your work."

"I've got some in my office and a little at home; you'll see it." I smiled at him, wishing that the moment on the bench, in the weird light of the tiny room, with the funny drinks and suggestive looks could last forever. I wished that James' last kiss could last forever. I sighed again and looked back to our spot as we left. It had been immediately occupied by an amorous couple who were putting our little public display of affection to shame.

James walked me back up to the studio without even offering. It was just a given for him to escort me there, as though it were part of his code to always see a lady safely on her way. As we walked, I tried to explain why any sudden drop in temperature would be a problem in a kiln the size of Max. He listened patiently, asking all the right questions.

"I'd like you to teach me to make something out of clay," he said finally.

"What, like in *Ghost*? No way. I'm not into the Demi Moore-sexy-clay-scene. It was too stupid."

"No! God. That's not what I had in mind."

"Good. I was beginning to question my judgment regarding dating you."

"Are we dating?" he asked, slowing his pace, still holding my hand and swinging me gently to face him.

"I... Um..." I began, stuttering.

"I love the idea," he said, saving me from myself.

"I don't know what we're doing. Dating, courting, getting to know each other, whatever it is, I um... I like it." I smiled shyly.

"I like it too," he said, pulling me in for one more kiss.

"I've got to go," I said finally, turning away, towards the studio building.

"I thought I'd come with you," he stated. "If that's OK."

"Why would you wanna to do that? I don't want to bore you."

"I won't be bored. I'll answer emails or make something elegant and inspiring out of clay. I am a big boy, I can entertain myself."

He smiled at me with such genuine affection that I couldn't say no.

"OK, but leave whenever you feel burning boredom searing the back of your brain." I smiled.

"It's a deal."

A moment later, we walked into Mayhem.

Ben and Claire were in a full-blown screaming match when James and I entered the studio.

"You must have left them open, Ben! How could you be so stupid?"

"I didn't, Claire! I had everything closed up tight. I would have had to open the dampers on purpose and I didn't do anything."

"God, all my work is in there. A whole semester of ideas. My senior thesis."

"Calm down, Claire," I said authoritatively from the doorway. I took off my coat and hung it up with my bag on the hooks at the door.

Ben and Claire stared me down and then looked at James. Ben couldn't help it. He rolled his eyes.

"Let me have a look. Claire, you and I both know that Ben wouldn't open the dampers during cooling. He knows better."

"Then how the fuck did it happen?" she spat.

"Let's go look and see." I mustered all my calm and walked towards the kiln room.

I examined the gas valves, checked that the dampers and peep holes were secure, looked at the temperature gage and shook my head. I was perplexed. Nothing was broken, everything looked fine.

"Thanks for noticing the damper was open. You probably saved the firing with quick thinking and vigilance," I told Ben. "Let's hope you caught it in time. We'll know soon enough."

"God!" Claire yelled, putting her hands into her hair and pulling at fistfuls. She turned on her heel and stalked out of the room.

"Was anyone else in here that you saw?" I asked Ben, after the tempest had subsided.

"No. Just me and the Goddess of Anger, there," he said gesturing to where Claire had just exited the room.

"Go easy on her. She's right, everything she needs to graduate is in that kiln."

"But I didn't..."

"I know you didn't," I replied firmly. "I trust you completely, or I wouldn't have left."

I stared at Max and chewed my thumb, a nervous habit I'd had since childhood. "Did you leave the studio at any time?"

"Yeah, I went to the bathroom a couple of times and grabbed a slice at Otto at around 10:00. When I got back, no one was here. I checked on everything and that's when I noticed that the dampers were out. What the fuck happened, Derrin?"

I took a breath, unsure whether I should voice my concerns yet. "Did you hear the conversation I had with Brent earlier before we went upstairs, by any chance?"

Ben looked sheepish. "I heard enough," he said quietly, glancing at James.

"He knows," I said, gesturing to James. "So you gathered enough information to know that Brent has a thing for me."

"Yes. And I heard you tell him to fuck off. I heard it all, I guess."

"OK. Can you write up a report with security right now about the incident? It's just a hunch, but maybe Brent was mad enough to do something like this."

"That fucker! That total asshole!" Ben looked as outraged as he sounded. His eyes bugged out and he had a wild, angry air. I realized I'd never seen this mild-mannered sculptor angry before.

"I don't know for sure that he did anything wrong. I'm not ready to make that leap. But I want to cover our bases. Go give a statement to security. I'll go down after you and check out the security footage to see if he was in here while you were gone. This sucks. I've never had anything like this happen before. I know it wasn't an accident. Un-fucking-believable."

Ben shook his head and I could feel James seething in the corner.

After Ben had gone downstairs and I had calmed my breathing and checked on the kiln again to make sure the temperature was stable, James came over to me and laid a hand on my shoulder.

"What would have happened if Ben hadn't noticed?"

"Everything in the kiln would have split and broken. It's called dunting, in clay terms. If it cools too fast, it cracks."

"You really think it was Brent?"

"I hate to think ill of anyone, but the look of hate that he gave me earlier was downright scary. I hurt his feelings and he's really angry. He also knows enough about clay to know this would be devastating. But to ruin everyone's work out of spite for me? What kind of person does that? It's so fucked up."

I took a couple more deep breaths, locked the back door so I would be able to see everyone who came and went through the studio. "At least Ben was being vigilant. There's a chance that things will survive. If he hadn't noticed, it would have been total ruin."

James hugged me and said, "If he'd do this to the kiln, what might he try to do to you?"

I hadn't let my mind wander down that thorny path yet. "I don't know, James. I haven't thought about it. I don't want to think about it."

When Ben returned, I walked down to security. The night guard's name was Andy, and he was a sullen sort, but good at his job. I asked him if Ben had talked to him. "I took a full report, Professor Derringer."

"Please, call me Derrin."

"OK, Derrin. Do you want to give a report now?"

I told him everything that had happened with Brent earlier in the day and then I quietly voiced my suspicions about the kiln. I expected a look of shock to appear on Andy's ruddy face, but it didn't. "Can I see the security footage for between 8:45 and 9:30?"

"Sure, it will take me a little while to pull it together."

"Flag it. Actually, flag the whole day's footage in the ceramics studio, if you don't mind. Maybe we have footage of the confrontation earlier. I want as much documentation as possible."

"OK, Derrin," Andy answered efficiently.

"Andy, please keep this all confidential right now. I don't want word getting around about any of it yet. Monday, I will file the reports with the office."

Andy nodded, and that was all the reassurance I required.

"Phone up to the studio when you have the footage. I'd like to see it for myself. I'll be here all night."

He nodded again. "Thanks, Andy," I said on my way out.

About a half an hour later, the phone in the studio rang. Andy had the footage and he wanted me to see it.

"I'll be down in a second." I hung up and turned to Ben, who looked every bit as tired as I felt. "You mind coming down and looking at the footage with me?"

"What about the kiln?"

"James, will you watch the kiln?"

"Of course, Elwyn."

"Elwyn," Ben said, shaking his head. "You're so *not* an Elwyn."

I smiled as I followed him out of the room.

The footage was shocking. Brent had unabashedly entered the studio while Ben was getting pizza, marched straight through, into the kiln room, and back out moments later with a smug smile on his face. It didn't prove that he had sabotaged the kiln, but it was damning evidence, nevertheless.

"Derrin, do you think he actually tampered with the kiln?" asked Andy.

Ben turned to look at me, anticipating my answer.

"It looks that way. Ben, this is the only time you left?"

"You know it, Derrin. God, why would he do this?"

"Angry people make bad decisions," replied Andy, shaking

his head.

"Should we confront him?"

"We don't have evidence of his actions in the kiln room, but he doesn't know that. Chances are, he had no idea that the studio was under surveillance, so we could show him the footage we have and see how he reacts." Andy thought like a police officer, and I appreciated it.

"I want to talk to President Baxter and get her opinion on the matter before we make the wrong decision. As I said, just keep this between us for now, act as though nothing has happened and on Monday when we open the kiln, we will watch his reaction. If nothing else, it will be amusing to see the shock of disappointment that we foiled his plans."

"Foiled his plans?" Ben laughed. "Sounds like a '60's comic book."

"Don't make fun of me, Ben," I scolded jokingly. "I've never had a real life villain to deal with before! This is new to me. Totally messed up."

"Totally," Ben replied.

"I will call President Baxter tomorrow. Get some rest, Ben. I'll look after things for the evening."

"OK. I'll just go clean up."

"Andy, in the meantime, can I see the footage of the conversation from earlier in the day? Did you find that too?"

"Yep."

He cued it up as Ben left and watching the silent footage was uncomfortable. Brent's body language was so aggressive and mine was so passive. I put my hands up in a "stop" position more than once. I took several steps backwards. I looked just like I had felt: like I was playing defense.

"It's so weird to watch myself like that," I said to Andy. "I look threatened."

"You were threatened, ma'am. This punk is threatening your safety and your career. We will handle it, don't worry."

I turned and looked at Andy, at his strong jaw and dark eyes. He had a naturally protective bearing that made him so good at what he did. "Thank you so much. Can we put a camera in the kiln room too, just for my own peace of mind? Or maybe locks on the door?"

"I'll see to installing both myself tomorrow."

"Again, thank you," I said. "I feel safer already." I smiled at him with genuine gratitude and left.

James was waiting for me alone in the studio when I returned. He had a partially shaped piece of clay in his hands. I smiled wanly; it was late and I was taxed. "So?" he asked. "Did the footage show anything incriminating?"

"Yes and no. It shows him entering the studio and the kiln room while Ben was out, but we don't have a camera in the kiln room. He was in there for a few minutes and then left looking smug. I'm just going to present all the information to the college president tomorrow and let her handle it. We got the conversation on video too, but no sound. My body language says it all, though. He was very aggressive. I don't know what she'll do about the kiln, but judging by his interactions with me, I don't think he'll be in my class anymore." I sat down on a bench next to James and leaned back against the wall. I took a deep breath. "This sucks," I said.

"Yeah," he replied, taking my hand. "It does. Are you OK?"

"Yeah," I replied, sounding stronger than I felt. I closed my eyes and let myself feel the warmth of James' fingers wrapped up in mine. "I need to stay here tonight," I said. "I'll call you tomorrow."

"What? No way. I'm staying with you. No way you're staying here alone tonight."

"Listen," I replied sternly. "This is *my* studio. This is *my* college. No one will make me afraid in my own environment. Andy is on high alert, don't worry."

"I'm staying, Elwyn. No argument. I want to."

"Fine," I said with mock exasperation. "I'm going to work, though. It's going to be a long night."

"Cool. I'll keep working on my sculpture of you."

I laughed and squeezed his hand. "I can't wait to see it finished."

James and I worked and played in the studio for hours, getting punchier and sillier the more tired we got. By the early hours of the morning, we were bleary-eyed and laughing uncontrollably. I can't imagine what Andy thought, watching us all night, but I hope he thought it was at least mildly amusing.

Ben returned at 7:00 a.m. with coffee for the three of us. I appreciated how considerate it was of him to come so early to relieve me. He smiled at James when he handed him his cup. "I knew you'd stay. Did she try to talk you out of it?"

James laughed and said, "Of course she did!"

"Glad you didn't listen. It makes me feel better. You're a good egg, Derrin, but you're kind of naive. Like a little kid, I guess. No offense."

"None taken, Ben. I guess I am naive. I never want to think the worst of people."

"That's part of what makes you who you are, though," interjected James thoughtfully.

"Go home, Derrin. I'll keep an eye on things for a while."

"OK, Ben. I think we're past the danger zone with the temperature, but I'd feel better if someone was here. Thank you so much. I'll come back for a while this afternoon to check on things, but we'll crack Max tomorrow morning, early."

"Awesome."

James and I collected our things and left, waving to Andy on the way out. Andy nodded professionally. We stepped out into the brisk morning air, breathing deeply, feeling restored. "May I treat you to a bagel for staying with me all night? A reward for good behavior?"

"Thanks," James replied. "I'll walk you home after. You need some sleep."

"It's a plan."

Bagels in hand, we headed to my loft a little while later. We arrived and went upstairs to eat. I unlocked my upstairs door and motioned for James to come in. He looked around with wide eyes. The morning sun was flooding into the space, creating the warmth that had drawn me to the loft in the first place. I showed him around. He picked up objects and books, examining everything like a little kid. I showed him the sliding doors that led to the small balcony terrace. By summer's end, it would be full of plants.

"I love this place," James said in awe.

"Thanks. Me too. I had an image in my mind of the perfect place to live in the city and this was it. I love the beams and the high ceilings and the wall of windows. It's home."

We felt silly from being so overtired. We joked around and giggled like children, finally eating our bagels. I felt so connected to James and I didn't want him to leave.

Finally, I mustered my bravery and said, "I'm going to sleep now. You should go home and rest too."

He hesitated a moment. "I still don't want to leave you," he returned, quietly, looking down at his hands.

"I don't want you to leave either, but you must feel as gross as I do."

"Let's just take a nap and then I'll go home when you go back to the studio."

I looked into his azure eyes, the morning sunlight was coming through them sideways, illuminating them in an otherworldly way. His face was so prepossessing, sleepy and perfect. I took his hand and led him towards my bed. We fell asleep in each other's arms, flooded in sunshine, enveloped in wellbeing.

By the time I returned to the studio, it was after one. Ben looked exhausted but now there was a lock on the kiln room door and a camera within. I felt better immediately. "Go home, Ben. I'll see you tomorrow. Thanks for being the guardian of the studio these past two days. It would have been total disaster without you."

"It would have, wouldn't it? See you tomorrow. Don't open Max without me."

"Wouldn't dream of it."

Students floated in and out of the studio all day. By the time I left, I had gotten a ton of my own work ready to fire. I loaded up one of the smaller, unnamed kilns and set it to fire automatically. It was a relief to lock the door behind me. I had made a sign for the kiln room door regarding the "new hours" and left my cares behind.

CHAPTER SIX

"One Moment in Annihilation's Waste,
   One Moment, of the Well of Life to taste -
   The Stars are setting and the Caravan
   Starts for the Dawn of Nothing - Oh, make haste!"

THE RUBAIYAT OF OMAR KHAYYAM
TRANSLATED BY EDWARD FITZGERALD

I walked down the street, heading back toward my neighborhood as someone came up behind me. I jumped, startled, and tripped on the loose brick. A hand grabbed my arm as I fell, only just keeping me off the ground this time. It was Brent and a wave of panic flooded through me as I stepped away, disengaging myself from his grasp.

"You OK?" he asked.

"Yes," I answered, feeling flustered and annoyed.

"Didn't mean to startle you."

"Didn't you, though?" I sounded more confrontational than I

had intended to. I was angry and exhausted and wasn't expecting to see Brent until the following day. "What, were you waiting for me out here?"

"No. Yes. I just wanted to see you."

"Why, Brent? I think we both made ourselves clear last night."

"You look awful. Rough night?" His tone made me think that he was trying to get me to say something about the kiln sabotage. I was tired, but not tired enough to give that away.

"Yep. I'm really tired. I'll see you tomorrow. We'll open Max bright and early if you want to join."

I was trying to hide my panicky nervousness, but all I wanted to do was run from this man. He tried to corner me into stopping by stepping in front of me.

"Derrin," he began, his eyes belying some animal urgency underneath that I could sense in my gut. "Please wait. I wanted to talk to you."

"Brent, I don't have anything else to say. I'll see you tomorrow." I sidestepped him and waved over my shoulder as I double-timed it down the street.

I didn't want to give anything away about the kiln and I was too tired to think straight in a conversation. I was relieved to see that he hadn't followed me when I turned a corner to head down to my street. I kept checking behind me as I walked, wondering if I should go a different route just in case. In the end, I went around the block, didn't see him anywhere, and headed into my building.

I bolted my door, took a shower and went straight to bed. I was toast.

When I awoke it was after 11:00 p.m. I checked my phone and saw two messages from James, the first telling me he'd had fun with me despite the circumstances, and the other saying goodnight. It had been written an hour before, so I thought that must mean he had gone to bed. I texted back that I was thankful to him for keeping me in good humor all weekend and that I would talk to him tomorrow.

I lay in bed after that, intentionally thinking not of the ceramics or student related drama of the past few days, but of the strange and almost immediate connection that James and I were in the thrall of. I hadn't stopped to analyze it recently, so I spent some time thinking about how much had changed between us in such a short time. I felt myself drawn to him more and more and I felt a distinct discomfort when we were not together. It was like having a youthful crush, where you just want to be with that other person non-stop. I didn't want to become a teenager all over again, nor did I want to treat this relationship immaturely. I knew that my feelings for James were intense, but I was barely ready to admit that fact to myself, let alone anyone else.

I fell asleep again and dreamed of dark water, lapping against a dock, distant shores illuminated with dancing lights, the sound of laughter wafting across a wide lake, a million stars reflected in the rippling water, like entangled souls searching for their mates.

I woke up with a jolt. I was disoriented and hot, twisted in my sheets and full of dread. It took a moment before the reality of why I would feel like this hit me. I lay back down, put my hands over my face and groaned. I would have to act a part today when we opened Max. I would have to pretend that nothing happened. I would have to discreetly watch Brent's expression as we assessed the firing. What was going to happen? How on earth would I deal with it? I do not have the right constitution for intrigue, I decided.

CHAPTER SEVEN

"With Earth's first Clay They did the Last Man's knead,
    And then of the Last Harvest sow'd the Seed:
Yea, the first Morning of Creation wrote
What the Last Dawn of Reckoning shall read."

THE RUBAIYAT OF OMAR KHAYYAM
TRANSLATED BY EDWARD FITZGERALD

I calmed myself down with some deep breaths, took a shower and made a large pot of coffee. I ate a quick hard boiled egg and toast and headed up towards Congress Street and to my fate.

I had emailed President Baxter the evening before, explaining the events of the weekend, and she had asked me to meet her at 7:30 a.m.. I headed to her office. It was a cloudy day, in keeping with my mood.

"Hi, Derrin," she said kindly when I entered her office. "Sorry about the unpleasantness." Olivia Baxter had been president of the College of Art for my entire tenure there. She was not only a great leader, but a good friend. Her frame was Rubenesque, curvaceous and comfortable. Her dark hair and velvety deep ebony skin belied her age, which must have been past sixty. Her outfits always had a burst of color somewhere, and her office was as put together as she was, pale grey walls, pale yellow velvet settee and simply framed modern art on the walls. One floor to ceiling window framed her and her desk in light.

"Hi, Olivia. Me too. Thanks for meeting."

"I reviewed the footage that Andy was kind enough to supply, and I read your and Ben's statements. I have to say, although this sort of thing rarely happens, you're pretty lucky to have had a witness and some video footage. It often comes down to hearsay and that puts a professor in a tenuous position."

My stomach lurched at the thought. "That happens?" Maybe I really was as naive as Ben had said.

"Unfortunately, it does, albeit not often. In my eight years, it's happened twice. Different circumstances, both messy. Glad we've got a witness this time."

"God, me too. It so easily could have happened when I was alone."

"So, we're going to allow you to open the kiln with the boy in the room to gage his reaction. After that, I will have a meeting at which Andy, the head of security, the head of admissions and the head of HR will be in attendance. We will question Brent and show him the footage. We will take a statement. We do not, however, have enough evidence to expel him, unless he confesses to the sabotage before we reveal that we don't have footage from the kiln room on the night in question. We do have enough evidence, with Ben's statement, to remove him from your class for the remainder of the semester, if you wish, based on his advances towards you. I will not expect you to allow him back into the studio."

"Thank you, Olivia. This sounds like the best outcome I could expect."

"You must be anxious about it all. Don't worry. We've got everything covered."

"Good. I'm going to go open the kiln now. I hope everything made it!"

"Good luck, Derrin. Thank you for your level-headed handling of the situation this weekend."

"Keep me posted, Olivia."

"I will."

I closed her door and headed downstairs, dread ebbing back into my heart. When I entered the studio, most of the students who had helped fire the kiln on Saturday were there for the opening. Everyone was excited and invested. Ben and I caught each other's glance. He looked as nervous as I felt.

"Hi, everyone," I greeted them. "Time for the great unveiling."

I sauntered back towards the kiln room, noticing that Brent was hanging back a bit, watching. I had a great idea, suddenly. "Someone want to film the opening for me? I can put it on the website."

Brynn offered, taking out her phone. I positioned her so that she would get Brent into the frame. The moment of truth: we cranked open Max's sliding door, inch by inch. Nothing was obviously broken. Everyone cheered as they saw the shelves stacked with gloriously intact forms. I started breathing again, having held my breath as I looked at the work. I smiled. Loads of lovely color, a great reduction. I glanced up at Ben, who looked as relieved as I felt, and then scanned the room for Brent's reaction. His eyes narrowed, he looked at me with ferocity in his eyes, turned and stormed out of the room.

"Brynn, if you can email me that footage right now, I'd appreciate it."

"Sure, Derrin!"

Everyone started unloading the kiln, talking excitedly, appreciating the beauty of each work they handled. Bowls with reds and blues, sculptures in shiny black, everything whole and undamaged. I walked over to Ben, stretched out my hand, and said, "Well done, superhero. You saved the day."

He smiled, looking incredibly relieved. We both shook our heads a little and laughed. I let the kids unload the kiln and got everything ready for my first class that would start at nine.

95

I texted James that the kiln had come out just fine and he was relieved on my behalf. He would be in Boston overnight, he reminded me, but wanted to meet for dinner on Tuesday evening. I agreed.

By the afternoon, Brent had been escorted into the studio to clean out his things. He didn't say a word to me. His amorous feelings had clearly transmuted into seething hatred, which was rather terrifying to feel. I didn't want to stick around after that.

It reminded me of an explosion I once saw. I was sitting in a diner in Boston's leather district, down the street from my first loft, almost ten years ago. My friends and I were eating a late dinner when suddenly, a manhole outside the window exploded in a fireball thirty feet tall and twenty feet wide. I felt the burn of the fire on my face through the glass. My friend Jeanine actually yelled, "Hit the deck!" The entire restaurant full of people threw themselves on the floor and, when it was determined to be safe, evacuated the premises. I was interviewed by a TV newswoman a short while later, and the only thing I could say was "That was fucking crazy." Thus began and ended my illustrious TV career. But it really was crazy and so was this. I felt like I had witnessed Brent's better nature consumed in an explosion of anger and I could feel the heat on my face from across the room. I knew there would be aftermath—he would not let this go. My stomach sank as I realized that I would have to watch my back.

I decided I wanted to know more about Brent, so when I got home I called a friend of mine in the ceramics department at Rhode Island School of Design, where Brent had alluded to attending. My friend's name was Samuel. He was a potter, he had studied with a Japanese master potter for many years, and he was very knowledgeable. He was also hilarious. I respected and cared for Samuel deeply.

"Hey, Derrin," he said, his voice low and deep. "Long time. What's up?"

I could just picture him on the other line, his wild, long, dreadlocked hair, his dark toned skin, his warm eyes. He had barely changed in years. I was flooded with memories of all our times together.

"Hi, Samuel. How's everything?"

"Been good, lady. Been good. Things around here are heating up, little frenzy before the end of the year. You?"

"About the same," I said. "I've had an interesting week, though, and I wanted to ask you a question."

"Shoot, sweetie."

"Does the name Brent Talbot ring any bells?"

"Holy shit, does it. Not mixed up with that crazy fucker, are you?"

"God, what did he do there?"

"Aw, you know. Just your average lunatic. He stalked one of his fellow students to the point of putting her on anti-anxiety meds. He sabotaged her work. He has an obsessive streak a mile wide. Great artist, but he's a crazy mother fucker."

"Man, I wish I'd known all that four days ago."

"What did he do now?"

"I think I might just be his new fixation. He told me he had a thing for me and I told him he'd have to let it go because he's a student. He got super angry and sabotaged our firing."

"Which kiln?"

"Max. Big gas kiln, almost a total disaster. We had one very vigilant student that noticed that Brent had opened the dampers during cooling. It could have been horrible. I think they'll probably expel him if they hear about the RISD things..."

"Actually, it's all off the record. The girl never pressed charges and he left of his own accord after he ruined her state of mind. Mission accomplished. Hadn't heard anything about him since."

"Great."

"Keep out of that guy's way, Derrin. I mean it. He's bad news."

"Thank you for the advice. I miss you, Samuel."

"Miss you too, sweetie. Come visit sometime. Floyd always asks about you. Maybe summer?"

"Maybe summer."

"Good. I gotta go. Talk to you soon."

"Thanks, Samuel. Say hi to Floyd for me. Take care."

"You too."

I hung up feeling overwhelmed. Brent was a bigger lunatic than I had given him credit for. It was very scary. I called Olivia to tell her what Samuel had said.

"Can't do anything about that if there were no criminal charges filed and he wasn't expelled. I can, however, suggest that you file an order of protection against him, so that if he harasses you, he could face criminal charges."

"Good idea, Olivia. I'll do it tomorrow."

"Sorry you've got to deal with all this stress. It's never easy."

"Thanks for your support, though. I appreciate it."

I hung up feeling drained. I lay back on my couch and looked out the windows. The clouds hung low over the little slice of harbor I could see in the distance. I loved my little view, watching the tankers and tugs come and go along the working waterfront always made me feel peaceful. Life went on below, never stopping, despite whatever turmoil I might be in.

My stomach rumbled and again, I realized I had not eaten much during the day. I made a quick gnocchi dish with sun-dried tomatoes, kalamata olives, garlic and spinach. In ten minutes, dinner was on the table. I poured a glass of wine, a nice Cotes de Rhone, and settled in to eat. James texted a little while later to say he missed me. I missed him too.

I felt exhausted. The emotional energy I had expended over the past few days had really taken its toll. I finished my glass of wine, poured another, and did the dishes. I was ready to curl up with a book and fall asleep reading. Instead, I got down some old photo albums of my time in grad school. It's when I had met Samuel and Floyd, who were already a couple, as well as a bunch of wild guys whom I still felt great affection for. We had such fun together, climbing all over the rooftops of Brooklyn, scampering around like feral children, drinking way too much and falling in love with all the wrong people. Good times. The pictures, although they were a fun reminder, did not do the time justice, and memory fades. It made me feel melancholy. I was so responsible now, so grown up. Watching the antics of the kids I taught made me feel so old sometimes, even though thirty didn't seem that ancient. I closed up the books, finished my wine, brushed my teeth and went to bed.

I lay awake for a long time thinking, letting the images of my old friends float through my subconscious, trying to keep worries about Brent out of the reverie. It was no easy task.

I paid the price the following morning, as bleary eyed and lethargic, I greeted the dawn. As I brushed my teeth, I looked at myself in the mirror once more. I didn't love what I saw and the old, familiar aversion to my reflection bubbled back up. I studied the woman before me and found exhausted eyes whose expression was careworn. In a sudden flash, I imagined the mirror in shattered shards, my reflection fragmenting. It was a very disconcerting experience. I blinked my eyes but the image was gone as quickly as it had come. I got done as fast as I could, taking no extra pains with my toilette so as not to prolong this strange interaction with the mirror.

CHAPTER EIGHT

"Dreaming when Dawn's Left Hand was in the Sky
I heard a Voice within the Tavern cry,
"Awake, my Little ones, and fill the Cup
Before Life's Liquor in its Cup be dry."

THE RUBAIYAT OF OMAR KHAYYAM
TRANSLATED BY EDWARD FITZGERALD

A dvanced Topics was my 9:00 class on Tuesday. I took a few minutes, however, knowing it wouldn't matter too much if I was late. I needed a little time to relax and make some phone calls, rather than rush out the door. I thought about what to say to my friend Carly when I asked her for Angela the soul reader's number. It sounded so odd to say "soul reader," but if that's what she was, it would be good to talk with her.

Carly answered cheerfully, as always. "Hi! Why have you been ignoring me?"

"I haven't been ignoring you! I've been preoccupied."

"Yeah? With what? What could be more important than our love?"

I laughed. "Nothing. You're right. I'm terrible. How've you been?"

"Despondent, waiting for you to call!"

"Better now?"

"Much!"

"Good. I'll take you out for lunch this week. When are you free?"

"Today."

"Fine. It's got to be early—I need to be back at school by 1."

"I want something expensive!"

"Only the best for you, my love."

"That's what I want to hear. So what's up?"

"I need the number of your mom's friend. You know, the medium lady."

"The medium lady? You mean Angela? She's a soul reader, Derrin. Not a medium."

"Is there a difference?"

"I have no idea!"

We both laughed, Carly gave me the number and asked me why I wanted to talk to her.

"I can't say right now, but when I do, you'll have a story and a half."

"Fine! Keep your dark secrets. See if I care!"

"See you at lunch. Sushi OK?"

"Only Miyake!"

"Yes, dear. Only the best for you."

"See you around 11:45."

"Kiss, kiss!"

"Bye."

This was going to be an expensive day.

I called Angela and her voice was soft and comforting, nurturing and kind. I liked her immediately. I asked her if we could meet sometime towards the end of the week or the weekend, since we'd be driving up from Portland. She agreed to meet Saturday, since we were friends of Carly's. She gave me directions and I hung up, pleased to finally check something off my list of things to do.

Next, I had to call my gallery rep in Boston. He was a total thug, but representation is representation, especially on Newbury Street. I had never gotten used to the plasticky tone of his voice, so practiced and so false. It still made me feel creepy. I told him about all the new work, emailed him some pictures and asked when he would like it brought down.

"Next month, sweetheart. We're in the middle of a major show right now, didn't you know?"

"Oh, yes. I remember. The Hundertwasser paintings. Love those."

"I will arrange for the sculpture space in back for you again, you'll be in there with some nice encaustic work by a little gal from Portsmouth. She's got a lovely touch."

"Mmm. Ok. Sounds great, Ed. Talk to you soon."

"OK, love. Can't wait."

The last phone call on my list was to the police. I wasn't sure if the phone was the right place to start, but if I had to go there I would. The police station was not exactly tops on my list of sights to see in Portland. The kind officer explained that the order of protection must be filed in person and that there must be some documented reason. I asked if a statement from the college would be enough and she said it would. I'd have to stop by and get a copy of the report.

At 10:00, James called. My heart leaped out of my chest when I heard the phone, I'm not sure why.

"Good morning, James," I answered, trying not to sound so excited.

"Good morning, Elwyn. How did you sleep?"

"OK. You?"

"Not as well as I did with you."

I blushed. I actually blushed. "Yeah, we'll have to nap together again soon."

He laughed.

"I called my friend's mom's friend," I said, trying to slip it in casually.

"The soul reader."

"Yes, Angela the soul reader. I still have a hard time saying that!"

"And what did she say?"

"Well, she sounds very kind and she's agreed to meet with us on Saturday. It's about two hours north, in Belfast."

"I love Belfast. Do you want to stay up there for the night?"

I don't know why, but his suggestion hit me hard, right in the center of my stomach. I felt longing and discomfort all jumbled up together in a big pit of confusion.

"Um, I hadn't thought about it." I tried hard to keep the panic out of my voice.

"It's fine if not. Just asking. There's tons of bed and breakfasts up there."

"OK," I acquiesced, "That's fine, I guess."

"If you're uncomfortable with it..."

"No! It's fine. I don't know what my problem is. It's fine."

"OK. Are you all right, Elwyn?" The concern in James' voice stopped me from spiraling into panic.

I took a steadying breath and said, "I'm fine. Really. It's just been a crazy couple of days. How's Boston?"

"Good. Investments are solid here, as usual. I've bought up a few blocks in Roxbury. I think they'll rehab nicely and turn a major profit."

"Blocks? Wouldn't that cost..."

"Yep. Twenty two million. But it's going to be worth it. Don't worry!"

"If you say so. I just can't picture that amount of money."

"Dunbar is a real investment firm, Elwyn. This kind of money is what we work with on a regular basis. This is pretty average."

"Like I said. If you say so. I still measure money in terms of bowls and plates, remember?"

He laughed. "I remember. Is my sculpture dry yet?"

"The one of me that looks like a Giacometti?"

"I don't know what that is."

"Modern sculptor, interesting textural figures and busts, never mind. It will take a while to dry. You made it pretty thick!"

"Keep me posted. I want to come back and glaze it."

"What color?"

"It's a secret."

"Dork," I laughed lightly.

"Yes. I am a dork."

"Still on for tonight?" I asked, feeling hopeful.

"Indeed. See you soon, Elwyn."

"Bye, James."

I hung up feeling like an elated teenager again. I could just picture James' smooth skin and flawless features, and those incredible azure eyes resting on my face, on my body... I was getting too worked up. I took another in what seemed like an endless series of deep breaths and gathered my things to leave. I'd meet Carly, teach my class and finally get to see James again. I held onto that thought like a kite on a peerless day, all fluttering joy, tugging me toward the cerulean sky.

CHAPTER NINE

"Ah, fill the Cup: - what boots it to repeat
How Time is slipping underneath our Feet:
Unborn TO-MoRROW, and dead YESTERDAY,
Why fret about them if TO-DAY be sweet!"

THE RUBAIYAT OF OMAR KHAYYAM
TRANSLATED BY EDWARD FITZGERALD

Lunch was, simply put, a revelation. Miyake is one of those restaurants that transcends regular food. It's worth it sometimes to treat a friend to something like that, and Carly deserved it. She and I had known each other for many years, and we had felt like the things we had in common ran deeper than most of your average friendships.

I didn't want to tell her about James yet, however, so I tried my best to focus on the drama at work. It was more than enough to occupy our time at lunch. Carly was horrified that Brent had set me in his sights.

"I am hoping he just lets it go," I returned.

"He won't. Guys like that never do. I shouldn't say guys, I guess. It's girls too. When people get obsessive and angry they are dangerous."

"I know, I know. I'm being careful."

"No you're not. You think you're being careful. What you're being is Derrin! You have no idea how to watch out for yourself!"

"Thanks for the vote of confidence."

"I mean it!"

"I know you do! But don't forget, I went to school in Brooklyn! Pratt is right on the edge of Bed-Stuy! It's not exactly the safest place on earth and I was fine. When I'm on high alert, my natural defenses kick in."

"All I'm saying is that you can't even begin to think like this guy. If he wants to hurt you, he'll get creative."

"I don't want to talk about it anymore. I'm losing my appetite, which is like a felony in this restaurant. What's going on with you?"

"I am precisely the same. Nothing changes. My internship is going swimmingly and I love what I do. I'm going to be a really good therapist for kids, I think. I can get them to talk. Apparently, that's a rare talent."

"We've always known you were talented!"

After lunch, we went our separate ways. I headed up to school and walked into the building, feeling content. It was a short-lived moment. Brent had watched me come in and came directly up to me. We were still in the main lobby and I shot Jerry the security guard a pointed look. He sat bolt upright and leaned forward. Apparently, he had been briefed.

"Derrin, can I talk to you for a moment?"

"Go ahead, Brent. What do you want to say?"

"Can we talk in your office?"

"No. I'm not comfortable with that. We can talk right here."

He shot a withering look at Jerry whose kind face hardened into a threatening grimace that I'd never imagined possible. "Fine."

We walked towards the bench in the front window and sat

down, only a few feet away from the security desk. Jerry was watching like a raptor from a treetop, waiting to strike prey. My stomach was tight, my body was tense, but I tried my best not to show any weakness or fear.

"Well?" I asked, with a hint of impatience.

"Why did you kick me out of your class? You know I love ceramics. What am I supposed to do now?"

"You should have thought about that before you opened the dampers on Max."

Brent shot Jerry a glance, his face betraying his surprise for just a moment before hardening into an angry mask. "I didn't do anything. I told everyone at that meeting yesterday. I didn't do it."

"You're lying to my face, Brent. I'm not comfortable with you in my class anymore after how you've behaved. I'm not comfortable with your feelings for me. I asked you to gracefully let it go and you've done the exact opposite. I'm sorry I'm involved with someone else, I'm sorry I don't share your feelings. Sometimes that's what happens in life."

"You're not sorry for any of it! You don't understand what you're doing. We're so alike. I just wanted you to give that a chance."

"Brent, I called RISD." I figured that if I was going to play my cards, I might as well play all of them.

I don't think Brent had expected me to mention his past. He looked shocked and stricken for a moment and again his face morphed into seething anger. I could feel its heat again, as menacing as the fireball in Boston. He barely concealed his fury as he said slowly, "I didn't do anything there either. What did they tell you?"

"Why don't you tell me?"

"I was in love with a girl and she didn't love me back. That's it."

"That's not how I heard it. You got obsessed with her and you drove her crazy. You won't do that here. I'm not some little girl, all insecure and weak. I'm telling you for the last time, just let this go and move on."

"I left RISD because of her! I went wandering around for a while until I felt better. And now you're railroading me out of my new school before I even have a chance to get credit for the semester."

"I am reacting to your poor judgment and bad behavior, Brent. You can't blame me for what you've said and done."

"You don't have any proof that I did anything."

"I don't need it."

"You think you're smart, Derrin. But I want you to know something." His voice was a low, hoarse, vehement whisper. "This is not over."

"What isn't over?" I asked loud enough for Jerry to hear.

"We could have worked this all out if you'd just understood how I felt about you."

"You can't fall for a teacher. It's against the rules. Besides, I told you. I don't feel anything romantic about you, Brent. I just don't."

"Why, because of pretty boy, there? Your new boyfriend? How long do you think *that's* going to last? He is way out of your league."

"Well, that's just mean. This conversation is over, Brent. I don't wish to speak with you again, and I will file a restraining order against you if I have to."

"Now who's being mean?"

"It's not meant to be mean. It's self-protection. Your anger is getting the best of you and I will not be blamed for your inability to control your feelings."

"Fuck you, Derrin," he said quietly.

"Did you want to say that a little louder, Brent?"

He stood up and gave me one more hard glare, his brown eyes almost black, his face contorted into such an extreme visage of hate I shuddered involuntarily. Finally, he stalked away, leaving me sweating on the bench.

"That's one troubled young man, Professor D.," Jerry said as soon as I stood up.

"Thanks for being witness to that little bit of crazy," I replied unsteadily. I knew Brent meant it when he said it wasn't over. Not by a long shot.

"Can I do anything for you?" Jerry asked kindly.

"You already did, my friend. Thank you." I reached out and shook Jerry's hand. He smiled in a very avuncular way, full of caring and protectiveness. I appreciated his loyalty.

I walked up to the ceramics room only to find yet another debate going on. Where had my peaceful classroom gone? How had things disintegrated into chaos overnight?

"What's up?" I asked, walking into the fray. I hung my bag and coat on the hook nearest the door and moved into the room.

"Nothing," said Brynn. She turned and walked away from the other students standing around.

"Is she OK?" I asked.

"She's fine. She lost something and she was blaming everyone else for it," replied Elaina.

"What did she lose?" I asked, feeling a little more concern about the situation.

"A nice bowl that came out of the firing. She had it on the shelf and now it's gone," said Josh. "She's blaming us for stealing it. Why would we steal something from her?"

"Thanks for explaining. I'll talk to Brynn."

I walked over and Brynn's tears had dried, leaving streaks on her delicate skin.

"Josh and Elaina told me you're missing an important piece of work."

"I am. It was right here," she gestured to the shelf that was marked with her name. "It was here yesterday."

"Come with me," I replied. As I passed through the room, I said over my shoulder, "Start work, demo in 15."

"K, boss," replied Josh.

"Where are we going?"

"We're going to file a report. Your bowl was stolen and I want you to tell Jerry the security guard exactly what happened, where you left it, the last time you saw it. Things are getting out of hand and I want an end to it."

I left Brynn with Jerry and walked back to the studio. I was pissed off and it was time to take action.

I opened the studio door and said, "I have an announcement." The kids gathered and I addressed them. "We have had some unpleasantness here recently. There have been two suspicious incidents, one regarding the kiln and now this theft."

"Theft!" I heard some of the students' murmurs.

"Yes, theft. Someone took Brynn's work. I want you all to be as vigilant as possible. Do not let anyone who is not in ceramics classes in the room. Do not leave your valuables around. Please keep in mind that Brent Talbot is no longer enrolled in ceramics, so this rule applies to him as well."

Students started glancing at each other with bewildered looks.

"Did he take Brynn's bowl?" Elaina asked.

"I am not accusing anyone right now. We're going to review the footage on the security cameras over the past 24 hours. I just want you to be more aware than usual. Take care of each other."

"OK, Derrin," they said quietly.

"I didn't want to worry everyone with all this, but it's better to know that there is something going on so that you can watch out for yourselves. If you have work you love, take it home. This space is no longer secure."

I turned around and headed for my apron. I put it on and put my hand in the pocket out of habit. Inside the pocket, I found a tiny drawing of myself. It was expertly done, very accurate and very disturbing. My expression in this tiny masterpiece was one of horror or shock, but even more disturbing than that, my eyes were left totally white, no irises, no pupils. As I stared down at the paper, I knew where it had come from without even thinking about it. Brent had been here and he wanted me to feel it. Well, I did.

Ben came up next to me and before I could hide the drawing he said, "Holy shit."

"Yep. It was in my apron pocket."

"He's insane, Derrin. That proves it. That is so messed up."

"I don't like to admit it, Ben, but it freaks me out."

"It should! It's super creepy."

"He is so talented, though. Look at these lines. Look at the shading. It's such a waste."

"Lots of psychos have made great art, Derrin. He's no exception on either front."

"I've got to show this to security. I'm wearing out the path between here and the front desk!"

"See you in a few."

I brought the drawing down to Jerry who asked me to photocopy it for him to put in the file. I wrote up a little report on finding it, copied it for Jerry and put one in Olivia's mailbox with a note. She should know just what we were dealing with.

The remaining two hours of class were uneventful. When everyone was gone, I grabbed my bag and coat and headed up to my office to put the disquieting little picture away. My keys were gone. Seriously, I thought. *What did I do with them?* I fished through my entire bag, I emptied out all the contents on the floor, and still nothing. Not in my coat pockets either. I walked back down to the studio and searched. Nothing.

I headed to the front desk and there was Jerry, and in his hand were my keys. "Someone turned these in just moments ago. Found them on the floor in the hallway."

"That is so weird. Which hallway did they say?"

"They didn't specify. Just said the hallway."

"I don't know how I lost them. What a weird day. Thanks, Jerry."

I left the building feeling very disconcerted. I was never careless with my keys. It felt baffling. I grabbed a latte from the coffee shop and sipped it as I walked home. I was ready for a night out with James, to stop thinking about all the fucked up things that had been happening. I put the needling fear out of my mind and pushed onward.

I had about an hour to kill at home, so I straightened up, watered the plants and did my hair and makeup. I cobbled together an outfit from a vintage sweater and a denim miniskirt. I had loved this skirt for years, and it still looked good. It was not too short and not too long and not too tight but just tight enough: the perfect skirt for a date. Shoes, however, were always a debate with me. Should I wear my signature Mary Janes? Or boots? I went with the boots since it was still rather cool after dark. It would be an excuse to wear tights.

Satisfied that I could do no better, I left the apartment and headed downstairs. James was supposed to pick me up and I couldn't wait. I sat outside on the little wall that surrounded the property next door and dangled my legs. I was thinking about that disturbing drawing, so I must have had a miserably worried expression on my face when James pulled up silently. Hybrids—you never hear them coming.

He hopped out of the car and came toward me. Without saying anything, he put his arms around me and hugged me tight.

"Thanks," I said, my voice muffled by his shoulder.

He pulled back, grasped my upper arms and kissed me on the forehead. "You alright? You looked mighty worried when I pulled up. Not having second thoughts about our date, are you?"

"No. It's not about you at all. It's just been a weird day, is all. I lost my keys earlier and someone turned them in at the desk. But I can't figure out how I might have lost them in the first place. They're always in my bag, clipped to the inside. I've not misplaced my keys in decades."

"Seems fishy to me," James said, thoughtfully.

"I know, right?" I shook my head. "Anyway, I want to go have fun with you. Where are we headed?"

"It's a surprise!" James looked giddy as a child. He took my hand and helped me hop down from the wall. "You look lovely, Elwyn. You are so cute."

"Gee, thanks," I said sardonically. "Like a fuzzy widdle teddy bear."

"That's not what I meant," he replied defensively. "I just think you're really adorable. I like how you dress. I like how you look. It's like how a little kid might dress for a date."

"God, that's even worse. I dress like a little kid. Wonderful. Listen. I don't own slinky red dresses or high heels. I just don't. Talk about feeling like a kid playing dress up—I can't wear that shit. This is as good as it gets. Sorry."

"Whoa, Elwyn, I said I *liked* it. I said I like the way you dress. It's unique. I don't think that saying you're cute should be taken like an insult."

"Sorry, I'm just insecure about my looks. I feel like you deserve some modelesque beauty in satin and Jimmy Choo's. I don't quite add up and I'm sorry."

"You are perfect. How many times am I going to have to tell you that?"

He kissed me on the head again, which felt kind of patronizing. I shook my head and got into the car. This was not how I'd wanted to start our date. I couldn't help myself though. Those ancient insecurities bubbled up out of nowhere sometimes. As usual, I couldn't get out of my own way. I felt guilty and sad. I slumped in the seat and stared out the window as my neighborhood passed by. I didn't want to fuck anything else up so I stayed silent.

James was quiet too. I knew I'd probably alienated him for the time being and I wasn't sure how to bridge the gap again. I closed my eyes, feeling desperate. I had never managed to keep a relationship going long term because of this shit. I knew I needed to apologize. I mustered my courage.

"James, I'm sorry. I'm working on trying to accept a compliment at face value rather than translate it as an insult. It's a real problem I have and I didn't mean to get snappy."

"Snap away, Elwyn. I like your feisty side. All I ask is that you make one assumption."

"What might that be?"

"That everything I say, I say because I care. I told you, I will never intentionally hurt you. And I'm sorry that the word cute has negative connotations for you, but I'll stand by my assessment. You are cute and that's all there is to it. You don't have to be some six-foot tall blonde model to be a beautiful woman. You're beautiful in the way that only Elwyn Beatrice Derringer can be beautiful."

"Thank you, I guess."

"You guess?"

"Yeah. Like I said, I'm working on it. So, what's it like to be beautiful in a more general sense?"

"What do you mean?"

"You know what I mean. You're gorgeous. So, what's it like?"

"I don't know what it's like to be anyone but me, Elwyn. I guess, in my experience, I get a lot of sexy looks from women, but that gets old. It's hard to know if people like you just for your looks or if there's something deeper. Unfortunately, I've had to figure that all out by trial and error."

"Poor baby."

"You can't do that. You can't ask a personal question and then ridicule my honest answer with sarcasm. It's not nice."

"God, I'm sorry. You're right. I asked. I guess that coming from opposite poles on the spectrum of good looks we have a very different set of experiences. It's true, I have always been able to assume that when someone likes me, it's not just for my looks."

"Apology accepted. You really have no reason to be so insecure, by the way."

"I am what I am, I guess." I looked out the window as we crossed over the bridge and headed south. "Brent told me you're out of my league."

"When did you talk to that guy?" James was outraged.

"He stopped me at school. It was in front of the security guard who heard the whole thing."

"I don't care. You shouldn't be talking to that psycho."

"I know. I didn't feel like there was any choice."

"There's always a choice. Just say you have nothing to say to him and keep walking."

"Next time."

"I can't believe they didn't expel him."

"I guess there wasn't enough evidence and he never admitted to the kiln sabotage."

"He's too smart. That makes him dangerous."

"I agree. I don't know what to do."

"You have to remain vigilant. And don't let him in your head. He played off your insecurity today. Telling you that I'm out of your league took your fear and gave it power. You have to tell yourself that everything he says is meant to hurt you, and then don't let it hurt you!"

"Easy, right?"

"No. It's not easy. But what else are you going to do?"

"I don't know. Restraining order, I guess."

"That sounds like a wise next step."

We drove south for a while, hugging the shoreline all the way into Kennebunkport. He had made a reservation at one of the seaside taverns. The night was getting cool, but we elected to sit outside on the deck overlooking the water anyway. They had propane heaters set up, so the cold was just manageable. We pulled our chairs closer together so that we could both take in the view. The clouds were glowing hot pink from the sun setting behind us, and the color's intensity played against the evening blue sky beyond. The riot of color was reflected in the waves below, each crest catching the magenta of the clouds, while the base of each wave stayed deep blue. It was breathtaking.

"I've always wanted to be a landscape painter," I shared.

"Why don't you?"

"I don't know. It's like how will I ever capture beauty like this? I can't even try."

"Guys like Thomas Cole and Frederic Edwin Church managed."

"You know your Hudson River School painters. Are you a Bierstadt fan too?"

"I am. I spend time at the Portland Museum of Art, and I actually read the tags."

"An academic!"

"An enthusiast. I know what I like. That painting of Mount Katahdin by Church is one of my favorite paintings of all time."

"It is luminous, isn't it? He painted it for his wife. It is actually a pretty romantic story."

"Of course you know the back story."

"I do. He was in his old age and he had been to Katahdin many times in his youth. He wanted to revisit the scenes he had loved so much one last time before he died, so he made a final trip up there. The sunset colors reflected on the mountain represent the sunset of his life. He wrote a touching letter to his wife when he gave her the painting. I'll see if I can find it." I took out my phone and Googled it. "Here it is. 'Your old guide is paddling his canoe in the shadow, but he knows that the glories of the heavens and the earth are seen more appreciatively when the observer rests in the shade.' He really loved her. Her name was Isabel."

"Wow. How sweet. See, Elwyn? The great loves in this world endure outside of time. Shall we take a picture of us with the sky behind?"

"Sure." We got up, went to the railing and James held out my phone. He snapped a few pictures in which he looked like a model and I looked like a groupie. I refrained from comment.

"Text one to me, OK?"

"OK," I replied, instantly sending him a picture.

After a delicious dinner, we went for a walk on Goose Rocks Beach, since it was sort of on our way home. The night air felt bracing, the moon had risen in the east and was reflecting off the water, bouncing tiny shards of moonlight around, expanding the light a millionfold. The rocks along the edge of the beach looked silver in the light, and James' skin glowed seductively. It was so evocative, somehow, that I just wanted to stare at him in that light forever. It touched a chord within me that I couldn't describe, something deep and emotional. I had to will myself to turn back to the water before he asked me what I was thinking. I didn't want to have to try to describe the feeling that had suddenly welled up within me, seeing him in that silvered light. He pressed me, however, so I took a moment to analyze it.

"I don't know. There's something about the silvery light of the moon against your skin that is hitting me hard in a part of me I can't describe. Like a passage from a favorite book that you just can't place

—it drives you a little nuts. Familiar yet unknowable at the same time."

"Silvered flesh in moonlight blazed,

Cool fire bathes the world in dreams

Of love, of loss, of the heart's great maze

Hands met in prayer, our souls redeemed," James recited.

"Do you have a poem for every occasion?" I jested.

"I just made it up," James replied shyly.

"How did you do that?" I was mystified by that kind of spontaneous eloquence.

"Just like you make things out of clay, I guess. Things just come to you."

"Do you remember the poems after you say them?"

"Most of the time. Especially if I write it down soon."

"Get the man a pen," I cried.

"You know it!"

We held hands and listened to the crash of the surf, reveling in the moment together. It was perfection.

"I wanted you to know something," James said after a little while.

"What?"

"I have been taking anti-anxiety medication since I was 10."

"Oh," I said, not sure how to reply.

"My dreams plagued me so deeply when I was a kid that the psychologists my mom sent me to see thought the nightmares were effecting my wellbeing. I was jittery and afraid, super clingy and pretty quiet. Not your average little kid."

"That sucks," I added, quietly. "Are you still having the nightmares?"

"They also put me on a dream surprising drug a few years ago."

"I'm so sorry. What's it like not dreaming? Just darkness?"

"It's weird. Like there's this void where my dreams should be. Like having a piece of my psyche excised each night like a cancer. It really does suck. It's not peaceful sleep."

"What are you going to do about it?"

"That's the thing. Since we met, I have been feeling sort of like I'm straining at bonds I can't see—like I'm working through the issues instead of hiding from them. The night we stayed up in the studio was the first night I've not taken the dream suppressants in four years. When we slept the next day, I experienced real, un-drugged, un-nightmare-plagued sleep for the first time in my entire life. Think about that, Elwyn. I have been either drugged or tortured in my sleep for thirty years."

"Jesus, James. How did you end up so normal?" I realized how offensive that must have sounded right after I said it. I put my face in my hands and said, "Let me try again. You seem very well adjusted for someone in your situation."

James was smiling. "You are so funny. Yes, I tried as hard as I could to be normal, even with the dreams. It wasn't easy."

"So, you had a good bit of rest when we slept together."

"Yes," he agreed.

"What about the past two nights?"

"I don't know. I was a coward and took the meds."

I laughed. "I think I would have too! It's scary to go back to a nightmare you're pretty sure will destroy your sense of wellbeing."

"Yep."

"So, what if we sleep together again and you try going without the meds?"

"I didn't want to rush things with you, but that thought did cross my mind."

"Oh," I realized, finally catching on. "You've already considered this."

"Yes, Elwyn," he continued, sheepishly. "But I don't want to do it unless you're ready to see me through a nightmare. It's kind of freaky, from what I'm told."

I could see what courage it took for him to tell me all of this. His life had been altered by the dreams of our past. I wanted to help him. I pictured him as a little boy, crying himself back to sleep, afraid to close his eyes because the dead woman was going to come back, afraid to tell his mother because she was so disturbed by it. It was horrible. "I'm sorry you had to endure all of that pain, especially as a child. I can't imagine. Let's try to get your nightlife on track, shall we?"

"Are you sure?"

"I am. I'm not afraid of you, James. Nothing you could do would scare me."

"Thank you, Elwyn. It would be amazing have a normal night's sleep. Being with you has given me a hope I never thought I'd have."

"Don't thank me yet," I quipped again. It was my new catch phrase. James hugged me to him sideways. I felt his adoration and gratitude flooding through his body and into mine like an energy exchange.

I shivered a moment later as the cold finally made its way through my jacket and sweater and into my very core. James kept his arm around me to warm me up. I shivered again and said, "I would stay here forever with you, but we'd need to start a fire."

"Not sure that's allowed, sweetheart. As I've mentioned, I don't really want to get arrested."

"Yeah, not the best way to end a date."

"Shall we?"

We turned to walk back to the car, and I was feeling kind of heartbroken to leave all that beauty behind. I took one last look at James' face in the light. Again, he caught me. He smiled, took my face in his hand and kissed me deeply, lovingly.

I let myself become enveloped in his intensity, I disconnected from space-time and tried to feel the quantum entanglement of our hearts that James had described just days before. I thought I could feel the powerful tug of what he described as an elemental force stronger than gravity. Maybe, just maybe, he was right.

CHAPTER TEN

"The Worldly Hope men set their Hearts upon
  Turns Ashes - or it prospers; and anon,
  Like Snow upon the Desert's dusty Face
  Lighting a little Hour or two - is gone."

THE RUBAIYAT OF OMAR KHAYYAM
TRANSLATED BY EDWARD FITZGERALD

J ames came upstairs with me and as we entered my loft I immediately knew that something wasn't right.

"What the hell," I said, plunging into the darkness. I banged my knee on the edge of a table. "Ow," I said under my breath. James was silhouetted against the light of the landing, still in the doorway.

"What's wrong?" he asked.

"I always leave this light on. Always. It's off. Maybe the bulbs blew." I flicked the switch and the kitchen lights came on, illuminating the apartment.

"Not the bulbs," James stated, as he shut the door and locked it behind him. He walked warily into the apartment. "Do you think someone's been here?"

"I don't know. I mean, those are substantial locks. I don't think people would want to stand out on the landing and pick two deadbolts and one doorknob lock. It would attract attention." I looked around to see if anything was out of place. Things appeared to be where I'd left them, but it was disconcerting to wonder. I moved to the bedroom and immediately I knew that my gut was right. Someone had been there. The bed was too tidy. "I feel like one of the three bears. Someone's been sleeping in my bed."

James rushed in and looked at the carefully made bedding. He turned to me, perplexed.

"I don't make the bed that neat. I never have. I'm more of a throw the comforter on to cover the messed up sheets kind of person. This is not my work." We walked around to the other side of the bed and examined it. We looked under the bed, in the closets, in the bathroom and this was the only trace that someone had been here. I felt sick. I loved my bed. I couldn't stand the thought of someone tampering with it in any way.

"I'm calling the police, Elwyn."

"No, James, don't," I pleaded.

"Why not? He's been in your house! He got into your home while you were gone, and God knows what he did in here. It's horrible and it's an invasion and you need to get the police in here."

I knew James was right. It was Brent's work. He dialed the number and within ten minutes, the police had arrived. Two officers came to the door, which I had left open for them. James greeted them and explained the situation. One of the officers came over and sat next to me on the sofa. She was pretty, probably twenty-five, hair pulled back in an efficient bun.

"Are you OK, ma'am?"

"Physically, yes, but I am very upset about this." I explained the situation with Brent, told her about all of the encounters and suspicions from school and then something clarified within me as I

124

recalled losing my keys earlier. I realized that Brent must have taken my keys and copied them while I was in the studio for three hours, then left them in a random hallway for someone else to find. He was conniving. "He took my keys today. He must have taken them and copied them." I explained the story to the policewoman.

James was listening now and said, "We should have realized that before he got in here. I'll call a locksmith right now."

"A man of action," I muttered. The officer smiled. "Can you fingerprint the place?" I asked her.

"Yes. We'll send a team over right away, but it doesn't look like he took anything."

"He might have, I haven't had time to thoroughly look." I scanned the place for missing objects and realized exactly what was missing. "The photograph of me and my father on my graduation day. It was in a shell frame on that bookcase and it's gone. I don't dust that often—let's see if there's a mark where it was."

Indeed, the dust had collected just enough to leave an empty silhouette where the frame had been.

"Burglary," the officer said to her companion, a man of around fifty. He called for investigators to come, and soon my home was bustling with police officers and detectives, searching for clues and fingerprinting everything.

The locksmith showed up about halfway through the circus and changed the locks. He gave me my new keys and I paid him exorbitantly for coming after hours. I was tired and pissed off and anxious. Even with new locks, I didn't want to stay alone after the hubbub died down. After the police were done examining my bed and had found a semen stain on the sheet that showed up with a black light, I had had it. They showed it to me with a sidelong look at James, as though he may be the culprit, and I shook my head. "We haven't had sex in this bed," I said, in a matter-of-fact tone. "It was the intruder."

"Thank you for your candor, ma'am," said the female officer softly. "I know this isn't easy."

"Thank you for your help. I would be much more upset if it wasn't for your work here tonight."

"It's our job."

When they left with all the evidence they could find, including the offending sheets, I looked at the jumble of bedding left behind. I felt miserable. "I can't keep that stuff. I never want to see it again." I headed to the kitchen and got a garbage bag. I managed to pick up the bedding with my hands through the bag so as not to touch any of it. I was so deeply disturbed and disgusted, I didn't know what to do to feel safe and uncontaminated again. He had jacked off in my bed. How disgusting. What a sick fucker.

We cleaned the apartment. We washed the counters and the bathroom and disinfected every surface we could find. When we finished, we sat together on the couch. I buried my head in my hands and finally let myself feel.

James moved closer to me and put his hand on my back, rubbing in small, soothing circles.

"What else did he do that we can't see evidence of? Did he find my birth certificate? Did he look at my baby pictures? Did he drink out my milk carton? It's disgusting. It's such a violation. Like if he can't have me, he will soil everything I love. It's so fucked up."

"Your office." James spoke quietly so that it didn't startle me, but he was right.

My heart sank. My office. He had had access to those keys too. "Fuck!" I heaved myself off the couch and called the security desk at the college. Andy answered. I told him about my keys and my suspicions that Brent would try to get into my office.

"I'm on it, Derrin," said Andy, reassuringly. "I'll review the security footage from today in your hallway and see if he's been in there."

"Thank you. Can we change the lock too?"

"Yep. First thing tomorrow."

"Thank you, Andy. Did you guys find anything about the bowl that was stolen out of the ceramics room?"

"Yes, we saw a hooded figure come in, cross the room, pick up the bowl and leave with it. Can't see the face, but from the size of the person, it could be our guy."

"OK. Thanks."

"Good night, Derrin."

"Good night, Andy."

I turned to James, who looked really drawn and tired. It was two in the morning by this time. "Thank you for thinking of my office. Lord knows what he would have done in there!"

"Yuck."

"Yeah, yuck. I don't want to stay here."

"It's your home, Elwyn. He shouldn't be able to make you uncomfortable in your home."

"Damn right, he shouldn't, but he did! He violated my space. I need to clean more before I can stay here, but I'm just too tired."

"Come over. I have an extra room if you don't want to sleep in mine yet."

I had never had such a mix of emotions roil through me. I was disgusted and furious at this situation with Brent, I felt hurt and violated. I also felt deep gratitude and affection for James, and beneath all of it, a wild attraction that I wasn't sure I would subdue when it came down to it. I measured my options and decided that I would accept James' offer, whatever might come of it. I thought of our conversation on the beach and decided that we might as well see if I could help him sleep, and we might as well start tonight.

"Thank you. It's late. Let me grab some things." I headed to my bedroom and bellowed, "God, did he go through my underwear drawer too, do you think? I am going to need new underwear. Let's just go. I'll borrow some boxers if you don't mind."

"How do you know I'm a boxer guy?" James asked playfully, trying to lighten the mood. "Might be briefs!"

"I can't wait to find out." Before I could let myself be embarrassed by the innuendo, I forced a little smile, grabbed my bag, and led us out the door, locking it in triplet behind me.

CHAPTER ELEVEN

"Alas, that Spring should vanish with the Rose
    That Youth's sweet-scented Manuscript should close!
    The Nightingale that in the Branches sang,
    Ah, whence, and whither flown again, who knows!"

THE RUBAIYAT OF OMAR KHAYYAM
TRANSLATED BY EDWARD FITZGERALD

James' house was pretty incredible. It was from the late 1800's, it glimmered with hardwood and marble in the foyer, and it smelled of lemon cleaner. The cantilevered staircase swept up the side of the great space and an antique chandelier hung from the ceiling. "Wow," I said stupidly. "This is awesome."

"It was a good buy. I lucked out. The guy that owned it before me went bankrupt in the crash and had to sell it at a time when no one was buying. My dad was still in charge at Dunbar and he had seen the crash coming. We were well prepared when most others weren't. I bought this, restored it, and I've lived here for six years. It's especially nice in the daytime—very sunny. I'll give you the grand tour tomorrow. Let me just get a couple of glasses of water and we can head upstairs."

"Thank you, James," I said thickly. "You are very kind to me and I appreciate it."

"Elwyn, I have loved you for over a century. I'm not about to stop loving you now that we've finally met!"

"That sounds a little crazy."

"Yep. It's been a crazy week. Come on."

We stopped by the kitchen, white cabinets, white marble counters, all gleaming, French windows banking the far wall that seemed to lead out to a terrace or something: it was a lush, beautiful space. I felt very small.

He got our waters and handed me one, then he led me up the stairs. "The guest room is here, if you want it. My room is there."

"Will you be offended if I ask to sleep with you tonight?"

"Why would I be offended?"

"Because of the conversation earlier. I would have slept with you anyway and not because of Brent. I want you to know that this is my decision." I felt weirdly embarrassed and stared at the rich carpet runner on the floor.

"Well, I *want* you to sleep with me, so it's a win-win. I especially want to hold you and help you feel safe again."

"You already do that." I smiled wanly and followed him into his room.

He found me a tee shirt and some pajama bottoms and held up some boxers with a smile. "You were right."

I laughed heartily, took the clothes he offered, changed and brushed my teeth with a new toothbrush he just happened to have. "For one night stands?" I asked, wickedly.

"Yep. 'Cause I'm just that type of guy."

We smiled at each other, turned out the lights and climbed into his bed. James held me close, kissed my head and we both fell deeply asleep.

I dreamed of the moonlit water again, this time it was the ocean and I was with James. A giant wave came toward us out of the distance, growing, threatening, ready to consume and destroy us. I screamed and started to run but the James in the dream held me fast, faced the wave and said, "Together."

I woke up as the wave crushed the life out of us and I gasped for air. I sat up in the bed, adrenaline racing through me and tried to calm myself down. I thought it was ironic that I should have a nightmare just as James was relinquishing his.

I shook my head and took stock of my surroundings. The room was suffused with pale morning light filtering through the translucent silk curtains that hung the length of the wall. It was a very peaceful room, done in dove grey and cream with a hint of ice blue here and there. Masculine, for sure, but tastefully so. I lay back down on the bed and the movement woke James. It was nice to see his morning face. He was adorably disoriented. Turns out, he wasn't a morning person at all.

"Uh," he groaned hoarsely. "What time is it?"

He put his hand over his eyes and shielded himself from the morning light. I leaned over and checked the clock on the nightstand. "It's 7:00 a.m.. We got as much sleep as we could have asked for, considering."

"Yeah. You shower first. I'm going back to sleep."

He fell back asleep without another second elapsing. I was in awe. Well, I thought, he deserved to sleep peacefully for the second time in his entire life.

I followed his advice and took a shower. I loved using the soap that smelled like James, letting it follow the contours of my body, just as he must have. I was feeling slightly turned on from the experience. I got out of the shower, grabbed my towel and dried off. I had brought the boxers with me and put them on. Then I put on my bra and wondered what to do about clothes. I had my date clothes, but I couldn't exactly work at the studio in a vintage sweater. I didn't want to wear any of my own clothes until I could wash them all, so I had left them home. That left James' wardrobe. I didn't want to wake him, so I wandered into his walk-in closet, wearing just my bra and his boxers, which were just big enough to slide down to the edge of my hips. I surveyed the well-organized racks and shelves around me. As I pondered the possibilities, James had gotten silently out of bed and from the closet door behind me he said, "I've never seen anything sexier than this."

I turned, startled and laughed. "Then what?" I demanded.

"Then you, standing in my wardrobe, dressed in my boxers and a little black bra. It is so hot."

I folded my hands over my body and frowned at him.

He shut the wardrobe door, saying, "Sorry. I didn't know you'd be in there or I would have given you some privacy. But some things can't be unseen."

I shook my head, smiling a little. I was glad he thought I was sexy.

"Do you mind if I take a shirt and sweater? I will try not to ruin them."

"Take whatever you want and use them however you may. They're just clothes."

"Thanks."

I chose a tee shirt that looked small enough to fit well and a hoodie sweater that was definitely too big. I put my denim skirt back on, grabbed some tube socks and put on my boots. It was good enough.

James got out of the shower and came into his bedroom wrapped in a towel, his bare chest glistening like some hunk on the cover of a cheesy romance novel. "Fair is fair," he said, as he grabbed boxers and socks from his drawer. He smiled a seductive smile over his muscular, wet shoulder, lord help me, and disappeared into his closet.

I inhaled deeply, groaned, and lay back down on the bed with my hands covering my face. Talk about sexy. He was unstoppably attractive. I wanted to stalk into the closet after him and rip off that towel, but I figured that wouldn't be very lady like. All in good time, I told myself. All in good time.

We ate a quick breakfast of fruit and yogurt and coffee together at the breakfast bar in the kitchen and I asked James whether he had slept well.

"I did," he exclaimed joyfully. "I think I even had what might have been a normal dream, although I'm not sure. It feels really good! Thank you so much."

"I am so glad! Will you stay off the meds, do you think?"

"I don't know. I think so. I'll take it day by day and see what happens."

After breakfast, we finished our tour of the house. The stone terrace outside the kitchen led to a lovely yard with a garden, all walled in by tall hedges and beautifully, classically landscaped. It was like something out of Architectural Digest, for goodness sake. It was breathtaking. We continued on to the library, which was inset like a crown of jewels with stained glass windows and mahogany bookshelves, comfortable leather furniture and a massive Georgian desk.

The living room and dining room were sumptuous as well, fitted with antiques and nice modern pieces, all aesthetically arranged and immaculate. "Do you actually live here?" I asked him.

He looked perplexed by the question. "Yeah, I actually live here. What do you mean?"

"I mean it's really immaculate."

"I have a maid. It's a luxury I allow myself. She keeps it tidy and dusted and clean. I can ask her to go to your place and help with the de-Brentifying that will need to happen. She's really good."

"That's a good plan. I accept. Thank you."

"You're welcome. It's hard for you to accept help. I know that. I'm glad you will, in this case."

"Will she wash all my clothes?"

"I'm sure she'll do whatever you want."

"I want to go to the mall and get new underwear. I was serious about that."

"Sounds like a fun excursion for a Wednesday night. Can I come?"

"Underwear shopping?"

"Sure."

"That's sort of a private thing, don't you think?"

"You're wearing my underwear right now, if I may remind you." He smiled in that seductive, steamy way that made me want to undress him right then and there.

"You think I am," I quipped. I turned to walk out the door and glanced back to catch his expression. He was amused and I was glad.

CHAPTER TWELVE

"Ah, Moon of my Delight who know'st no wane,
  The Moon of Heav'n is rising once again:
  How oft hereafter rising shall she look
  Through this same Garden after me - in vain!

THE RUBAIYAT OF OMAR KHAYYAM
TRANSLATED BY EDWARD FITZGERALD

The day dragged by. Classes were fine, Brent didn't show his face anywhere, and by the afternoon I was ready to be done. No amount of coffee had been able to touch my exhaustion.

I decided to let James take me to the mall, but when it came down to actually buying underwear in his presence, I just couldn't do it. I told him I'd meet him on the couches outside the store. I bought twenty pairs of pretty undies, something I'd never done in my life. The woman must have thought I was insane. I smiled at the thought that she'd go home and tell her husband or wife that some crazy girl had bought twenty pairs of undies. So funny.

I bought two pairs of jeans, four tee shirts and a sweater as well, figuring that I would at least have something to wear that Brent hadn't contaminated. I met James at the benches, where I found him in conversation with an elderly man. They were talking about investment banking and technology. The man had been waiting for his wife who apparently always took too long buying clothes for the grandkids who didn't need clothes. We said goodbye to the gentleman and headed out of the mall.

"Do you want me to take you home?"

"I guess," I said sullenly. I had been dreading this moment.

"Elwyn, you can stay with me as long as you want to. In fact, I really enjoyed having you at the house. You'll want to go home eventually. My maid Karen will come and clean for you tomorrow. I've arranged it all. She'll be there at 8:00 a.m.. Come home with me again tonight and tomorrow, we'll go meet Karen, explain what needs to be done and by tomorrow evening you will return to a freshly cleaned, Brent-free home. Sound good?"

I hesitated. I hated asking James for so much. He'd already done enough. "Are you sure?" I asked, feeling awful.

"I wouldn't have offered if I didn't mean it. Come with me. We can cook together."

"Can I use your washing machine?"

"Sure."

"OK. I don't like bothering you though."

"It's not a bother, sweetheart. It's a pleasure. I want to be with you."

"I want to be with you too."

"It's settled. We like being with each other. Go figure."

I giggled a little and tried to make myself feel less sullen.

"Besides," James continued, "this way, we can continue the great sleep experiment."

Before long, we were cooking pasta in James' kitchen, chopping garlic and veggies and searing chicken. It was so natural and so fun that I forgot that I was in someone else's house. I felt very much at home.

I tried not to think about Brent. I wanted to let myself be in the present with James, to focus on this new relationship we were creating. I wanted to know everything about him. When we finished eating our dinner, we sat on the little settee near the French doors to the terrace.

"Tell me more about your mom," I asked, as James poured me another glass of wine.

"Should I lie down on the couch?"

"Unnecessary."

"She's great, I guess. Once I stopped telling her about my dreams, she eased back a bit on the mother hen thing. She must have just thought it was a phase or that my overactive imagination had moved on to less disturbing things. I tried really hard to please her. She's a really kind person and I love her. What else do you want to know?"

"I want to know everything. What was your eighth birthday like? What did you excel at in school? Were you good at sports? Art? Music? I just want to know you better."

"You will. We will know each other inside and out, my dear. I have no doubt of that." James smiled at me. After a moment of thought, he said, "I was good at math and track. I can run really far without really trying too hard. And I learned to sail when I was really little and I've loved it ever since. There's nothing like being on the water. It's so peaceful and exhilarating at the same time."

"Did you grow up in Portland or in one of the other towns around?"

"Cape Elizabeth. My parents still live there. Very idyllic. I'll take you soon. They'll like you."

"What's your dad do in retirement?"

"He comes to the office in a three piece suit and tells everyone how to do their job."

We both laughed. "That doesn't sound much like retiring."

"It isn't, but I think the thought of letting it all go is too much for him to bear. It is every bit as much his child as my sister and I are."

"What's your sister's name?"

"Annabelle."

"She must have loved that name, growing up."

"Yep. She's cantankerous and quick to anger, most likely because of the name. Kids were ruthless with her."

"Kids often are," I replied, wistfully, thinking of my own difficult years at school with a name like Elwyn Beatrice.

"They are. She's really strong, though, probably also from her experiences early on. She learned to stand up for herself and fight, if need be. I remember one time this kid tried to lift up her skirt. We were in elementary school—she was probably in 4th grade. I was in 5th. I saw it happen from across the playground. By the time I got over to her, ready to kick the kid's ass, she had him pinned to the ground. His nose was bloody and she was yelling, 'Apologize!' It was terrifying. No one messed with her after that."

"Yeah, a moment like that goes a long way to earning you respect at that age."

"I never had a fight at school. Never needed to. I had learned to control my feelings and hide my nature from so early on that I never let myself get that worked up about the stupid shit kids did."

"That must have been so hard, though. Hiding how you felt all the time."

"I don't know. It was self-protection, I guess. I knew no one wanted to hear about my crazy dreams, about the deep feeling I had that I was in the wrong time, about the fact that everyone I met seemed like a shadow compared to the woman I held dying every night. If I shared any of that, I knew instinctively that it would be the end of my social life at school, whatever that was worth."

"Keeping up appearances."

"Yep. Just so I didn't have to confront the truth of who I was. For a while, in high school, I think I even managed to convince myself that I was this well-rounded, average teenage kid. My psyche shut up for a while. But it didn't last."

"What happened?"

"I started drinking, hanging out with the party kids. They all did drugs, but at least I knew enough to draw the line there. This one night, the girl I'd been going out with wanted to drop acid. I told her no. I wasn't interested. She was insistent and I finally caved."

"Oh, shit. That must have been horrifying."

"Yep. Everything changed for me that night. All of my nightmares came flooding back and attacked like a zombie bride. It terrified all my friends, it terrified my parents, I ended up in the hospital and when I finally came around I tried to explain that my girlfriend had really wanted me to trip with her, but my wild actions while I was high were enough to end my relationships with all but my closest friend. He understood that I had been flayed by the experience and he didn't have the heart to abandon me. We're still close."

"What's his name?"

"Foster. He is the VP at Dunbar. You'll meet him too. Soon."

"Have you told him about your past life?"

"A little. He knows that I have weird dreams and that I think they're connected to my past. He doesn't pry. He got married a few years ago and has three kids. We only see each other at work now, for the most part."

"How crazy. I can't believe your girlfriend pressured you like that."

"Believe it. She was a terror, in retrospect. She didn't care about me at all. She just wanted to be seen with me, to use me to make herself look better. She taught me that pretty on the outside isn't always pretty on the inside."

"That sucks."

"How about you? What are your parents like?"

My stomach clenched at the idea of having to talk about my family. James had just shared so much of his past with me I knew I couldn't skirt the issue. I didn't want to. I took a deep breath, poured us each another glass of wine, and said, "My mom does humanitarian aid for a non-profit. She's pretty strong and throws herself into her work. She moved to South Sudan to work with refugees after my father passed away last year. She says it gives her life meaning."

I swallowed hard, trying to ignore the lump in my throat that always appeared when I tried to talk about my dad's death.

James pulled me into an embrace and held me close. "I'm sorry about your dad, Elwyn. I really am."

I let myself be comforted by his warmth, his smell, his empathy. He kissed me on the head.

Eventually I sat up and said, "Everyone loses people they love, James. I'm no exception. I think of him every day of my life, but he helped shape me into the person I am. I am thankful for that."

"You are a brave woman, my dear."

"Hardly," I replied, not feeling very brave.

"No, really. It couldn't have been easy for you to lose him."

"Let's talk about something else."

"OK," James replied gently, thinking for a moment. "What was school like for you?"

"Ha! School. I really hated it when I was little. I had a few friends and they were awesome, but we weren't the popular kids. Eventually, though, it didn't matter. As soon as I discovered art, it became my way of dealing with life's ups and downs. My disappointments. My longings. My fears. My sadness."

"That's why your art is so evocative, Elwyn."

"When did you see my work?" I couldn't remember showing him much of anything. There was only a piece or two in my loft and a few unfinished things on the shelf in the studio, but they weren't indicative of my usual style, more production stuff.

"I Googled you," James confessed. "I looked at every piece of artwork you've ever had in a gallery. I bought one." He said it so quietly, so sheepishly, that I could not help but laugh out loud.

"You did not!"

"I did. I should have told you. I didn't want to seem like a creepy stalker. But like I said, from that first moment in the market, I knew I was connected to you somehow."

"Which piece did you buy?" I was totally floored.

"It's one from your show in Newport. It's called 'Flooded.' The elegant shape with the back blown out like that just got me right here." He pointed to his solar plexus.

"That was my favorite. I didn't want to sell it but the asshole at the gallery said it was part of the series and that it needed a price. I set it so high I thought no one would ever pay that!"

"It's coming next week."

"You're crazy," I laughed.

"Maybe," James said, smiling self-consciously.

"Well, I'm flattered."

"You don't think I'm a stalker?"

"No, I guess not." I smiled, then I confessed very quietly, "I Googled you too."

I looked up sheepishly and when our eyes met, we both burst out laughing.

"I'm glad you like my work," I admitted. "It's every bit a part of me as my skin or my blood."

James leaned in and kissed my neck. "I can taste it on you," he said, seductively. "Your creativity runs through your body, pulsing like energy. It really is a part of you. I can feel it."

I had never before had a man understand this aspect of me. Brent thought he did, but all he really understood was his own desires and feelings. James, however, understood me in the most essential way. I was astounded. Lots of people had complimented my work. Some of them had said it moved them, or that it spoke to them. Some of them tried to flatter me into bed. James, however, was the first person who understood that the things I made were a part of my life force. That my creative drive was part of my electrochemical make up. Cellular. Sub-atomic. I kissed him back.

"Let's talk about something happy," I said when we surfaced a while later.

"OK. Happy. Happy. I'm thinking. Got it. I was the best man at my sister's wedding."

"That's so sweet!"

"Yep. She told her husband that he could have his own best man or woman if he wanted, but that she was taking me. I stood behind her, with her bouquet in my hands as the two of them joined in marriage."

"You didn't have to wear a dress though, did you?"

"No. She let me wear a tux. It was unconventional, but in retrospect, I can't imagine why it would have been any other way. Why do we always divide things by gender?"

"I really don't know. I've always resented it."

"Me too. Same with Annabelle. She wore this elegant dress, full of lace and a long train, with flip-flops. It was hilarious. She said that if her husband didn't have to wear heels, neither would she."

"I am going to like her! I can tell."

"She's going to like you too. She's fiercely protective of me, though. Just be prepared for the third degree."

"I can't wait."

James and I opened another bottle of wine and headed outside to the back yard. By the end of the night we were purple lipped and silly, chasing each other barefoot through the grass. I couldn't remember ever being so content. He caught me and we rolled to the ground, toppling over each other, laughing like little children, when in a sudden flash, a new memory came to me.

It caught me so unexpectedly that I gasped. "Did I hurt you?" James asked breathlessly.

"No," I whispered. "It's just... Give me a second."

I lay down on the grass and closed my eyes, praying that the memory would last, as I tried to grasp it head on rather than allow it to dissipate like a dream in the sunshine of morning. I managed to hold onto a thread of it, just enough to tell James what I had felt and seen.

"I had this weird sense of déjà vu or something just now. I was running in a wide park, the same one as that crazy dream I had after we first met. I was barefoot, being chased by a young man, no more than sixteen. I was in a long dress with petticoats and I had hiked them up in front and was holding the bunched material in my hands as I ran through the grass. There were trees surrounding me, weeping willows and apple trees and the woods off to the side. Up the hill was a brick manor house. There was a swing hanging out of one of the willows. It was a golden day, warm and safe, and I felt flooded with love."

"Wow," James gasped. "I've had flashes of memory from some-place like that too. I feel like we knew each other from the time we were young."

"Maybe that's why I feel like such a giddy teenager around you."

"Maybe." He leaned up on one elbow and reached over to put his hand on my stomach. He gently glided it around to my back, pulling me towards him softly, slowly, until we were facing each other sideways, lying under the stars.

"So you remember happy times from our lives then?" I asked, looking into his eyes.

"Not as vividly as my recurring dream, but little flashes here and there. But I want you to remember of your own accord, like this memory, not because I tell you."

"I want to know more, James. I want to share what you feel. This little glimmer, just now, it's not enough. I want the whole story."

"Let's see what Angela has to say on Saturday. It's only a couple more days."

"OK," I said, feeling kind of crestfallen.

James leaned forward and kissed my nose, then my forehead. He moved closer, rolled me onto my back again and kissed me deeply on the mouth. His tongue explored me, his hand held my back and his weight upon my chest felt sublime. He slid his leg over mine and moved it up my thigh. My heart was beating impossibly fast, my body was responding to his seduction of its own accord. I wanted him; he wanted me. What could be wrong with that, I asked myself?

We made out under the stars for an age, feeling each other's bodies pressed together, our limbs in a tangle, pausing to look into each other's eyes and diving back into a passionate kiss. It was excru-ciating and exhilarating and again, I wanted to stop time in its tracks and hold James against me for an eternity.

Eventually it got too cold to be outside any longer, so we walked hand in hand towards the French doors leading to the kitchen. Warm yellow light spilled out onto the stone like the golden blood of some rare animal. I was definitely a bit drunk and my sense of caution had been excised, left on the dewy grass, under the moonlight, to do as it would. Without inhibition, I led James by the hand through his own home, up the stairs and to his bedroom, where I had so desperately wanted to undress him that very morning. This time, I followed through on my desires.

"I hope you were a boy scout," I said seductively.

"What? Why?" James asked, amused, as I pulled his shirt over his head.

"Be prepared."

"Oh!" James actually blushed. I couldn't believe it. It was so endearing that I had to smile. "Side table drawer."

He moaned as I slipped my fingers under the waistband of his jeans and undid the button and slid down the zipper.

"Elwyn," he said softly. "What..."

"Shh. Don't say anything." I kissed him deeply as I held him close to me. I felt him hard against me and all I wanted was to have him on top of me, inside me. And then I froze. I couldn't do it. Not yet.

Instead, I thought, there are a lot of ways to be close, never mind sex. I lifted his tee shirt over my head, unbuttoned my skirt and let it fall to the floor. I crawled up onto his bed, still wearing his boxers and my bra. He smiled.

"So sexy," he breathed, as he moved forward onto the bed, crawling towards me, inch by inch.

"I changed my mind," I said. "About the sex. I'm not quite there."

"Oh," he said, moving back a tad, trying not to look disappointed.

"That doesn't mean I don't want to be close to you and to do, you know, other stuff."

"You really are cute. Other stuff?"

"Other stuff. You know."

"No, I don't know," he toyed with me, laying next to me with his arm bent and his head propped up on his hand, looking bemused. "Tell me exactly what you want me to do."

I giggled and whispered something audacious in his ear. "Your wish is my command, m'lady." Indeed, it was. I couldn't believe how responsive he was to my body, and how responsive my body was to him. We thrilled at each other's touch, reveled in each other's mouths, desperate for each other's pleasure to fuel our own. It was the most intensely sexual experience I'd ever had, and we hadn't even had sex. I was elated. Talk about having your cake and eating it too.

The morning came too soon. We lay naked in each other's arms, me on my stomach, him on his side.

"Tell me about this," James asked me, tracing his finger along the gold and red firebird tattoo on my back.

"It's a phoenix," I replied. "I got it last year."

James gently kissed my back along the lines of the tattoo.

"It's for your father, isn't it?"

"Yes."

"It's beautiful," he mused. "I can see that you loved him deeply. You miss him a lot."

"His death left a hole in my world that I can't seem to fill," I replied, not wanting to continue the conversation. It hurt too much.

"I understand. That's how I've felt for over a hundred years. Leave it to you to find the exact image to reflect that cycle of pain and rebirth."

I rolled on my side to face him. "You've endured so much pain. Living with memories you weren't sure were yours, trying to live your life on a new path while the past dragged you back."

"Yes, but I learned to work around the pain, like a torn ligament or something. It's always hurt, but unless you hit it just the wrong way, you can live with it. Sometimes, though, the intensity of it has bled through and it has been very destructive."

"Your fiancé?"

"She didn't understand. The dreams—I explained them to her once and that was a mistake. Or, maybe in retrospect, it wasn't. Maybe we'd still be together and then I'd be torn about being with you, trying to choose between past or present love. She didn't love me enough to see past my waking up in a sweat, panting like a dog, almost every single night, popping anti-anxiety meds. I got on the dream suppressants soon after we ended things. She left thinking I was crazy. I had begun to wonder if she was right."

"If she was, then we're both crazy." I smiled.

"We're not." He was so certain, so steadfast, that I believed him.

"No more pain," I said, gently caressing his face. "No more pain for either of us."

"It's a deal, Elwyn. No bad dreams last night, by the way. Not one. Since we've met, I've had just a few flashes of memory, here and there, like images in a dark subway tunnel that are lit for just a moment and then fade just as fast, flickering by like an old film. Nothing about the end, though. It's as though sharing it with you, even though I didn't mean to, drained out a festering wound. It's finally beginning to heal."

"I'm so glad," I told him. I leaned over and kissed his shoulder.

"We need a plan for next time around, you know. I don't want to wander around looking for you for another hundred years," James stated emphatically.

I laughed and smiled into his eyes. "You mean in our next life? Good idea. It will need to be a specific time and place. Like Christmas Eve under the Eiffel Tower."

"Exactly. And the years will tick by, and we will pray that we're the same age then too."

"What if I don't remember again?" It was a terribly sad thought.

"You will. And if I have to spend the remaining 364 days of every year searching for you, I will."

He kissed me on the forehead. I smiled sadly. He kissed me on the lips. We sunk back into each other's embrace, filling each other with a lifetime of the love we had missed out on the last time around.

CHAPTER THIRTEEN

"But leave the Wise to wrangle, and with me
    The Quarrel of the Universe let be:
    And, in some corner of the Hubbub coucht,
    Make Game of that which makes as much of Thee."

THE RUBAIYAT OF OMAR KHAYYAM
TRANSLATED BY EDWARD FITZGERALD

Jerry and Andy kept a vigilant watch over me and the ceramics studio. Olivia hired an extra security person to walk the halls and to monitor things. At any other time in my career, I would have thought this was overkill, but I was beyond thankful to her.

I was actually nervous that Brent had made no moves against me. I had thought for sure that he would be harassing me around every corner and following me around, but I couldn't find any evidence of it. Curiosity was getting the better of me, however. I wanted to see the rest of what was in the sketchbook that he had snatched away from me when I had been in his painting studio.

Ben had been there, so I decided to talk with him about the drawing of the gun. "Do you think the whole notebook is full of drawings like that?" I asked.

"Probably," he answered. He was working on the surface of his big sculpture, which he had finished over the weekend. He had a rasp and between strokes he said, "I mean, did you see the paintings? All those body parts? They were so f'd up!"

"Yeah, but beautifully done at the same time. How could that be the stuff in someone's mind? We all create from the subconscious. His must be the seventh circle of hell!"

"Wouldn't want to look too close, D. He's worth forgetting about."

"I know, but part of me just can't seem to let it go. Like that little drawing he did of me. It was so messed up but so perfect at the same time. Like his idea of love, I guess. I just don't know what must have happened to him to make him like that."

"He should be on major meds. Maybe lithium."

"Do they even give people that anymore?"

"How the hell should I know? Derrin, let this go! Stop thinking about him. Focus on staying safe and getting me through the semester."

I loved Ben. His sense of humor was always just under the surface. "Did you hear about grad school yet?"

"Not the one I want, unfortunately. I got into New Paltz, though."

"That's a great program. I'm so proud of you!"

"Your recommendation was really great. I don't think I ever properly thanked you for that."

"I only write letters like that for students like you."

"No one is like me," Ben replied dramatically. We both laughed. Then he said, in the most serious tone he could manage, "I'm actually worried about you."

"Don't be. It's going to be fine. But I do want to see those notebooks. I just feel like they're a window into his psyche, you know?"

"Not a place I want to visit, like I said."

I'm not sure why, but the idea that I needed to look at Brent's sketchbooks had really grown on me. It got under my skin in a big way. I talked to Olivia about it and she reminded me that they were his private property.

"I know, Olivia. But I think it would help for me to see them. I think they're the key to his motivation."

"Well, the studios *are* open spaces and everyone has access to a locker. I guess that means that anything left out is meant to be looked at, right? Take Andy with you and have Jerry keep an eye out for Brent. Take a look, Derrin, if you really need to. Just be careful."

"Thank you, Olivia. I will."

That evening, I told Jerry and Andy my plan. They looked at each other like I'd lost my mind. I admit, I was a little obsessed. Andy and I went upstairs and Jerry watched the doors and the security camera feeds at the front desk. They both had their radios handy. When we got into the studio, it was deserted. I headed towards the back, to where Brent's space was. There were the notebooks, stacked in messy piles on the desk. I picked one up, looking at Andy. He looked away, as though he didn't want to see me transgress this invisible boundary.

I was glad that Andy was there, however, because what I saw in the notebooks frightened me stupid. It's hard to describe the imagery in those pages, other than to say that it was fucked up beyond belief. Horrible images of women strung up, guns from every angle, faces frozen in fear or pain, and each drawing was rendered with the accuracy of a photograph, yet imbued with the expressive lines of Egon Sheille. I was startled into silence. Andy stole a glance at me and I held up a picture of a woman who had been autopsied. "This is what we're dealing with, Andy. I just needed to see for myself how disturbed the boy is."

"Judging from that, very. Please don't show me anymore. I don't want that stuff in my head."

"Andy, I do believe that's the longest paragraph you've ever spoken to me. I'm growing on you, aren't I?"

He actually cracked an infinitesimal smile.

I closed the notebook and picked up another, which was very much the same as the first, with one notable exception. The people weren't in modern clothing. They were dressed in Victorian era clothes. Chills of fear gripped me on the deepest level. My heart froze. I knew I shouldn't, but I took out my camera and started snapping pictures of the sketches. If Brent was obsessing about Victorian scenes of violence, the connection was just too uncanny to ignore. I couldn't analyze it just yet, I decided. It was just too insane. I focused on documenting as much as I could, but when I came across my own face in one of the more disturbing pictures, I had to call it quits. It was a drawing of me crying, viewing myself through a cracked mirror, with a shadowy shape of a man's body behind me. My stomach turned at the sight. It was time to get out. Andy walked me back downstairs and I thanked him profusely.

I was beyond shaken when I walked back into the studio. Ben shook his head when he saw me. "Derrin, I told you not to take a walk through his psyche."

"Fuck it, Ben. I'm already there!" I took out my phone and showed him the last picture, the one of me in the cracked mirror.

"Holy shit. Man, that's fucked up. Look at that. It's like he saw it —like he really saw it in life. It's insane! God, Derrin. I never want to see you look like that."

"Me neither. For the first time in my life, I am really scared, Ben. He's a lunatic. The rest of the sketchbooks were just as crazy."

"What are you going to do?"

"I really don't know. I think my plan of 'hope for the best' seems a tad naive, though."

"Uh, yeah, it does. Do you think it's time to call in the police?"

"He hasn't done anything to me, though."

"Why wait?"

"I will get a restraining order tomorrow."

"Good."

That night, I went back to James' house feeling pensive and nervous. By unspoken agreement, we had just stayed at his house all week. His maid cleaned my apartment, washed all my clothes and brought me some things that I asked for. She was a gem.

As I walked through his front door that night I was especially anxious because I knew that I couldn't win on whether or not to show James the drawings. If I did, I would worry him unnecessarily. If I didn't, it was tantamount to lying, and I didn't want to lie to him.

He took it like I expected. He went through the roof. I can't explain what would possess me to feel a sense of guilt about his reaction. After all, I hadn't drawn the fricking things. I just felt so responsible for James' happiness and wellbeing that it seemed like I had hurt him, which in turn hurt me.

"I'm so sorry. I didn't know whether I should show them to you or not, for this exact reason. You have enough to worry about."

"No, you did the right thing. I definitely wouldn't have wanted you to hide them. They are horrible, though. I can't believe that stuff is in his head. Do you think he has a gun? Do you think that he remembers some past life like we do?"

"I don't know. It's like I needed to understand more deeply by looking at the sketchbooks, but now that I've seen them, I don't understand anything at all. And I totally wish that I could un-see them. That mirror one is so creepy."

"It is. It really is. Did you ever tell him that you don't like mirrors?"

"No. I've never told anyone but you." I blushed as I said it, thinking that James would think less of me for being such a sap. Of course, the opposite was true.

He put his arms around me and hugged me tight.

"Elwyn, I want to keep you safe. You need to get a restraining order against him. Please."

"I will, James. I promise."

That night, my dreams were of darkened gardens lit by lanterns, fireflies flashing about the bushes and my James paddling us across a pond in a rowboat. It suddenly turned dark as all the lights went out, and I was gripped with a deep sense of fear. I awoke in a sweat, wishing I knew which of James' pills were the dream suppressants, because I surely would have popped a few.

Friday passed uneventfully. I worked in the studio, James worked and we met in the evening. We packed an overnight bag and went to bed early.

James and I drove north towards Belfast early on Saturday morning. It was the kind of spring day you look forward to all winter in Maine. It felt fresh and full of possibility. We took the highway up to route one in Bath and then drove the picturesque remainder of the journey, noticing all the cute places on the way.

"Wiscasset," I pointed out. "The Prettiest Village in Maine."

"It is cute, I guess," James replied.

"No, that's what the sign says. 'The Prettiest Village in Maine.'"

We both giggled a little. "Way to toot your own horn," James commented.

"If you made yourself a sign, what would it say?"

"Happy man."

I smiled. It was a wonderful thought that he was happy, in part because of me.

"How about you?" he asked.

"Cutest Ass in the County," I replied, in jest.

"Mmm. Cute ass indeed."

We both laughed.

As we came closer to Belfast, I started to fidget.

"You OK?" James asked me.

"Just nervous."

"Why? What's the worst she's going to say?"

"That we're both delusional."

"Exactly! That's not so bad. At least we're delusional together, right?"

"I appreciate your humor, but really. What if she just looks at us like 'Are you two kidding?' and sends us on our way?"

"Do you think that's what's going to happen?"

"I don't honestly know. I'm nervous because it sounds so insane."

"Maybe she sees this kind of thing all the time. Let's just stay calm and see what happens."

"Fine," I said, feeling a little surly.

We drove up to Angela's office. It was in an old brick building overlooking the harbor. We walked past a gallery, entered an unremarkable door and headed up a long, narrow flight of stairs. We turned and headed up the second set of stairs and ultimately the third. Her office was at the back, on the top floor. Her name was on a sign on the door. We knocked, and I could feel James' nervousness and mine feeding off each other.

Angela opened the door and smiled at us. "Come in," she said in a very regular sounding voice. Her tone was kind.

"Thank you," I replied, stepping into her office. It was light and airy after the darkness of the stairwell. She had windows on the entire back wall with a view of the harbor. "That is a lovely view!"

"Thank you," Angela said, looking out over the water. She had plants hanging in all the windows. There were two soft-looking couches facing each other across a low vintage table. The space was welcoming and comfortable. Angela motioned towards the sofas and asked if we'd like water or tea.

"I'm fine," I replied.

"I'm going to get you a drink," Angela stated, looking amused. "I was wondering if you'd prefer water or tea."

I blushed. "Tea, thank you."

"And for you?"

"Tea also," said James. "Thank you. Would you like a hand?"

"I'm fine. Be right there, the water's boiling."

Angela came back to the couches from the little kitchen area bearing a tray with three teacups and a teapot. It was a nice set, probably Japanese mid-century. I smiled and thanked her as she handed me a cup of green tea.

"So, you're Carly's friend?" she asked without preamble. I nodded. "Great. I love Carly and her mom. Brenda and I have been friends for decades. But the two of you, it's clear you've known each other for much longer than that."

I felt James start next to me. I reached out and took his hand, never taking my widening eyes off Angela. Her face was open, her hair was soft blonde, her pale blue eyes were extremely kind. She smiled at us reassuringly.

"You've come today without telling me anything about your-selves in advance, but I think you're here because you want me to tell you what you already seem to know, is that right? That you were connected by an extremely deep love in a past life. You missed each other last time around, too. It's a shame. Lots of people miss each other. James, you've been plagued by memories of your life with Elwyn, correct?"

"Yes." His voice was unsteady, barely hanging on. I squeezed his hand.

"Elwyn, you don't remember anything specific, do you?"

"I have one of James' memories imbedded in me now. We shared it sort of accidentally."

"The memory of your tragic and early death, correct?"

I was shaken to my very core. I had told this woman nothing. I had told Carly nothing. Yet Angela knew it all. I nodded in affirma-tion, unwilling to trust my voice.

"It was a violent death." She looked pained. She paused for a moment while James and I breathed rapidly in nervous anticipation of what she would say next. "I can tell you the whole story of your love, if you want me to. I see your past lives quite clearly; they are etched in your very souls. And your love is a transcendent one. It stretches back eons, by the way. The Victorian dilemma is only the most recent of your connections. Until now, that is. I hesitate, however, because once we know, we cannot unknow. Elwyn, I worry that James' memory of your past together is more fully formed than yours. I do not want you to resent it or feel like we have planted an old life inside your mind that you have no tangible connection to. I leave it up to you both. There is no rush, by the way. Your story isn't going anywhere." She stood up and said, "I'll give you a moment together to think about how you'd like to proceed."

With that, Angela, the soul reader, left the room. James and I were dumbfounded. We were speechless. I burst into tears. We held each other tightly and I sobbed with relief and sorrow and loss and redemption and reclamation all at once. James was overcome with emotion as well, relieved that finally someone had validated what his own dear heart had known for so long.

When I regained control of my emotions again, I looked at James and said, "You knew! You knew and you were so brave to finally bring us back together. How you must have suffered all this time. Thank you for never letting go of me."

"How could I let go, Elwyn? We really are connected. At our very cores." He held me tighter.

"What should we do? Should I let Angela tell us the story?"

"I don't know, Elwyn. I think this one's largely up to you, like Angela said. Do you want to know or not?"

I felt so torn. I had hoped that my memories would just flood into my psyche as my relationship with James unfolded. The connection I felt to him was not in doubt anymore, but the evidence was lacking. Angela could fill in all the gaps for us, but was it cheating? I just didn't know what to do.

I finally settled on the idea that knowledge is power. I wanted to know.

Angela came back into the room moments later, probably having sensed that the timing was correct and that I had come to my decision. She didn't ask the verdict.

"This chapter of your story begins in 1874. Elwyn, you were born to a family of merchants by the name of Weller. Your name was Joyce, but people called you 'Joy.' I can see that your family life was a happy one. You and James met when you were but children, as your two families became acquainted. You spent your childhood rolling around together on the grass like puppies. You grew together in the love that is born out of an ancient connection between two souls who are lucky enough to land in bodies of nearly the same age, in the same time, and in the same place. It is incredibly rare and so beautiful. Your love for each other grew in this time and place, nurtured by sunshine and family, and happy times.

"During this time, however, another man fell in love with you. James was away at school and your family fancied the connection you would make with this other man, should you marry him. They invited him to your family house, which was in the country, a very idyllic setting. They entertained him, hoping you would find him attractive. You, however, had no interest. Your father was not a cruel man, but he had a business empire to look after, so he was persistent. He thought it would be better for your stability to bring two wealthy families together by marrying you to him. The man's name was Clifton Slate.

"When the two of you met, you knew instantly that he was dangerous. You tried to tell your father, but he wasn't listening. He thought your puppy love for James was getting in the way of good judgment. You were correct, however. Clifton Slate was dangerous and cruel. One evening, while he was staying with you, he came to your room while you were getting ready for a dinner with your two families, and he tried to attack you. You got away and threw a heavy jewelry box across the room at him, missing and shattering your dressing table mirror. The sound brought everyone running to your room, where he was discovered with you pinned down to your bed, screaming.

"Your father of course called off the engagement, severed his business relationship with the Slate family and recalled James to your side.

"You married James soon after, as you were both of age. James was to carry on the family law business. James, you attended law-college in London and the two of you moved there with the blessings of your families. You were happy together and spent most of your time in each other's embrace. Joy liked to go for walks to explore the city, but James, you knew that the safety of your wife was in question, for Victorian London was far from safe, so you accompanied her on these jaunts. Are you positive you want to hear the rest of the story?"

"This is the part we both know," I replied. "When James shared his memory, we lived it—all the pain of it—together."

"That must have been shocking," Angela commented, sadly.

"Yes, it was. I ran away from him, I'm sorry to admit. I thought he was crazy."

"Don't be sorry, Elwyn. You did what anyone would have done," James soothed.

"Yes. These are difficult truths. Shall I tell you the rest of the story?"

"Please," we both said in unison.

"You were walking one clear night, passing over a bridge to get a view of the starlight sparkling on the Thames. You were ensconced in a kiss when a man approached you. It was dark and you did not see until it was too late that it was Clifton Slate. He had a pistol and he was aiming it at James. Joy pled with Slate not to hurt you. Clifton was raging, yelling insults and profanities. You never let go of each other's hands. Clifton shifted angrily, his body language was menacing. He changed his target from James to Joy. James, you protested with your whole body, trying to persuade Slate to calm down. That is when the gun went off, Slate ran away, and Joy was left to die in your arms. She had been shot high in the abdomen. The life ebbed out of her, flooding the stones around you, filling your heart with the most extreme form of loss that humans can know. The loss of your soulmate."

I was sobbing again by this point, James had his arm around me and I could feel his body racked with emotion by this time too. We were quite a sight. Angela's eyes were brimming with tears as well, she clearly felt connected to our story.

"James, you have spent two lifetimes searching for Joy and now you have found her. Elwyn, your heart and soul know that you belong with James. Do not let the fact that memory slipped away as you died change the fact that you are connected. You are linked in the deepest way that two souls can link. It transcends memory and time and place."

"Thank you," James said thickly, his voice choked with emotion. "My entire life has been spent haunted by these memories. You have laid these ghosts to rest."

"Sweetheart, you *are* the ghosts," Angela said lightly. "And you should do anything but rest."

We all laughed together, a much-needed catharsis, utterly full of joy.

"You knew that Elwyn's name was Joy. What was mine?" James asked finally.

"Why, it was James. It's always been James, strangely enough. Sometimes, parents just name their children the right thing."

"Wow." He was so happy to finally have answers.

"There's so much more to your story, you know, but I think you've had enough for one day. Will you come back to me sometime and we can explore some other past lives?"

"We would love to. What can we do to ensure that we meet again in the next life? Or can we?"

"We can talk about that too. I have a couple of tricks."

"Great. We were worried about that."

"Don't worry. You have bigger fish to fry right now." Angela looked at me pointedly.

"I do," I replied. "Am I in danger, Angela?"

"You are."

My heart sank like a stone, my stomach felt like lead. She leaned over and put her hand on mine. "Do not fear, Elwyn. Fear is your only enemy. Face this man head on and take him down. Do not let anything come between the two of you this time," she gestured to James as she spoke, "after so much searching."

"How? How am I supposed to protect myself?"

"Think like a fish," she replied, enigmatically.

James and I left Angela shortly thereafter, our heads swimming, our hearts brimming. She had corroborated our connection, validated our feelings and shown us that the path forward, although challenging, was not impossible.

We drove directly to our bed and breakfast, checked into our room and made unstoppable love for the first time in this lifetime. We scrambled against each other with urgency, pressing our bodies together into one, climaxing to the point of madness and fury, the energies of the universe drawn down into our elemental connection like a collision of atoms, bursting into wild, untamed power, consuming us with the force of our love.

Then, we slept sound as babes, still in love's embrace, glued together with the mingled sweat of our bodies. When we woke up, I was ravenous. It had grown dark, I had no idea what time it was. I figured it was somewhere past dinner but long before breakfast. My stomach protested vehemently. James looked at me longingly again, as though he could feast on me alone and be perfectly sated.

I gazed into his sweet, loving face, thinking that even if he looked like a harpy eagle, I would still love him from the center of my being. Hearing Angela's validation of our connection, which we had both felt from the first instant, somehow propelled us past the boundaries that people usually set up when they first get together. I felt as though all of those walls were being stripped away, along with my inhibitions and insecurities and fears, to be replaced by the purest love I had ever known. I smiled, and James smiled back. No words necessary.

"Let's forage," he said eventually.

"Before my stomach stages a revolution," I agreed. We giggled.

We got dressed and checked the time. It was after 9:00 p.m.. There was a little pub in Belfast, which amused us with its irony, so we drove back towards town. The lights were on, and the Saturday evening festivities were just getting underway. We found a little table in the corner from which to watch the musicians and enjoy the view.

We ordered Guinness because, when in Belfast! We laughed at our silly little joke and drank our stout. We ordered potato nachos, a traditional food of most Maine pubs, and held hands and cuddled in the booth unabashedly. I know I didn't imagine the looks he got from women around the bar, as well as the curious looks that they would give me, a cross between jealousy and wonder. How on earth did such a homely girl snag such a hot guy? But we had been snagged from the start, it seemed. Maybe James' entanglement theory really was the answer. I had forgotten to ask Angela.

We spent the evening at the pub, headed back to our b & b around midnight, and fell back into our bed, desperate to hold each other again. This time, we moved slower, reveling in the connections between our bodies, tasting every surface, pushing every boundary. We came together almost simultaneously, unable to contain our groans of delight. I could not get enough of him.

Morning floated in, silent as owl's wings, cool and calm and utterly full of joy.

"Maybe we shouldn't go back, James. What if we just start over, somewhere else, just us. No one will know what became of us."

"Like in that Postal Service song—'we'll give ourselves new names.'"

"Except that yours is always James!"

We laughed at the absurdity of our musings. "We like our lives in Portland, Elwyn. We can't run away. We will resolve all this stuff with Brent and move on. Together."

I knew in my heart that it would not be so easy, but I agreed nevertheless.

We drove back to Portland slowly, stopping at every little town and antique store that caught our eye. It took all day. The closer we got to home, however, the more my sense of foreboding about Brent settled in. I hadn't heard from him in days, but I knew his anger had not dissipated with the passing of time. Still, the euphoria I felt at James' and my newfound understanding of our past had not lessoned even as reality flooded back in. I was in awe of our feelings for each other. Mutual love is such an incredible experience—it had given me a whole new perspective on my existence. I knew I could believe in it—there was no more room for self-doubt. If James and I were supposed to be together, what was there to question? It was downright liberating. We got back to Portland around six, foraged in the fridge at James' house for some dinner and ultimately walked over to my place. It was time for me to face my fears.

It felt weird to go into this home that I loved, knowing that it had been violated by Brent, but I trusted that James' maid had done her best to clean the traces of him away. I walked in as boldly as I could, surveyed the clean, neat space and exhaled. It would take time, but I did not want to exile myself from my own space.

James and I sat on the couch, looked out the windows at the swath of blue water sparkling in the distance between buildings. It was just enough of a view to feel luxurious.

"I need to get plants for my balcony next weekend. Want to come?"

"I would come anywhere with you."

"How about London?"

He froze. "I hadn't thought about it."

"Do you think that going there will help me see the memories better?"

"Do you need to? I thought we were OK. I thought Angela had helped you through that need."

"I guess she did, but some part of me still wants to remember it all for myself. It's like amnesia, I guess. I feel something's missing and I want to reclaim it."

"I understand. I just don't know. London would be hard for me, Elwyn."

"We don't have to, it was just a thought. Don't worry. I'm fine. I could live the rest of my life without remembering, and it would be OK, as long as you're with me."

"I am with you, my love. You heard Angela, we're connected even farther into the past than the Victorian incarnation of our selves. I wonder what other lives we lived, who we were and how we met. It's amazing that she can see all that."

"If we hadn't had our mind meld, I'm not sure I could have let myself believe it. The mind revolts against such strange and fantastic ideas, you know."

"But you do believe her, don't you?"

"I do."

"Good. I love you, Elwyn." He spoke earnestly, fervently.

I breathed in those words as deeply as I could. I decided to let myself say them in return because it was true. Why hold back? "I love you too, James. Apparently, I always have!"

"I want to introduce you to my family. Is it too soon?"

"Too soon? We've been waiting over a hundred years. No reason to put it off."

"You seem excited about this whole new phase for us."

"I am. It's like part of the reason I've hated dating is the uncertainty. I've been insecure, lost and defensive in every relationship I've ever had. I was at sea. Now, all that uncertainty has dissipated. We're supposed to be together. What is there to feel insecure about? I am who I am, you are who you are, and you've travelled through time and space with the most horrific memories, just to bring us back together. What more could a girl want?"

"Flowers?"

"Like I said, we can go plant shopping next weekend." I smiled widely, unselfconsciously, and nestled into his embrace, where I spent the remainder of that wildly erotic evening.

CHAPTER FOURTEEN

"Oh, Thou, who Man of baser Earth didst make,
    And who with Eden didst devise the Snake;
For all the Sin where with the Face of Man
    Is blacken'd, Man's Forgiveness give—and take!"

THE RUBAIYAT OF OMAR KHAYYAM
TRANSLATED BY EDWARD FITZGERALD

B rent had been questioned about stealing my keys and entering my apartment. He denied everything, according to the policewoman who called me. Her name was Officer Simmons. She was the one who had helped out in my apartment during the investigation.

"I wish we could have gotten some fingerprints, or something. The DNA we took from the stain on the sheet was not a match to anyone in the database. Unfortunately, we can't just go asking suspects for their DNA without a warrant."

"That's too bad," I said, feeling a little despondent. "I was hoping this would be easier to manage."

"It won't be. In my experience, if he wants to hurt you, he will try very hard to hurt you. He seems like the cat type of criminal, though."

"What does that mean?"

"He wants to play with his victims first. He wants to taunt you, to get you angry, to torture you a little bit before he pounces. This is psychological warfare."

"It's so messed up."

"Yep. Just watch your back, Miss Derringer."

"I intend to."

"Call me if you need anything, please. You have my direct line."

"I really appreciate it, Officer Simmons."

"No problem."

I hung up feeling kind of sick to my stomach about it. I didn't want to rely on James to protect me, I had to figure out how to keep myself safe. What would Brent do next? It was Monday morning and it was time to head to school. James had already left. We had stayed the night at my loft and woke up as happy as two people can be. Our intimate exchanges were not limited to the evening, as we both woke up feeling amorous. I couldn't believe how much I wanted James or how deeply. I shook my head to try and clear my thoughts of the morning's acrobatics.

It was not long before I found out what Brent's next move was. By the time I reached work, I had gotten a lot of weird looks from people I passed—more than I usually did, anyway. It didn't register that there was anything unusual or disturbing about it until I saw the look on Jerry's face.

"Good morning, Jerry. Is everything all right? Everyone looks weird today."

"You don't know what happened, do you?" he asked.

"Seriously, what's going on, Jerry?"

"Oh, Derrin. It's bad. Real bad."

"God, what? Just tell me?"

He pulled out his phone, opened his College of Art email account and showed me an email that had been sent that morning. It contained a video. A very intimate and graphic video of me and James making love in my bed only hours before. I felt like I'd been hit in the stomach by a truck. I almost fainted. I grabbed the desk for support.

"How did he do this?" I asked.

"Who? It came from your email account, Professor D.. You must have sent it on accident."

"What?" I hollered. I didn't know how to handle the outrage. "I didn't do anything! This was Brent's work."

"Oh, my goodness. Of course. I'm so sorry I didn't see that right away. You'd never do anything so crazy. We need to manage it quickly before everyone on Earth sees it."

"Jesus." I couldn't think straight. Brent had gotten into my email, he had installed a secret camera in my apartment and now he was trying to sabotage my career. I had never felt more ill. "Call the head of IT. We need to do something right now."

While Jerry called the IT department, I called Olivia at home. I explained the situation and she was silent for a moment.

"This is bad, Derrin. I'm so sorry. You must be mortified."

"I am beside myself, Olivia. I don't know what to do. Jerry is helping me get in touch with the IT guys to take it off the web, but once shit is out there it's out there. Oh, poor James."

"I assume James is the person caught in flagrante with you?"

"Yes, he's my boyfriend. God, this is horrible. Help me, Olivia. Please!"

"I will be there in thirty minutes. Go to my office and take some deep breaths. Or scream a bit."

I laughed, despite myself. "Thank you."

I hung up and called James, my heart in my throat. How was I going to explain to this respectable businessman that his naked ass was out on the web having hot and heavy sex with an ugly brunette? Fuck.

He picked up immediately. "I am so sorry, James."

"About what, sweetie? Are you OK?"

"I am not OK. That fucker put a hidden camera in my bedroom." My voice choked.

"You're not saying..."

"I am. He emailed everyone at school the video of us from last night. And he emailed it from *my* account!"

"Holy shit. I'll be right there."

"No! Don't come. It would just be worse. It's being handled the best it can be. The IT guy is on it, apparently. He's retracting the email from all boxes, but if someone downloaded it, which they probably all did, then I can't control where it ends up. Probably on a porn website. Jesus, I feel so sick."

"It is really bad, but don't worry. It won't help."

"I know, but I can't help it. That motherfucker."

"He really is a motherfucker." James paused for a moment and said, "He plays his hand quick, though, doesn't he? He can never wait."

"But he plays well. He always has an idea for how to mess with me. This is diabolical. The sheets were just a distraction from the fact that he had hidden a camera. How many do you think there are? I can't believe this. I need to call the police officer again."

"OK. I'll check in on you a little later. You sure you don't want me to come there?"

"It would just make me feel worse. I'm so sorry you're on the internet in such an embarrassing way."

"I don't think it's that embarrassing. It's just sex, honey. Everyone has sex."

"I guess. Thanks, James."

"Talk to you later, Elwyn. Be brave."

I did not feel brave. I went up to Olivia's office where the team from IT met me soon after, laptops in tow, along with the head of security. Officer Simmons showed up a moment later with a woman from their cyber-crimes lab. She looked at me shyly.

"So, how did he get into my email account?" I asked since no one else was talking.

My IT guy's name was Gus and he typed furiously on his laptop while he answered. "Did you leave your office open?"

"No. But he stole my keys last week and copied them, he must have entered my office the same exact way he entered my home: through the goddamned door."

"We have found footage of someone entering Derrin's office Friday afternoon, matching the description of the person who stole a bowl from the ceramics studio the same day, incidentally. The lock on the office door was changed the following morning as soon as we realized it had been compromised," said the head of security.

"Did you have your password written down in your office or something?"

I felt like a total idiot. Of course I had my password written down. I can't remember stuff like that to save my life! I had it written on a piece of paper in my desk drawer. "Yes," I admitted sheepishly. "It was on a sticky note in my desk."

"Well, that's how he got into your account, I guess. I have retracted the email and shut down your account. I'll build you a new one later. What I'm trying to do is track where the email was sent from. It wasn't your IP address."

"OK," I said, flustered. "So?"

"So, that means you definitely didn't send it."

"I know that."

"Well, now everyone knows it. I'll work with Gus on this," said the detective from cyber-crimes. She sat next to Gus and they worked together quietly.

Officer Simmons said, "I've had the guys call Brent in for questioning again. I think if we could get into your place we could find the camera and possibly trace the feed. Also, fingerprint the cameras."

"He's good at covering his tracks," Gus interjected.

"Talented artist, cyber-criminal and psycho, all rolled into one. Great profile if he ever wants to do some online dating," I joked. No one laughed. I buried my face in my hands as I sat on Olivia's comfy yellow velvet settee.

The only good thing to come of the ordeal was that I finally filed the paperwork for a restraining order against Brent. He was not allowed within 50 feet of me—it would have been more had he not attended the college I worked at. Somehow, just having that piece of paper filed made me feel better. He would be served notice the following day.

By the afternoon, an email had been sent out to the school informing everyone that it would be a crime to send, share or view the pornographic email that was sent out earlier in the day, and that they should delete it at once in order to comply with the law, as well as with the policies of the school.

I was given the day off from my classes—Olivia didn't want me to have to face everyone just yet. "Let the fuss die down," she had said. We'll see, I thought, and went home.

The police questioned Brent, who, of course, admitted nothing. I was told that charging Brent would take time, that he had covered his tracks really well. He had several cameras hidden around my house. The police combed the entire place and swept it with EMF detectors three times. James said that no one on his end had reported any fishy emails, and no one was looking at him any more strangely than usual. I was relieved that at least Brent hadn't sent it to James' work. Maybe he just didn't know where that was yet. It occurred to me that James should be watching his back too. If Brent wanted to hurt me—I mean really hurt me—he would go after James.

How was I going to stop this guy? I lay on my couch after the police left, and stared out the window, letting a cup of tea go cold, as I pondered the question. I was in for a fight, that much was obvious. I had been caught off guard three times, now. Four, if you counted the stolen bowl in the studio, although I think he did that just to be spiteful. It was disconcerting to think that I had no idea what he would try to do next, nor any clue how to stop him. How could I get some of his DNA? It would surely link him back to the DNA evidence, and therefore, to the cameras, at least.

I could trap him into meeting me, perhaps, and get him to admit everything. I'd have to give it some thought and run it by James. I had never been a very good chess player, much to my dear dad's chagrin. I think he'd hoped that once he had taught me the game that I would be a natural and challenge him. Alas, I sucked. We rarely played chess after that.

Carly called around six and I answered. She knew that something was going on from the tone of my voice. I told her about Brent and the video and she was horrified, but curious. "And who might the gentleman in the video be, pray tell?"

"I'm fine, thank you for asking!"

"Of course, you're fine. The real issue at hand is that you're having sex with someone and I didn't know."

"His name is James. We met a couple of weeks ago."

"Whoa! That's unlike you, Derrin. Normally you tease a guy for a while first before you jump his bones."

"Yeah, well, this moved a little faster than normal. I really like him."

"You must. When do I get to meet the hunk?"

"I don't know. Soon. We can go out for drinks Friday, if he's free."

"It's a deal."

I didn't have the courage to tell Carly about the past life stuff yet. I knew that if anyone would believe it, it would be her, but I just wasn't ready to explain.

James showed up around 7:00 p.m., I had made a salad with some roasted chicken in it. We ate, although I mostly just pushed food around on my plate. I hadn't been hungry since the early morning. James lay down his fork and stared at me.

"What?" I demanded.

"I'm worried about you," James answered. "This has been rough for you and I just want to make sure you're OK."

"Let's see." I pretended to pause and think about it. "Um, no. I'm not OK. Students saw a video of me having sex with you. Colleagues saw it. Everyone saw it. It could be on a porn sight right now."

"What can we do about it, though? I mean, it's done. Let's think about what the next move is, rather than dwell on something you can't undo."

"Easy for you to say. This is easily the most horrible, embarrassing thing that's ever happened to me. In this life, at least."

We smiled halfheartedly at each other. I was lucky, I guess. James was not flustered by the incident. In fact, he was staying stronger and steadier about it than I was. It was reassuring.

"What if I trick him into meeting me and get him to admit everything? Do you think that would do it?"

"No, I don't trust him anywhere near you," James stated vehemently. "I don't want to give him more opportunities to hurt you. Besides, he's not about to admit to anything. Let's just think about it for a few days."

"A few days? Every few days, he does something egregious. Something new that gets under my skin and causes havoc."

"I know," James replied sadly. "I wish I could protect you better."

"That's not your job. That's my job. I should be protecting myself. I shouldn't have been so cavalier at the beginning when I first felt threatened by him. I just don't know. The police are not helping; the school is only doing damage control. I can't attack him because there's no solid evidence against him, and then that would make me the criminal."

"It's a catch 22, like I said. So let's stop thinking about it for tonight and there will be some clarity once we put it out of our mind. Problem solving has always been like that for me—the less I think about it directly, the easier it is to find an answer."

"OK, but I'll need alcohol for that. Let's get drunk." I felt my inner punk emerging. I was tired of being a victim. I wanted to fight.

James and I agreed that driving wasn't an option for this particular adventure. We settled on walking to the dive bar a few blocks from his house. It was a neighborhood place that had been there, in that incongruous spot, for over seventy years. It looked like it too. It smelled as stale as I thought it would, the decor was of the wood paneling variety, patinaed by ancient cigarette smoke and time, yellowed and unappealing. Black and white photos stagnated on the walls in random places, depicting Portland in past times. Hard liquor was the only way to go in a place like this.

James ordered scotch and soda; I did the same. I told him about the restraining order and he was relieved that it was filed. After our second drink, I leaned back in my scarred, black leatherette chair, enjoying the rusty squeal of its shot spring and sighed. "That's better." I looked at the stained ceiling: concentric rings of water damage spread from various, invisible epicenters, telling a story that no one cared about. "I never imagined I'd be a porn star."

James choked on his drink as he laughed. I doubt that was what he had expected me to say. But what could I say? The situation was untenable.

"I'm glad I'm your leading man," he replied, after he had stopped coughing.

"This is just a stepping stone to a promising future. Just like Paris Hilton. Maybe it will launch my modeling career."

We both laughed again. James took my hand in his. "We could branch into art films from there. Black and white, avant-garde. Bleak and melodramatic. Like a mix of Fellini and Bergman. All the scenes would be done in the nude."

"Didn't know you were into the antique film scene."

"Well, this is a nice springboard into a new career, like you said. I told you I was looking for a change."

After a third drink, I was seeing more humor in the situation than I had thought possible earlier in the day. What was the point of feeling oppressed? That was what Brent was trying to make me feel. Why should he have all the power? Power, I thought. *That was the key.* "I want the power back," I said, sounding non-sequitur.

"What power?"

"My power. I want to be the master of my situation. The controller of my destiny. I am an artist. I am a creator. I want to reclaim that power for myself."

"Brent is a strange person," James mused. "He got mixed up along the way and he can't process the world like everyone else.

What is his motivation? He wants what he can't have. He wants to possess you. He wants to possess that power you're talking about, Elwyn. He wants to suck it out of you. He thrives on it."

"But it's mine, and he can't have it," I retorted, childishly.

"Exactly. It's yours. But what if we pretend to give him what he wants?"

"What?"

"We let him think he has the power. Maybe it will defuse him and he will lose interest."

"How?"

We stared up at the disgusting ceiling for ages, thinking about this new question. The brown rings were telling a story, and that story was becoming clear to me. "He is like the water source responsible for those rings. You can't see it working behind the ceiling tile, but you can see the evidence of its effect. The source is insidious and damaging, but invisible. Brent's strength is his invisibility. His motivation is gaining power. His goal is to destroy me."

"Exactly. Wow. What disgusting imagery," James replied, examining the brown stains anew. "Understanding your enemy is the first step in destroying your enemy."

"Sun Tzu?"

"What?"

"'The Art of War?'" I asked, trying to clarify.

"Never read it. Sounds apropos, though."

"Never mind. So, what are our strengths?"

"Creativity, happiness, love... How about goals?"

"Survival. That is my strongest desire. I want to survive, this time around, so that we can be together, James."

James squeezed my hand and then he kissed it. "OK. Survival. So, when a cornered animal wants to survive, what does it do?"

I paused for a moment as chills played down my spine. I spoke the words slowly as they came to me. "It plays dead." It was an epiphany.

"Right. So, you play dead."

"What, like fake my own death?"

"Ha! That would do it, but then, how would you teach? No, I was thinking something a little less dramatic."

"Like pretend that I've had some emotional breakdown? That he finally pushed me to the precipice?"

"Exactly. Do you think that Olivia would play along?"

"Sure! I know she would."

"The question is, how do we convince him?"

"He wants that outcome. It won't be hard to convince him that he's won."

"Maybe we can find new careers as strategists. We could contract with the government."

"No thanks," I said and we both laughed.

We didn't have a plan, exactly, but I felt at least like we were on the track to a plan. I was excited. I was also tipsy. After drink four, we left. We wobbled home, holding each other around the waist, giggling and acting like kids. Luckily, it was a short walk. We started a fire in the fire bowl on James' terrace when we got back to his place. We sat on the cushioned glider and made out with playful attentiveness. When the fire finally died out and we went inside to bed, I whispered, "Thank you, James."

"For what, Elwyn?"

"For reminding me about what is important. I know we can win."

"Of course we can win, babe. We're in love."

CHAPTER FIFTEEN

"'Tis all a Chequer-board of Nights and Days
  Where Destiny with Men for Pieces plays:
  Hither and thither moves, and mates, and slays,
  And one by one back in the Closet lays."

THE RUBAIYAT OF OMAR KHAYYAM
TRANSLATED BY EDWARD FITZGERALD

James was a pretty optimistic person, for one who had been plagued by nightmares of a dying woman his entire life. He woke up smiling at me and the first words out of his mouth were, "It's all going to work out fine."

"I hope you're right, James."

"Of course I'm right," he said sweetly.

We both had headaches, but James had been nightmare free for almost two weeks and the previous night was no exception. James got us ibuprofen and made toast. I was relieved that we at least had a vague idea about how to move forward regarding Brent. I texted

Olivia to say that I didn't want to come in and that I would explain later.

She told me to take the day off and not to worry at all. James offered that I stay in his house while he went to work. I could imagine nothing more pleasant, so I thankfully agreed. I made some coffee, headed out to the terrace with a blanket and settled myself down on a chaise lounge in the sun.

Despite the peaceful surroundings, searing anger welled up within me as I pictured the video of James and me in our most intimate of moments. It galvanized my resolve: I was prepared to formulate a plan.

First thing, I decided I needed an accomplice on the inside. I thought about all the students in the ceramics department, and although I hesitated to confide in anyone, Ben already had a pretty clear idea of what was happening. Ben could disseminate information within the college about my fragile mental state. He could also get closer to Brent than I dared to. I didn't want to put him in danger, and I didn't want to put him in a situation in which he would be uncomfortable. Maybe I could just tell him that I was feeling pretty destroyed after what happened with the video and hope that he spread it around, but I thought that it would need to be more direct than that in order to have the desired impact.

Brent was masterful. He had a command of technology that trumped mine handily. I couldn't get to him on that front, even if I had an idea. I also had to be careful about what else I said or did that he could watch. I wondered if he had bugged my bag—I felt very paranoid, suddenly, that he could track me to James' house. I went inside, locked the patio door and called Officer Simmons.

"Simmons, here," she answered.

"Hi, Officer Simmons, it's Elwyn Derringer. How are you?"

"OK, ma'am. You hanging in there?"

"Yes, thank you for asking. Did you guys sweep my bag for bugs or cameras, when you did my apartment?"

"Yes. We were very thorough."

"Thank you. That's a relief. Listen, I have had an idea and I wanted to run it by you."

"Go ahead."

"I was thinking that I should pretend to give Brent what he wants—that way he loses interest in me and leaves me alone. I think that he wanted to destroy me since he couldn't possess me, so maybe we pretend that he did that."

"What do you mean?"

"Well, if there was a rumor about attempted suicide, or a mental breakdown or something that got around at school, maybe he would be put off the infatuation. Like a power play that he won."

"I think it would do too much damage to your reputation to have that stuff out there. Think about how everyone would look at you from then on. I always find it's best not to lie."

"I've thought about it. Maybe the attempted suicide goes too far, but everyone has breakdowns, especially artists. I don't think the negative effect would last long or have much impact, especially if the president of the school was in on it."

"Maybe, but I think Brent is going to want more. I think he's going to want a final blow, if you know what I mean."

"God, I hadn't thought about that."

"Criminal minds are surprisingly tenacious. They want closure. They don't want to leave loose ends. You mentioned that he had harassed a student in Rhode Island. Do you know her name?"

"I will call my friend at RISD and ask."

"Let me know and I'll run her. See what I find. Might give us a clue on how far we need to go in order to shut him down. Keep thinking about it, Miss Derringer, and I'll keep fishing around. I think that our best bet is to get his DNA to prove that he was in your home, but we don't have enough evidence to get a warrant. And I don't want to use you as bait."

"Scary thought. I could wear a wire, get him to admit what he'd done?"

"He won't. Let's leave that as a last resort, OK?"

"OK. Thank you so much for your help."

"It's hard not to be able to help more, ma'am. Really. I want to put this guy away so he can't hurt people anymore. Please, just keep in mind that he is very dangerous. Be careful."

"Thank you, Officer. I appreciate your help and concern."

After we hung up, I was so disturbed. Brent was unstable and Officer Simmons was right. He was very dangerous.

I called Olivia and asked her what she thought of the mental breakdown idea.

"Are you sure you want to put your reputation through that?"

"After what it's been through this week, a mental breakdown pales in comparison. I'm a porn star, remember?"

"God. It's such a rotten situation. OK. We'll try this out. Maybe he'll leave you alone. Maybe he'll go away after this semester and move on to some other place."

Olivia's words settled into my mind slowly and as they did, the vast implication of that idea hit me full force: "Move on to some other victim, you mean."

"One can only assume, Derrin. But at least you'd be safe."

Anger welled up in me again. How could I let Brent do this to anyone else? How could I be so selfish? How had I not realized that just getting myself out of his sights might put some other hapless woman there next? "Maybe safety isn't the priority here. Maybe ending his reign of terror is. Ending his career as a criminal once and for all, whatever it takes, and maybe getting him some mental health treatment."

"Derrin, I care about you and I don't want your life or wellbeing endangered."

"What if they are endangered this very moment?" I asked. I told her what Officer Simmons had said about him wanting a final blow.

Olivia, a very composed and compassionate person, sighed deeply. "What a disaster. A dangerous man is at large on my campus and I don't have enough evidence against him to kick him out. I am not happy with this situation." She paused, the tension mounting. "OK. We will work together to end it, Derrin. Whatever that means. But promise me you will not take any unnecessary risks."

"I won't. And I'll work with the police, if I can."

"OK. I support you one hundred percent, whatever you decide to do."

"Thank you, Olivia. You're a great administrator and a wonderful friend."

"Don't make me blush, Derrin. Talk to you later."

We hung up and I called Ben.

"Derrin!"

"Hi, Ben," I answered. "Things OK in the studio? Sorry I'm not there."

"Things are crazy. Everyone is worried about you."

"They don't think I belong in a 'Girls Gone Wild' video?"

"No one gives a shit about the video. Kids my age think of sex tapes as lame publicity stunts. Maybe you were just trying to promote your new gallery show."

I actually laughed. This is why I liked Ben. "You are hilarious. It's actually a pretty good idea!" We both laughed.

"So, I'm assuming you didn't post it yourself?" he asked.

"God! No! I think it was Brent."

"Of course. That makes sense. In his fucked up sort of way, I guess."

"Are you alone? I have a favor to ask you," I said eventually.

"Shoot, D."

"I am hoping that you can spread a little rumor for me. Tell a few people that I've had a mental breakdown and that I'm thinking of resigning. I want it to get back to Brent."

"God, are you OK, Derrin?"

"Yes, Ben. Really, I am."

"Then why would you want to spread a rumor like that?"

"I'm hoping that Brent will lose interest in torturing me now that the target is proving easier than he thought. More than likely, though, it will force his hand. He will make his next move and maybe this time, we can catch him."

"OK. Everyone knows you and I are close, so it would make sense for me to know how you're doing and everyone keeps asking.

Brent is friendly with one of the freshmen in Ceramics 1. I will make sure he hears about it."

"Perfect. Keep your eyes and ears peeled, and if anything happens that you think is suspicious or of interest to me, please tell me as soon as possible."

"I'm on it."

"Also, Ben, please be careful. Brent is dangerous."

"OK. You be careful too, Derrin. We need you around here."

"I will be back as soon as it's safe."

"I'll keep you posted on my progress."

"Awesome. You rock, Ben."

"I know."

We hung up and I was exhausted from all the phone calls and intrigue. People live like this? Too much drama for me. Give me the quiet life of a transcendental romance any day. I didn't need to live a crime thriller too.

I had one last call to make, and it was to Samuel at RISD.

"Hey, Derrin! To what do I owe the pleasure of two phone calls in two weeks?"

"Our mutual friend has pulled a pretty aggressive stunt." I explained about the hidden cameras and the sex video. Samuel was the second person to have the same reaction.

"And who might your hot-blooded beau be?"

"Seriously? He's my boyfriend. I like him a lot and this was sort of a hard way to start out in a new relationship."

"I'll bet, sweetie."

"So, I need the name of the girl Brent fucked with last time around. The student he tortured."

"I can't do it, Derrin. That's all confidential."

"Please, Samuel. I won't win with this guy unless I have ammo."

"You're putting me in a very hard position. I could lose my job. Imagine if it got out there that I had shared confidential information about a student with you?"

"I know. I wouldn't ask unless it was totally necessary."

"Jesus. Do not let this get back to me. I mean it. I will deny it full force."

"Samuel," I said, taking a breath, "I love you. You know I love you. I would never do anything to hurt you or jeopardize your career. But you also know I wouldn't ask unless I needed to."

He exhaled heavily and paused a moment, clearly torn. "OK. Her name was Delia Ordalinsky." I could picture Samuel shaking his head, now that he had told me. "This sounds like a tough time, Derrin. I hope this helps."

"It will help. You are amazing, Samuel. Thank you so much."

"Good luck."

"I'm going to need it. Love to Floyd."

"He's going to kick your ass if I get in trouble!"

I laughed, picturing it. "Thanks, Samuel."

"Any time, sugar."

Now that I had the name, I called Officer Simmons again and gave it to her. She asked how I had gotten the name, and I told her that I was friends with some students that had graduated from RISD a few years ago that remembered the situation. It was a lie, but I needed to protect Samuel.

She said she'd investigate and get back to me.

I had worked up an appetite. I made myself a salad and another pot of coffee and settled down at the sunny table near the French doors to eat. I was feeling positive about the possibilities, about the actions I had taken, about the way things were headed. This time, I would not let down my guard.

I decided to take the afternoon off from thinking about the situation. I had put wheels in motion, there was little left to do for the moment.

I went to James' library room. The stained glass was luminous in the sunlight. What a fantastic space. It had so much character. I'd been so distracted by James that I hadn't come in here again since the first tour. Now, I looked through all the many books, leather bound and beautiful, and chose a Victorian volume of children's fairy stories. It had been illustrated by Edmund Dulac, one of my favorites. I couldn't believe that James just happened to have this rarity in his collection. I would have to ask him how he came by it.

I read the stories and studied the illustrations, eventually growing sleepy in the oversized club chair. I had nodded off when my phone buzzed.

It was a text from a number I didn't know. It said, "Poor baby. You OK?"

Even though it was not a familiar number, I knew it was from Brent, and I got chills thinking about him teasing me. I also wasn't sure how to respond. News travels fast in a tiny art college, I thought viscerally. I was hesitant to engage. Then I thought of Brent moving from city to city, emotionally torturing and physically hurting other people. Other women. It has to stop, I told myself, and I texted him back.

"Who is this? I don't recognize the number."

Nothing for a few minutes. I thought maybe he'd given up.

I called Officer Simmons. "Yes?"

"He texted me from an unknown number. What should I do?"

"How do you know it's him?"

"I just know." I read her the text and my reply.

"Give me the number."

I did. She ran it through her computer. "It's a burner," she said. "He's good."

"What is a burner?"

"Don't you watch TV? Untraceable phone, usually paid for in cash."

"Oh."

"I don't think you should engage. I just looked into Delia Ordalinsky. She's dead."

"Holy shit! Sorry. God. How did it happen?"

"Suicide."

"Jesus."

"Really. I don't think this is a good plan. Block the number."

"Thank you. I'll let you know if anything else happens."

"OK," she replied and hung up.

My phone buzzed in my hand and I jumped. It was him.

It said, "How can I help? I am here for you."

I texted back, "No one can help, Brent. My career is ruined."

"Don't lose hope, Derrin," was his reply. "See, we are connected. You knew it was me. Meet me and we can talk about everything."

I wrote, "I don't want to see you. I don't want to see anyone. This is horrible. I've never been more upset. Are you happy? You hurt me back for rejecting you, and you hurt deep."

"You can't prove that I had anything to do with that video."

"Except that you did and we both know it. I don't have to prove it. You hate me!"

"I don't hate you," he texted, "It's the opposite. I'm in love with you. We belong together!"

"Then you know nothing of love. We don't hurt the ones we love," I reminded him. "Brent, please understand, I am not interested in dating you. Have you received the restraining order, by the way?"

Nothing. No reply. That shut him up, I thought. I wondered if I had succeeded in making him think I was despondent. I doubted it. I thought that I had come off more angry, which was true. I sucked at playing a part and I knew it. I wasn't about to trick him into believing that I was about to jump off a bridge. He knew me a little better than that.

I thought about Delia Ordalinsky. I thought about him driving her mad, doing crazy things to make her question her sanity, instilling fear and sadness in her heart and ultimately making her so miserable that she would kill herself. Unless he had killed her, but I didn't have any evidence of that. He just wanted people to all be as miserable as he was. I hated the thought of him doing this again and again to women all over the country. I wanted to stop him.

How had he gotten to be so messed up? How could a person be such a great artist and yet so deeply disturbed? What had attracted him to me, of all people? I couldn't figure it out. His drawings were so intense – so personal—they clearly told a story, but parts of that story were muddled and parts were clear. Was he haunted by something that had happened in a past life like James had been? James and I had been proving what power those past lives could have over our present state of mind, so maybe Brent was plagued by something that he just couldn't remember or deeply understand. And if that was part of the answer, shouldn't I have some level of compassion for him? I needed to step back and think more clearly. I decided to take a walk.

Portland is a Victorian town. It's full of beautiful details from the 1800's—they lend the whole town character. I looked up at the stately homes in the West End, surrounding James' house. His neighborhood was full of architectural gems. I admired the slate mansard roofs, the rounded third story tower rooms, the wonderful brick and stonework—each building told a story of style and crafts-manship that I just loved thinking about. I also started imagining the lives of the people who had inhabited those homes when they had been built. The fine dresses, the perfect posture, the piano being played in the evenings as everyone gathered around to listen.

These were the lovely images of Victorian life that I had roman-ticized. Yet, what about the arranged marriages? The abusive men? The broken women who couldn't even vote for a better life or a kinder future? It was a fight we were still trying to win, I thought, rather angrily. It wasn't a simple matter of pretending we were equal, it was actively working to live equally. Brent was trying his hardest to dominate me, just as Slade had wanted to dominate Joy. The connection seemed to create a buzz in my mind that I just couldn't reconcile. The two names vibrated against each other some-how. Or maybe it was just my phone vibrating in my pocket. I smiled as I took it out to see who was texting me. It was James.

"Just checking in," it said.

"Doing fine—out for a walk," I responded.

"Love you," he texted.

"Love you too," I answered, my smile growing wider as I imag-ined him in his sun-drenched office, surrounded by people who worked for him and admired him, but who would never understand him as I did. That was love.

If love could fix the issues James had had before we met, if it could repair a lifetime of pain and damage done to him by the memories of our love and of my death, maybe love could fix Brent's heart too. I couldn't imagine that a heart could be beyond repair. Maybe I needed to think about the problem in a new way. Hiding wouldn't work, lying about my mental state and trying to get him to admit his crimes wouldn't work, maybe honesty and compassion would. Maybe I could help him get the mental health help he needed to be a whole person again.

CHAPTER SIXTEEN

"And this I know: whether the one True Light,
  Kindle to Love, or Wrath consume me quite,
  One glimpse of It within the Tavern caught
  Better than in the Temple lost outright."

THE RUBAIYAT OF OMAR KHAYYAM
TRANSLATED BY EDWARD FITZGERALD

James returned home to the scent of dinner cooking. I had roasted some salmon with capers and made jasmine rice and veggies. He smiled instantly upon seeing me in his kitchen, wearing his apron.

"It's a good look for you," he said. "I could do without the pants, though."

"Oh, my, you've come home in a randy mood."

"Yes, my love. I want some home cooking and some sweet loving."

I shook my head at him and threw myself into his arms. We held each other for a long moment. Finally, knowing that it would be like ripping off a Band-Aid—better fast than slow, better sooner than later—I told him about my latest epiphany.

James froze. His demeanor changed instantly. "You want to meet with him to try to convince him to get mental health counseling? No. I'm sorry, Elwyn. I don't think it's a good idea for you to put yourself in harm's way, naively thinking that you can fix him. You would be placing yourself at his mercy—and he doesn't have any. Baby, I don't want to lose you again. I can't."

"I know, James, but think about this: the girl that he was fucking with in Rhode Island? Her name was Delia Ordalinsky and she is dead. Dead, James. Suicide. Brent is dangerous and completely insane. He has to be stopped. This is the best chance we have of doing that."

"It's exactly what we decided not to do!" James raised his voice; he was clearly getting worked up. "We agreed that you would just act like you were having a break down so that he would back off. We just got the restraining order in place. Meeting with him in any way is too dangerous. He's too fucking smart. He's going to hurt you. Trust me, Elwyn. He's ten steps ahead of you."

I didn't want to cry, and I didn't want to raise my voice. I could see from James' expression that I was in danger of losing this battle. I needed to present a clear and convincing argument for wanting to put myself in Brent's vicinity. My voice was soft but steady. "I've made my decision, James. I have to do this, because if I can save him, I should."

"Elwyn, it's not safe," James began vehemently.

I interrupted him gently. "I know. But he's obsessed with me just like he was obsessed with Delia. It has to stop and I know I'm the one who has to stop it. Love was the answer for us, James. I refuse to believe that fear is the answer now just because it's easier. If someone could have stopped Clifton Slate before he shot me on the bridge, it would have saved you lifetimes of pain. How could I live with myself if Brent hurts or maybe even kills someone, knowing that I didn't do all I could to help?"

Silence. I had played the Joy card, even though it meant hurting James, and it was gut wrenching. The last thing I had wanted to do was hurt him, but I couldn't see another way. He turned away, his expression one of excruciating pain distorting his pale, angelic face and he headed upstairs alone to change.

We ate dinner in silence. I could barely chew and swallow my food, I was so knotted up inside. I cleared the dishes and James washed them. When we were done, I took him by the hand and led him back to the library. It was dark but for the streetlight coming through the stained glass, casting eerie silver-blue shadows on the walls and bookcases. I turned on the lights and retrieved the Dulac book I'd fallen asleep with earlier.

"Where did you get this book?" I asked.

James took it and smiled faintly. His features softened, he stroked the cover. "Annabelle gave it to me."

"Why?"

"One of the stories in here reminded her of me. The one about a little boy who falls asleep and ends up in a different world within our world."

"Is that how she saw you?"

"Elwyn, until I met you, that's how *everyone* saw me. It's how I had begun to see myself. I am lost in a parallel world of loneliness and loss without you. Now that we're together, the world makes sense. It's everyone else whose perceptions of time and love are too narrow. You and I embody what it is to transcend time and space for love. Please don't ask me to sacrifice that willingly, not when I've finally found you again. It's too much. I just want to keep you safe."

His words were so honest, so achingly tender, so full of the loss that he had experienced through three lifetimes. Tears spilled down my cheeks as I pulled him into my arms. "Oh, James."

"I can't lose you, Elwyn. I just can't. Please. That idea you had about running away? I'm in. I'll sell everything I own and we can give ourselves new names."

I sobbed in his arms, knowing that I would like nothing more, and knowing that I needed to climb this formidable mountain first before I could earn that unfettered joy. Joy. What a crazy fucking world.

Finally, when I had regained my ability to string words together, I looked at him and said, "After we convince Brent to get the help he needs, and when I am satisfied that he won't hurt anyone else, I will do anything you want. Anything. I'll toss all my pottery into the sea and say goodbye to everything I've ever known, just to sail away with you. But not until we make sure Brent is under control. I can't let him hurt anyone else. I need to do this."

"I know." His eyes were brimming with unshed tears. "It's pure selfishness on my part to ask you to do anything less."

"Our first part of the plan worked. I haven't told you yet. I called Ben and told him to spread a rumor about me having an emotional breakdown and about me thinking about resigning. I talked it over with Olivia and she was on board. It didn't take long for the story to circulate and that's when Brent texted me."

"Wow. He doesn't waste time. I guess if he senses your weakness, he will try to contact you again. Although, who knows how this maniac thinks? If he does, maybe that's when you subtly explain that you think his work and his actions belie a mental instability and you want him to get help because you care about him."

"That's kind of what I was thinking. I believe that he won't be able to stay away from me, even with a restraining order."

"God, Elwyn. I really hate this. It gives me a terrible sense of foreboding to put all this power in the hands of a madman."

"Don't give in to the fear. I can't and neither can you."

"God loves the brave, Elwyn."

"Well, let's be brave. Together."

"Can you at least tell the police your plan? Then, maybe if he admits what he did but won't get help, you can at least have the police arrest him."

"I can agree to that. I would feel safer that way."

That night, I had a dream unlike any other I'd ever had in this lifetime. I was sitting in the sunlight, watching its dappled progress across a wide swath of green grass. I could hear laughter in the distance. I felt a sense of overwhelming joy. Joy. "Joy!" I heard the word louder and louder as someone yelled it. I realized they were calling for me. Coming closer. My heart did a funny leap in my chest as I sprang up from my mossy spot and hid behind the closest tree. "Joy?" As the voice came closer, I leapt out from behind the tree and into the embrace of my lover. "James," I cooed, as he kissed me on the mouth.

The idylls of Victorian country life were not fiction. The sun blessed us in that moment, enveloping us in a dewy golden light that stood outside of time. James kissed me and it was as though he touched my very soul. My body soared, full and elated, a winged angel full of hope and promise and the very essence of love. I awoke still full of that glowing moment, poised on the edge between two worlds bridged by one love.

I needed to survive. I needed to see my way through this mess and into a time of peace. James and I deserved that. I could not let history repeat itself. I would not.

CHAPTER SEVENTEEN

"The Moving Finger writes; and, having writ,
Moves on: nor all thy Piety nor Wit
Shall lure it back to cancel half a Line,
Nor all thy Tears wash out a Word of it."

THE RUBAIYAT OF OMAR KHAYYAM
TRANSLATED BY EDWARD FITZGERALD

I reluctantly climbed out of bed, leaving the down comforter and James' sleep warmed body behind in exchange for the cold floors and crisp air of a spring morning. I headed to the kitchen to make coffee and looked at my phone while it brewed. Brent had texted again. "You can't restrain love."

My stomach clenched as I thought of willingly delivering myself into his clutches, with a flimsy idea of helping him see reality and getting him help. It was such a bad idea, but I didn't see any alternative. I thought about what to write back.

I couldn't think of anything yet. It could wait.

I put the phone on the counter and watched my own hand shake as I poured my coffee. I am not a victim, I told myself. A new mantra for a new day. I said it over and over in my mind until my hand stopped shaking and the coffee flooded into me. I relished its warmth, a contrast to the chilling air around me. It was only just six. The sun was rising, as it always did. The earth rotated on its axis and revolved around the sun and the sun would burn the cold away and fill the world with its life-giving warmth, and everything would continue on. Wars and peace, famine and strife and joy and love and every state in between. And what did it matter in the end? We would just come back and do it all again. The cosmic revelation brought my little plight into perspective so that when the sun peeked above the tree line, I accepted its gift of radiance, pulled it into my very being, and resolved not to be weak or sad or insecure any longer. I am incandescent, I told myself. *I am a being of light, meant to share the light, not cower in the shadows. Fear, be gone.*

I headed back upstairs and nestled in bed next to James, this time sitting up against the headboard and drawing his warmth into me as he slept. I had brought the Dulac book with me and was reading the fairy tale that his sister had said reminded her of him. I read it in all its heartbreaking sweetness, truly hoping that the boy would be returned to his family in the end, and then asking myself why I felt that way. Wouldn't he be happier among the fey fairies, where he was understood? I was torn. It was just a fairy tale, I reminded myself.

I glanced down at James who stirred beside me. I closed the book and placed it on the bedside table. I slid back under the covers and stroked James' fair hair. He looked so peaceful, so young, and my heart filled with gratitude. This man loved me, he had loved me for an age, and I loved him. Whatever else happened, we had been given a rare gift. I breathed him in and let that love envelop me in its flawlessness. I closed my eyes and slipped back into a dream, knowing full well that the day would start soon enough, despite me.

This time, my dream was dark. It was broken shards of glass reflecting a scene of anger and fear. I saw my own eyes, red-rimmed and tear-filled, and the shattered, chaotic scene surrounding me. I saw Slate and my father yelling in each other's faces, I saw my mother's arms around me, I saw the bruises on my bare arms and my torn gown, and the remains of a necklace of pearls that had been ripped from my neck as Slate had tried to force himself upon me. I saw all these things, a passive observer, like I was watching a film. When my attention drifted from my own sad eyes to the scene behind me, Slate met my gaze with hatred so deep it was animalistic. My heart froze within me. Then his face flickered, and instead of looking into Slate's eyes, I was staring into Brent's eyes, filled with the same wild, all-consuming anger that he had when I had seen him last. I bolted awake.

James woke up as he felt me jolt in the bed next to him. I told him all about my dream of the altercation in my Victorian bedroom, of my father and mother, of Slate looking at me with vehement hatred, of him morphing into Brent. James held me closer than I could have asked.

"I don't want to be afraid of him. I can't be afraid of the past. It's gone."

Then, I told him of the garden dream I'd had in the night, and how he had called out for me. I told him about the kiss we had shared, and how real it had felt. He held me and kissed my head. "I remember," he whispered. "I remember that day. I looked everywhere for you and there you were, hiding in the ferns. You dove out from behind that tree into my arms and I had never felt more complete happiness."

"Joy."

"Indeed. That you were."

"Do you ever wish we could go back and do it again? Maybe not move to London?"

"I spent a good portion of my childhood wishing to live in the past. It doesn't do any good, Elwyn. We exist now and if we dwell on the past we do not move forward."

I smiled wistfully, imagining the little boy with the big blue eyes holding all the love of two grownups lost in the past, in his child-sized heart. How did he bear it? I held him closer and kissed the dip where his clavicles gave way to vulnerable flesh below. He groaned as I explored his tender spots with my mouth. I wanted nothing more than to enfold him at that moment, to hold him, to have him, to give him everything of myself, to lose ourselves together in this present perfect.

Afterwards, I lay in his embrace, thankful for every single moment of our time in love, praying that it wouldn't end in tragedy again, this time around.

CHAPTER EIGHTEEN

"And if the Wine you drink, the Lip you press,
End in the Nothing all Things end in - Yes -
Then fancy while Thou art, Thou art but what
Thou shalt be - Nothing - Thou shalt not be less."

THE RUBAIYAT OF OMAR KHAYYAM
TRANSLATED BY EDWARD FITZGERALD

S immons offered a plan when I told her of my idea. I wasn't sure
it was a good plan, but it was something. She told me she didn't
want me to go to the police station, fearing that Brent was going to
be monitoring it. She assured me that the safest thing for me to do
was stay put and let the officers come to me. I directed them to the
back gate of James' house. They came in an unmarked car in plain
clothes, but they looked so official anyway that they were unmistak-
able. I unlocked the gate in the high brick wall and led them through
the garden and yard to the house. We sat with the curtains drawn, all
the while hoping that they had not been observed.

Simmons introduced me to her two colleagues. "This is Detective Anders and Lieutenant Berger." The former was a woman about my age with kind eyes, translucent, milky skin and auburn hair. She could have modeled in commercials for shampoo, I mused. She was just so pretty. I smiled. Berger, in contrast, was a wide man with mottled skin, scarred worse than mine, and a meaty jowl that shook when he moved. He must have been close to sixty. He was a brow mopper, I noticed, sweating profusely, despite the fact that the room was only 64 degrees. He returned my smile, though, and I was at ease with them immediately.

"Here's the plan, miss," Anders began. "We know that the suspect has contacted you. We are aware that you wish to help him seek mental health counseling. On the off chance that he provides concrete evidence of his crimes against you, however, with either a verbal confession to one of the crimes or the statement of intent to commit further crimes, we will apprehend him. He won't willingly give up this information, and I doubt you can coax it out of him, but it's worth trying if it yields anything we can use, including a sample of his DNA. If he asks you to go with him someplace, you can't go. You will do what you can from the secure location we're setting up. We're working with a coffee shop downtown to bug a table so you don't have to wear a wire."

"So how do you hide the fact that you're bugging the place?"

"Trade secret," Anders smiled shyly. "Suffice to say we piggyback on the Wi-Fi signals already coursing through the air and hide in there."

"Cool. What am I supposed to do if he insists on leaving?"

"Let him leave. Do not go with him under any circumstances."

"OK. What if he threatens me?"

"We will arrest him immediately. We'll have undercover agents posted around. One will be a barista in the coffee shop, one will be outside pretending to be homeless. Another will be in a car down the street. You get the idea."

"I do. You'll hear him if he threatens me and make your move."

"Yes."

"OK. I am only going to try to talk him into getting help, though."

"You couldn't get him to admit anything if you were actively trying to do so. If you just talk, though, the possibility exists that he will say something incriminating that he didn't mean to say."

"What about the DNA?"

"He might take a sip of coffee or water, or run his fingers through his hair and leave some behind. If he does, we'll collect the samples and see if we can get the DNA from his saliva or hair."

"OK. When are we doing this?"

"Tomorrow. Plan to see him in the morning."

"I'll text him now."

I picked up my phone and started typing. "We need to talk."

"Where?"

"Speckled Ax coffee shop, tomorrow morning at 9:00."

Faster than he could have written the words, he replied, "See you soon, Derrin."

Chills gripped my nervous system as I shuddered. I held out the phone to the three officers. "Done. He'll be there." I was suddenly gripped with insecurity. Was I doing the right thing? I would never have the answer for that question, but my resolve had been galvanized. I needed to try to help him, or at the very least, stop him.

Anders instructed me to put on a light blouse or dress with no sleeves so that it would be more obvious that I was not wearing a wire. She suggested that I be as subtle as I could, because he wouldn't take kindly to the suggestion that he was crazy.

"Who would?" I asked, trying to lighten the mood. "Do you have the name of a psychologist I can recommend to him?"

They said they'd get a name and call me later. Then they left.

James came home early from work bearing a couple of bottles of fine Prosecco. I had texted him earlier to warn him that tomorrow was the day I would meet Brent. James hadn't texted back. Instead, there he was, on the threshold of his home, kicking off his wingtips and stalking towards me as he did on the day we met, his eyes full of unfathomable emotion. My heart started racing just looking at him.

"I wanted to be with you. I decided to finally be a manager and make everyone else do the work. I'm all yours."

"Thank you," I replied lamely, as he kissed my forehead. I slid my hand around his waist and we walked to the kitchen. James put the bottles in the fridge and I kept my hand around his body, praying that it would be enough to keep me afloat.

"Can we sit and talk for a little while?" he asked, his voice serious and quiet.

"Yes, of course."

"I called Angela today," he said without preamble, once we were seated in a sunny spot on the couch.

"Oh," I replied dumbly, not sure what I thought about this revelation.

"I wanted to go see her again with you before you met the madman, but you're moving too fast. I needed to ask her some questions."

"Did you like her answers?"

"No. I didn't. She won't read futures, she said, even though they can be as clear to her as the past."

I admit that my heart sank a little, knowing this. "OK," I replied without affect.

"She did tell me that no matter what happens, you and I are meant to be together. We need to draw our strength from that, Elwyn. Past, present and future, all tied into one neat knot. Nothing will keep us apart forever, sweetheart. We will always come back to each other. We always have and we always will. OK?"

Tears were flowing freely now, my love for James was the most powerful element in the universe at that moment. "I understand," I answered. "I am so thankful for that."

"I am too. Eiffel Tower on Christmas Eve. Do you understand?"

"James, please. Don't."

"Elwyn, I don't want to wait another lifetime searching. I want a plan next time!"

"I'm not going to die, James. Please. Don't worry. I won't let him hurt me!"

"I trust you, my love. But I will never, ever, trust him."

We held each other for a long, quiet moment.

"Christmas Eve, then. I will always know it's you."

"And I you, my love. I would know you with my eyes closed. The universe wants us together, Elwyn."

"I just can't fathom how it all works."

"Elwyn, if you want to understand the nature of the universe, look no further than your precious human heart. You are the universe, my dear, and so am I. We are made of stars and we will end up being consumed by a star. And in the meantime, we're meant to be together. It's an elegant dynamic, if you ask me."

"Entangled souls."

"Yes. Entangled souls."

We lay in each other's arms for a long while before either of us dared to speak. When I could finally use my voice I asked, "How was work?"

"It was good. I'm close to the end of this deal in Boston and I'm very hopeful."

"Sounds like a lot of effort."

"Everything worth doing requires effort."

"Yep."

"Speaking of which, are you nervous you won't have time to make work for your show in a few weeks?"

"Wow," I replied, flabbergasted at his ability to remember everything about my life. "I haven't thought about my show at all! Luckily, I have enough work made. It's all in the studio in crates already. I had a few new things I wanted to slip in, but it's no emergency if I don't."

"I'm glad you show your work in big cities. It deserves to be seen."

"Thank you," I replied, feeling overwrought.

"Seriously, Elwyn. I know I've told you, but your work is lovely.

It is graceful and disarming and powerful all at the same time. It's so personal. I'm proud of you."

"Would you respect me if my work wasn't as good?" I joked.

"Absolutely not," James said with a mock serious tone. We burst out laughing. "I respect you, Elwyn. That respect comes from more than just your beautiful mode of self-expression, though. It comes from your courage and tenacity."

"I am stubborn!"

"You are. I wouldn't have it any other way." He squeezed me to him, and I could feel the desperation beneath his bantering facade. It broke my heart all over again. "Tell me the plan for tomorrow," he said eventually, his tone just a little too cheerful.

I breathed in deeply and said, "It's all set. The police are going to surround the coffee shop and they have the place bugged, just in case he freaks out. It's foolproof."

"Nothing is foolproof."

"As long as I don't leave with him, which I won't because he's crazy, I'm safe."

"No one is safe, Elwyn," James spoke gravely. "Not in this world and certainly not sitting across the table from a psychopath. But I trust you. Godspeed, my love."

"Thanks, James. It will all be over soon, I hope."

I felt James shudder beside me, but his face did not belie his trepidation.

"Let's spend the evening naked," I suggested, hoping to distract him.

He turned slowly to face me, eying me the whole while with a mix of love and lust and wonder and sadness. "Now that's a good idea," he whispered low, shifting his weight to all fours on the couch and leaning over me like a wild tiger. I longed to be his prey.

James unbuttoned my thin blouse as he kissed my neck. He kissed all the way down my bosom; my body arched at the tantaliz- ing, sweet yearning I felt as his hands slid down my back, applying just the right amount of pressure. I wanted him to take me again and again, everywhere, in every way. I wanted to feel our bodies melt into one being. I abandoned my senses to him and let myself be adored. I wanted to remember this ecstatic moment for the rest of my life, and for all of my lifetimes to come. I never wanted to forget this man and his love for me again.

CHAPTER NINETEEN

"For in and out, above, about, below,
    'Tis nothing but a Magic Shadow-show,
    Play'd in a Box whose Candle is the Sun,
    Round which we Phantom Figures come and go."

THE RUBAIYAT OF OMAR KHAYYAM
TRANSLATED BY EDWARD FITZGERALD

I dressed the following morning with deliberate care. I followed the advice of Detective Anders and wore a lightweight, sleeveless black shift that cut deeply in front, making it obvious that I was not concealing a wire. I hoped it would be enough to put Brent at ease, although why anyone would suspect I was wearing a wire I couldn't imagine.

James and I were subdued, having reveled in each other so fully the night before had left us with little left unsaid or unfelt. Now, we just existed side by side, awaiting a fate we could not predict.

James drove me up to Congress Street. I had decided to say

goodbye to him a few blocks away and walk the rest, just so Brent didn't see James. I thought it would be better this way. The second he parked the car I was seized with regret over my decision to meet Brent. It suddenly felt terrifying and wrong. What was I thinking, I wondered, trying not to panic. I didn't let it show, but inside, my heart pounded against my ribs. James and I said our farewells; he kissed me once on the lips and once on the forehead. "I will see you soon, angel. Call me the second you can and I will come for you."

"Thank you, James. For everything. I..." I hesitated, not wanting to sound trite.

"It's going to be OK, Elwyn. I love you. Always have, always will." He tipped our foreheads together tenderly.

"I love you too, James. See you soon."

I hadn't wanted to look weak in front of James, but as I saw his taillights recede, it hit me that I was on my own for this task. I burst into tears, wildly angry that I had put myself in this position, furious that at long last I knew love and that it had been threatened from the moment it first bloomed. I was livid that any human being would dare come between me and that long-deserved happiness. I wanted joy. I wanted love. I wanted life. And I wanted this nightmare to be over.

I kept crying as I walked, abandoning myself to the grief. I slowed down and wiped away my tears as I approached the coffee shop. I decided not to look around for the police, but I kept my head tilted forward and entered.

I ordered a latte from the policewoman cum barista, wondering if she actually knew how to make one, sat down at the assigned table, and waited impatiently for my worst nightmare to show up. He was right on time. He walked in, dark eyes glittering with unconcealed interest. He nodded to me and walked past, up to the counter, and ordered a coffee.

I waited patiently, not letting my nervousness get the best of me. Brent added milk and sugar to his brew and sauntered over, nonchalant.

"My, you look nice, Derrin, despite the red eyes. Have you been crying, honey?"

I couldn't help myself. I narrowed my eyes at him and prepared to answer in anger. Then I thought of James and remembered that I was there to help this damaged man before me. I lowered my gaze to my cooling latte. I took in a deep breath and looked at Brent again. His expression gave nothing away.

"How's school?" I asked.

"Really? "How's school?'" he mocked as he sank into the chair across from me. "You kicked me out of your ceramics class, which I loved, two weeks before the end of the semester. It was really mean."

"I'm sorry, Brent. I know how much you love clay. I just couldn't have you so close with your feelings for me so obvious."

"My feelings for you," he began, leaning back in his chair, extending his legs below. They brushed against mine and I shuddered. "Let's see. You didn't give a goddamn about my feelings for you a week ago. What changed?"

"I think you're deeply obsessed with me. I think you were obsessed with Delia Ordalinsky. She's dead, so you had to find someone else. We need to talk about this and move on. Love and attraction need to be mutual. In this case, they're not. If you're having a hard time coping with that, maybe you should talk to someone."

"What, like a school councilor? No thanks."

"Your work is so dark, Brent. You clearly have a lot of violent images in your mind and in your heart. Art is a great way to get those out, but if your relationships reflect all that pain and damage, you'll never find the love you're looking for."

"How profound, Derrin. You're a real philosopher."

"Don't make fun of me, Brent. I care about you and I want to help you. You need to heal your heart. You need to find a peaceful, respectful way to love another person. You can't smother them, hurt them when you're angry, insult them or make them live in fear. That is not love, Brent. That's not how love works."

"Oh! Now you're a love expert. Nice. You've been with your

new boyfriend for what—three weeks? At the most? And you're teaching me about love? You didn't teach me anything about ceramics, and you're not about to teach me anything about love. You don't know the first thing about love!"

He'd shouted those words and I jumped in my seat at the intensity of his voice. He violently rubbed his face and his eyes, pulling back his unruly hair in mounting anger. "Let me tell you something about love. Love grips you by the stomach and clenches so tight you want to die. Love drives you to create something to take a little of the pain away. Love makes you want to hold on to her, to possess her so hard that you could rip her heart out and shove it into your own chest."

I was stone still, watching in horror as all of Brent's wild madness bubbled over. If I didn't take my chance now, I would never get another one.

"Is that *love* what you wanted me to feel the power of? You wanted to show me how intense your feelings are—how much you are hurting—by hurting me?"

"Yes!" He yelled it. "I wanted you to know how much you had hurt me!"

"That video did it. You showed me, Brent. You showed me how much you're hurting. I understand it now."

"That video, Derrin..." He stopped, suddenly aware that he was incriminating himself. "That video," he continued more calmly. "I have to admit, I was pretty surprised you posted something so private on the internet. Let alone emailing it to everyone. Did you do it to hurt me?"

I had not been expecting this turnaround. He really was conniving. I had lost that round.

"I didn't post it, Brent. You know that."

"It's career suicide, Derrin. People don't easily forget that kind of transgression, let alone from a professor. Your boyfriend, James, is it? He really seemed to be giving you what you want, everyone saw that. No need to rub it in just to prove that you had a man already."

I glared at him angrily. I just couldn't help it.

"Yes," Brent continued, "James really seems to understand your body. Your orgasm was inspiring to watch. 'Ah, ah, ah!'" His cruel tone and vulgar mocking of one of my most personal moments took it too far.

"Fuck you, Brent. Don't you mock me."

"No, Derrin. Why would I mock you? You're right. You're too perfect and sweet to be made fun of. All I'm trying to say is that Mister Macho might understand you sexually, but I understand you as an artist."

"Do you?"

"I do. You create out of a deep sense of loneliness. Your work shows your insecurity and repression, years of struggling to be some-body in a world already flooded with greatness. You're trying, Derrin, but you need someone to push you to make good work great. To make your mediocre ideas spark to life. To challenge you to dig a little deeper into what it means to be an artist."

"And I suppose you're the one who could do that?"

"Yes. You know that my work is inspired. You know that I have the kind of talent you've only ever dreamed of. You want it."

"Tell me more about what I want. This is enlightening."

Brent glared at me hard. He leaned in and grabbed my wrist, pulling it closer to him, grasping it with desperate intensity. The strength in his hands was unnerving. My whole body tensed, my eyes involuntarily darted to the green haired barista at the counter whose body was facing me in an act of solidarity. I had forgotten the police were even there. It gave me courage.

"Brent," I said, trying to pull my hand away from his grip, "Brent, you need help. Do you see what you're doing to me right now? You're hurting me! You can't control your anger. You can't control your emotions. You're obsessed with me and you think that's love but it's not. You need help and I want you to get better because I believe, with my whole heart, that you could be a really great artist someday. You just need to get yourself under control."

Brent glared at me angrily, violently releasing my hand, and said, "So you want me to check into a mental institution? Get the help I need? What about you? You hurt people and you don't even care. You're the one who needs help."

"What the fuck are you talking about? I am not the one who's been sabotaging kilns, stealing keys and breaking into people's houses! Those are not the actions of a sane man."

"You pretend to care about me, but you only care about yourself. You don't even really care about your boyfriend. You're a selfish bitch. Don't you dare try to tell me that I'm crazy." He rubbed his face again, sort of an obsessive gesture at this point, like he was trying to rub some horrid vision out of his eyes.

"I'm sorry I don't love you, Brent. But I do want you to be happy. You can learn to deal with your big feelings better. Maybe then you'll grow up and see that you're not the only person in the world who can't have something he wants."

"No," he said, almost inaudibly. "I'm not." He reached into his pocket and pulled out a phone. He turned it on and showed it to me. It was a picture of James and I, walking together, in the West End, just a few nights earlier. The next photo showed us entering James' house. So, Brent did know where James lived. My heart suddenly seized up with fear. James. Was James OK?

"Why are you showing me pictures of me and James?" I demanded, trying not to belie my panicking heart.

"Because you're such a pretty couple."

With that, he picked up his un-drunk coffee, put it in the dish bin and left.

I sat in stunned silence. All I had to show for this encounter was a cold latte and a reddening bruise around my wrist where he had grabbed me. I had utterly failed.

CHAPTER TWENTY

"Up from Earth's Centre through the Seventh Gate
    I rose, and on the Throne of Saturn sate,
    And many Knots unravel'd by the Road;
    But not the Knot of Human Death and Fate.

There was a Door to which I found no Key:
    There was a Veil past which I could not see:
    Some little Talk awhile of ME and THEE
    There seem'd - and then no more of THEE and ME."

THE RUBAIYAT OF OMAR KHAYYAM
TRANSLATED BY EDWARD FITZGERALD

The police offered to give me a ride home but I declined. I just wanted to be alone. Officer Simmons reassured me that I had done all I could and that at some point Brent would slip up and we would catch him. I agreed unenthusiastically.

I started walking, lost in my own thoughts, not quite ready to call

James and admit that he had been right. Brent was crazy, but he was not stupid. He wouldn't just say, "Gee, Derrin. You're right. I *do* need help! Take me to the institution of your choice." I don't know what I had been thinking.

I shook my head. I was naive and a total fool. How sad. He knew where James lived, as well. That was scary. This was a total mess and I had no more ideas about what to do. When in doubt, I thought, get back to work. I hadn't touched clay for days and it was starting to get to me. I needed to center. I needed to think. I called James to let him know that I was OK.

"Sweetie, how did it go?"

"It was a pointless mess. I don't know what I was thinking."

"I'm sorry. Can I take you out for lunch?"

"No, I'm going to go to the studio for a little while. Can we have dinner instead? Maybe Noodle House again?"

"Sure sweetie. I'll meet you there at 7:30 p.m.."

How could I ask for a kinder man in my life? How could he be a lovelier person? Something was nagging at me, though. Then, it hit me. I should have told James about the fact that Brent had photographed us in James' neighborhood. I tried to call him, but he didn't answer. I texted it instead, glad to have remembered.

The studio noises literally screeched to a halt the moment I walked through the door, as though it was an old western movie and I was the villain. I had somehow forgotten to be embarrassed as I entered the studio. I had entirely forgotten about the video, that is, until I saw the looks on everyone's faces. I was supposed to be distraught and instead I was sauntering into the place like the Queen of Clay. I smiled at everyone and said, "Nothing to see here, just your average, every day, local celebrity!"

A few people laughed. Some of them just looked down at their work, unsure what to say. I thought I'd better make a speech.

"Sorry I've been out of the studio for a few days. As you can imagine, the video that was sent from my account came as quite a shock to me. It was an egregious violation of my privacy and I'm really pissed off. But what's done is done and I can't undo it. So, if you will assist me, I'd like to put it behind me and move on with the rest of my life! We have to wrap this semester up in a matter of two weeks. Wet work ends this weekend. I'll post a timeline for finishing everything and getting the studio cleaned out. Thanks for under-standing and being patient."

There was a good ten seconds of silence and then a little voice at the back of the room said, "Welcome back, Derrin." It was Elaina.

"Thanks. I'm happy to be here."

After that, several brave people came and talked to me for a few minutes. I eventually got back to work, and it felt really fricking good. About an hour later, Ben walked in and said, "Derrin! I didn't expect to see you yet. Everything OK?"

"Thanks again for your help, Ben. It's as good as it's going to get for now. Everything looks ship shape in here, my friend. Thank you for holding it all together for me."

"Well, it wasn't easy, but anything for you."

We both laughed. "Are you ready to graduate?" I asked him.

"No! I have a ton left to glaze. I am bisquing the big sculpture this weekend. After that, it's just finish work and setting up the senior show."

"Awesome. I'm excited for you."

"I heard back from Pratt—I'm in for grad school!"

"Wow! I'm so excited for you!" I hopped out of my seat and shook his hand. "Are you going to do it? You'll love New York. It's so much fun."

"I think so. I could use a change of scenery. Besides, the drama around here is getting thick."

We both laughed again and then got back to work. I was thankful to have Ben around and I'd miss him very much.

Around three, I left and walked home. I took a shower, and since I had a few minutes, I lay down in the sunshine on my couch. Before I knew it, I was asleep, sucked deeply down into a dream of the past. I was Joy, in my bedroom again. This time, the mirror was whole. I was putting on my pearl necklace. I heard the door open behind me. I looked up to see Clifton Slate's reflection in the glass.

"What are you doing here? I'm dressing for dinner."

"I wanted to see you. You look lovely."

"Thank you, but I need a few more moments of privacy, please."
Joy's voice was unfamiliar to me, but her feelings were my own. And
we were terrified. My heart raced, my hands were sweaty. I hated
being with this man and my body was reminding me just how much.

He walked towards me and I stood up, feeling like a cornered
animal. My hand automatically grasped a heavy metal jewelry box
on the dresser behind me and as Slate circled around, I walked backwards. He rushed towards me suddenly and I threw the box. It flew
just past his face and hit the mirror, which shattered loudly. I
screamed as he lunged and forced me to my bed with his heavy
body, hands gripping my delicate wrists.

I woke up still screaming, fear prickling my skin. Its visceral
intensity must have its own energy signature, I thought. I gasped for
breath and tried to calm down as adrenaline pulsed through my
veins. He had wanted to hurt me. He would have hurt me if I hadn't
thrown that box and screamed, I realized. My hands were shaking. I
breathed in deeply to calm myself down to think clearly.

An idea had begun to coalesce in my mind. Even after several
minutes, I couldn't shake the dreams about the broken mirror. I
combined the one I just had with the one from the early morning. I
tried to put it all together like a scene from a movie. I had thrown
the box through the mirror accidentally—I had been aiming for
Slate. He dodged it and came at me just in time for me to see my
own reflection shatter. The pieces didn't fall away, however, and I
watched in the splintered glass as Slate overpowered me. I screamed
and saw the door open behind us. He had me pinned to my own
bed, and it took two grown men to drag him off of me. His anger was
primal and overwhelming. I sat petrified, trembling on my coverlet,
watching them drag him away. I looked away only to see my pain
and fear reflected in that broken mirror as the shadow of Clifton
Slate was removed from the scene. In my morning's dream,
however, just as he had looked at me, Slate's face had morphed into
Brent's.

The revelation was physically painful. How could I have missed it? How could I be so stupid?

No, no, I thought. *It can't be*, and yet it was. I had been so clouded by my love and my new life with James that I couldn't see the true nature of the danger that lay right before my very eyes. My phone lay on the table next to me. I reached out with trembling hands and I called James. He answered, his usual cool and calm self.

"Hey sweetheart."

"Hi, I need to tell you something important."

"Shoot, honey."

"Jesus, don't say shoot. It's him. It's Brent. He is—oh my God, how can I put this without it sounding mad—I think he's Clifton Slate. In fact, I know it. I should have seen it sooner—it was the mirror. Remember that sketch with the broken mirror I showed you the picture of? It was me—it was Joy reflected in the glass. Angela said that when Slate attacked me in the past life I threw a box at him and broke my dresser mirror. I just had this horrible dream of when Slate attacked me and when I woke up, I finally put it together. It makes so much sense. It's him. He is connected to us, just as we're connected to each other. James! What are we going to do?"

"Stay calm, Elwyn. I'm coming."

"No! Don't! He's somewhere near here—I know it, now that I know it's him. I'm in my loft but I think he's out there. James, we're not safe. You're not safe."

"OK. We need a plan. We were going to meet for dinner. What if I picked you up and we drove? It's not so easy to follow us in a car."

"I just think he's watching me. Or you. Maybe you. God, I don't know. This is so insane."

"Stay calm, my love. We're going to figure this out. Get a taxi and meet me at my house."

"OK. I'll be there soon. Be vigilant, James."

"I will. You too."

"James, I'm scared."

"It's going to be OK, Elwyn. I love you."

"I love you too, James."

I hung up and dialed the number for a taxi. Within fifteen minutes, I was being driven to James' house. I reached his lovely home, paid the driver and got out of the taxi. As I started walking towards the front stairs, I noticed a figure out of the corner of my eye. I turned and looked, but it was gone. It wasn't quite dark yet, as it was only 7:00 p.m., but dark enough to be creepy. I walked up to the sidewalk and saw James on the other side of the door. He opened it and started to come through it. And then, my world as I knew it collapsed in on itself.

Just as James skipped down the steps and hugged me, I saw Brent step out of the shadows next door. He was all in black, and his eyes were menacing and cruel. I drew a startled breath as Brent started towards us, but James saw him and put himself between. Brent said, "Get out of my way, pretty boy. Derrin and I need to work some things out." The deep anger Brent felt was palpable in the calm evening air.

"Just calm down, Brent." James' voice was commanding. "The restraining order says you cannot come within fifty feet of her."

Brent reached into his pocket and pulled out a handgun. It was the same one he had drawn in his sketchbook. I spoke, my voice trembling, "Brent, put that away. Please. I know what you're dreaming about every night. You were a man named Clifton Slate over a hundred and thirty years ago. We were supposed to get married, but I didn't love you. You wanted to be with me—to possess me—but I was already in love with another man. You were so angry and jealous that you killed me in that past life. Please, Brent. Don't repeat the past!"

"How do you know about my dream?" he demanded, his voice high and intense. "I've never told anyone about that dream. Not since her." His hand holding the gun shook uncontrollably.

"Who, Delia?"

"Don't you talk about her!"

"Delia must have wanted you to get help too, didn't she? She might have loved you, if you had listened to her. Brent, please. It's not too late this time."

"I mean it. How did you know about my dream? You can't know. It's not possible."

All this time, James had positioned his body between Brent and I. Neither of us dared move, although I couldn't imagine the scene had escaped the attention of the neighbors heading to their own homes. My hand was on James' arm and I was gripping him for dear life.

"This is all your fault," Brent shouted, waving the gun at James. "If you hadn't showed up, she would have loved me!"

"No, Brent. I wouldn't have. I've told you that. But you were right about something. We are connected. Let's just do it better this time around. We don't have to end in hatred. We can end this moment in peace."

"There will be no peace for you, Elwyn," Brent said, his voice eerily calm. He lifted the gun and shot my James. Then, Brent turned the gun on himself and as I screamed "No!" at the top of my lungs, he pulled the trigger.

James and Brent collapsed at almost the same moment. Brent lay bleeding from the head on the sidewalk a few feet away, his dark eyes had already turned to glass. James had fallen backwards and as I threw both my arms around his body, we collapsed to the ground together. His head rested against my chest. He looked up at me in the same way I had looked up at him a hundred and thirty years before; his eyes had a stunned expression. My tears fell on his dear face. The screams of passersby who had witnessed the whole thing filtered through my consciousness. Sirens grew louder.

Time snapped back into place suddenly and I held James tight to my breast, rocking back and forth with him in my arms. "Don't you die, James! Don't you die. I love you. Please. Don't leave me. I love you!" I whispered these words to him as I held him close. Sobs racked my body between each word. His blood had saturated my clothing, my hands, my psyche. I held my dying love, just as he had held me, and my heart was torn asunder.

CHAPTER TWENTY-ONE

"Lo! some we loved, the loveliest and best
    That Time and Fate of all their Vintage prest,
Have drunk their Cup a Round or two before,
And one by one crept silently to Rest."

THE RUBAIYAT OF OMAR KHAYYAM
TRANSLATED BY EDWARD FITZGERALD

Entanglement theory is a strange thing. The forces that act on one entangled body have an identical effect on its entangled twin. Having your soulmate shot through the abdomen at close range creates a pain that is equal to the pain of the gunshot wound itself. It gnaws, it burns, it sears through flesh and leaves a hole equal to that left by the bullet. The sadness of holding James' limp body was like dying, a fact I happened to understand firsthand.

The EMTs were at the scene in mere moments. They rushed James and I to the hospital, which was only a few blocks away. They whisked him away from me on a stretcher, down clean white corridors lit with long fluorescent bulbs, James' beautiful face as white as the surroundings, bleached of all life, livid red streaks of blood along his divinely handsome cheeks. At that moment, I didn't know if I would ever stare into the azure depths of his eyes again. I did not know if I would hold him in life or in death. I did not know what to do with myself now that his fate was in the hands of the doctors and nurses who worked frantically to save him.

I stood still in the hallway, oblivious to the world around me, soaked through to the bone with James' blood. I cannot imagine what I looked like, nor do I have any idea how long I stood there, catatonic. Eventually, a nurse took me by the elbow and led me to a bathroom where she instructed me to wash up. She shut the door and left me alone in the bathroom to confront my visage. I couldn't see much of my own skin through all of the blood on my hands, my face, my clothes. Wash up? There is nothing to wash, I thought. *This is me, now. I am only his blood.* The flickering florescent lights made the whole image seem surreal. The contrast of red against the few pale slices of skin I could still see shown like fresh scars in reverse. There was no thought, no feeling, nothing left but my reflection in blood.

I was totally paralyzed by my own image. I flashed suddenly to the scene in Brent's studio, body parts from his distorted paintings and disturbing drawings, rendered with the loving care of a medical illustrator and all the insanity of a serial killer. I saw my own haunted eyes, splayed body parts, everything detailed and objectified. Now, reflected in the mirror before me, I saw that my body was Brent's final canvas, and he had painted it with James' blood.

The nurse must have contacted a social worker, for the next thing I remember was being assisted in undressing and washing James' blood off my body and hands. She dressed me in someone's scrubs, as they were the only clean clothes around. She led me, comatose, to a waiting room where she put a cup of coffee in my hand. I don't remember speaking to her, but I was thankful for her presence, nevertheless. An eternity passed. My mind passed out of time and place, my love for James was the only life left in my veins.

A hundred and thirty years ago, I had been shot and died. This day, James had been shot and lived. Modern science may not be able to explain why love is the connecting force in the universe, but it sure can work miracles on a human body in distress.

The following morning, I was led to a room in the ICU. There before me was the living James, his pale skin glowing in the fresh light of dawn. His eyes remained closed as I approached. I was unsure whether I should rejoice—unsure whether this was a mirage. Was my mind tricking me? Had I finally had a full on break with reality? Or could my James be breathing, living, on the hospital bed before me? I took his hand in mine. It felt warm. My heart, that had not beat in hours, started beating again. I lay my face upon his sweet hand and silently wept.

"Do me a favor, Elwyn." James' voice was so quiet I could barely hear it.

"What is it James?"

"Don't let any more psychos fall in love with you, OK?"

I laughed and cried, as all the tension and fear and sadness and regret and despair of the past days, the past lifetimes, ebbed out of me, to be replaced with pure, unadulterated Joy.

"OK, sweetheart. I won't."

CHAPTER TWENTY-TWO

"Here with a Loaf of Bread beneath the Bough,
  A Flask of Wine, a Book of Verse - and Thou
  Beside me singing in the Wilderness -
  And Wilderness is Paradise enow."

THE RUBAIYAT OF OMAR KHAYYAM
TRANSLATED BY EDWARD FITZGERALD

W eeks later, when James was sufficiently recovered from his physical wounds, including the fractured ribs where the bullet had torn through his precious body, and the lung it had also damaged, we drove north. Neither of us had needed to say it, but we wanted to see Angela again. Somehow, it felt like it would bring closure to the emotional wounds from which we were still suffering.

James had been quieter and more withdrawn than he had been since I had met him. There was no difference in the depth of his love for me, it was just that he was deeply shaken by his near death experience. Having his body become the receptacle for someone else's wild anger and violence had wrought a change in him that I felt deep guilt and responsibility for. If not for me, Brent would never have hurt him.

Anger and sadness had flared volcanic within me from time to time, as I was gripped by the memory of James bleeding in my arms. During those moments, I was unable to keep my feelings inside me. How could Brent want to hurt people? Why did he thrive on suffering? How had I let James become his final target? Brent was dead, I would remind myself. He couldn't hurt anyone, anymore. I needed to take back control of my own emotions, my own fate. I reclaim this body, I told myself again and again. *All this pain will fade.*

Insecurity used to nestle in my heart like a broken bird. I used to feel the oppression of my ugliness weighing me down. I had had it all wrong, I realized. I was a transcendent being, incandescent. A phoenix finally rising from the ashes of my own failed attempts at life, at love, at art. Fiercely, I had fortified my heart within my breast. Brent could never touch that protected piece of me. I had it so guarded against all storms. I had practiced the art of closing off my essential being so effectively that it had suppressed some of my creative instincts, my ability to love myself, my ability to love James. But nearly losing James had destroyed those fortifications once and for all. I had felt them fall away, stone by stone, leaving the raw tissue of my being exposed to the furies of time and loss and finally reclamation. I desperately scrambled to emerge whole from my past and resolved to take the future by the balls.

As we drove to Angela, I shared these thoughts with James for the first time. He hadn't known about the blood that had soaked into me, about the fact that I had stared at myself in the mirror, thinking of Brent's disturbed paintings. I explained how I was trying to move into the present so that the past could no longer hold sway over my heart. James reached out and held my hand fiercely as he drove, the sunlight streaming from the east into the car, alighting upon our joined hands, a blessing on our love.

"I'm so sorry you had to go through all this, angel," he mused. "You are so brave."

"You are the brave one, James," I said vehemently. "You stood steadfastly between Brent and me, thinking that it was me that he would shoot. I should have known! I'm so sorry I didn't protect you."

He gazed at the road ahead, pensive for a moment. "You and I need to stop telling each other we're sorry, Elwyn. We're lucky to be here and we have to let it all go now."

James was quiet for a moment. Then, as if making a decision he was still unsure about, he explained how his mind had wandered out of time while he was waiting to die in my arms.

"It is curious," he admitted. "I really thought I was dying. I felt life flowing out of me, ebbing away as the light faded from the sky. Time became elastic. I was aware of the present passing, but of the past and future too, all tied together, a cosmic fabric. I saw through your eyes, into your heart where I felt your pain, and then on to a deeper connection between us that gave me strength. It was such a shock to hear the sound of the sirens. It was the sound of hope, though I didn't dare believe it."

"Hope. That's the story of your life, I guess. You've never given up hope."

"Or Joy," he said, smiling at me.

Angela's office was once again flooded with sunshine when we arrived. It was like opening up the door to a star, blazing and blinding, glittering bliss. It lit her golden hair from behind, making her look even more ethereal than usual.

"My dears," she greeted us. "Come in."

We entered her warm space, instantly enveloped in peace, and sat down together on her couch. "Water? Tea?"

"Tea," we said in unison. "Thank you."

Angela brought the tray to the table. Today's tea was different. It was herbal and floral as though she had distilled summer into the pot. I breathed it in and smiled.

"You are so much more at peace today, Elwyn. After everything you've been through, that's quite a feat. I'm happy for you. James, let yourself join her."

I looked at him not expecting to see such worry upon his lovely, kind face. "What is it?"

"I am still full of fear, Angela. Elwyn," he said, turning towards me, "I love you more than anything, past, present and future. I know that I want to let go of my past—our past—and live happily with you in the now."

"But," I said, uncertainly.

"But I don't know how."

Angela spoke softly. "Your inner child is afraid, James. In your heart, you're still a little boy having dark dreams he can't make sense of. Your reactions, therefore, are those of that scared little boy."

James looked down at his knees and nodded his head.

Angela continued. "Of course, you need a little help moving into the present. When you two met, this time around, you went into protection mode instantly because of Brent, because of your past loss of Joy. You've been kept in protection mode for the entirety of your relationship so far, because Elwyn was threatened."

"Yes," I agreed. "That's true."

"So, you've never had to see yourself as a vulnerable person, you've been so busy being a protective man." Angela looked off to the side, her eyes went dreamy for a moment. I could tell she was 'seeing,' in her own special way, all of what surrounded us but we could not sense. Eventually, she nodded and focused on James again. "We must reassure your lost child," she continued. "The little boy needs to know that he is safe and loved. The little boy needs to know that the man is in charge now, keeping the heart of the little boy alive and loved and nurtured."

Tears streamed down James' porcelain skin, glinting briefly prismatic in the sunlight, as they dropped into oblivion. "How? We are so vulnerable." He spoke in a whisper.

"By loving yourself as deeply as you love Elwyn. By letting go of the pain of growing up misunderstood. By giving yourself permission to grieve a lost childhood. By knowing in your deepest places that you are finally whole and that your love is transcendent."

"I believe in you," I said softly, squeezing his hand, which I still held.

"So do I," agreed Angela.

He looked up, first at her beatific smile and then at me. He breathed in deeply. "I understand," he said. "I've been dealing with that little child I was for a lifetime, hoping he would just go away. I see now that he won't go anywhere because he's just a part of me. I can't push the past away, but I can put it to rest."

"Yes," Angela reassured. "Acknowledge him, hug him and let him go play outside." We all smiled at each other, wistfully, thinking of the little child that James once was, finally being freed of an adult pain he couldn't understand. "May I place my hands on you, James? I am a Reiki healer as well."

James inhaled and looked up at Angela. "Of course," he replied. He closed his eyes as Angela stood before him and placed her hands on his head and then his shoulders. Then she lifted her hands above him, and worked with his energy to bring him back to balance. Tears streamed down James' cheeks from his closed eyes as he allowed himself to be realigned. After some time, she sat down, still maintaining her peaceful expression.

"I sense now the depth of the fear you experienced when you were shot. That experience has taught you something, however, whether you realize it or not."

"I was scared out of my mind, Angela," James admitted.

"Rightly so. Your fear was justified. You came very close to passing into the next life. What we can learn, however, from such a brutal experience, is that sometimes you are not in control of your destiny. Surrender is inevitable, for all of us, at some point or another. Your inner child is angry about being made to feel afraid, James. And the adult in you is angry to be made vulnerable. Both of you need to understand that it is OK to be afraid and vulnerable sometimes. Do you know what saved you?"

"The doctors, I guess," James replied, perplexed.

"Of course, the doctors saved your body, but without your hope and love, you wouldn't have held on."

James squeezed my hand hard.

"I love you so much," I said. "Please forgive my not putting it all together until it was almost too late."

"There is nothing to forgive, Elwyn. I am just thankful that it's over."

"Times of peace are ahead, my loves," said Angela, quietly. "Well earned, deeply deserved peace."

"I thought you didn't tell futures," James said with a mock accusatory tone.

"Not when I can't see them," she replied. "When you called me, I saw the danger facing you both. I didn't see, however, whether you could escape it. That is not something I can let myself say to another. I can, however, let myself say that I remain inspired by the two of you, and that your love will transcend this lifetime, as it has so many others. Blessings, my dears. Blessings that you will always find each other, balance each other, and bring the light of your love to the world around you."

"Thank you, Angela," I said, starting to mist up again. My heart felt so open, so strong, so renewed. James, I had every faith, would get there too, in time.

We left Angela and continued our drive north. We made it all the way to Acadia. The weather was warmer than we had expected. We drove around the perimeter of the park, absorbing all the beauty into us, letting the Maine summer—so long in coming, so refreshing when it did—renew us deeply. From the top of Cadillac Mountain, we held hands and surveyed the vast, unending horizon before us. The ocean tugged at my depths, calling me to her. I knew James felt that desire as well. I recalled his mention of a yacht in a conversation we had had on our first date and it made me smile.

"I've changed my mind about something," I said.

"What's that, Elwyn?"

"I will swab your poop deck, if you want me to."

James laughed out in a clear, melodic tone that carried for

endless miles into the heart of Acadia's forests, bouncing and scattering off the waves of the Atlantic crashing far below, and just like a butterfly's wings beating on the other side of the world, it's ripple in the fabric of the universe gilded the course of our fates, as our two entangled souls continued their age old dance.

EPILOGUE

"Ah Love! could thou and I with Fate conspire
    To grasp this sorry Scheme of Things entire,
Would not we shatter it to bits - and then
Re-mould it nearer to the Heart's Desire!"

THE RUBAIYAT OF OMAR KHAYYAM
TRANSLATED BY EDWARD FITZGERALD

I looked around, my eyes tearing up in the frigid air. I had been told that Paris was never freezing cold this time of year, yet here I was, standing under the Eiffel Tower, in the wrong coat, wondering how I could be so crazy. The drive to come here had just been so strong, so intense. Something had willed me here. As the lights started flickering and dancing on the Eiffel Tower above me, a man approached. His azure eyes locked on mine and suddenly we both smiled. Somehow, I finally understood.

"Merry Christmas, James," I said, falling into his embrace. This was why I had come. I was whole once again.

———

THANK YOU FOR READING

———

Did you enjoy this book?

We invite you to leave a review at your favorite book site, such as Goodreads, Amazon, Barnes & Noble, etc.

DID YOU KNOW THAT LEAVING A REVIEW…

- Helps other readers find books they may enjoy.
- Gives you a chance to let your voice be heard.
- Gives authors recognition for their hard work.
- Doesn't have to be long. A sentence or two about why you liked the book will do.

ACKNOWLEDGMENTS

I owe a deep debt of gratitude to Erica Blair Reilly for her critical eye and her fearless honesty as the first reader of this book. It would not be half what it is without her.

Thank you as well to T. and E. and S. for allowing me the time and space to create.

Thank you to the real Angela. You are a light in the darkness.

I also wish to thank Professor Matt Wilt for all your help with the details.

Lastly, thank you to my sister, my mother, and my father for their support of all my creative endeavors.

CREDITS

I would like to acknowledge the following businesses, restaurants and historic sites that I mentioned in the novel. They are all important to me personally, in some way or another.

- Allagash Brewing Company
- Geno's Rock Club
- The Holy Donut
- Longfellow Garden
- Miyake
- Otto Pizza Restaurant
- The Portland Hunt and Alpine Club
- Portland Museum of Art
- Portland Public Market
- Rhode Island School of Design
- Speckled Ax

Finally, I would like to say that taking a walk with "The Rubaiyat" of Omar Khayyam, Translated by Edward FitzGerald, was a wonderful experience.

———

Don't miss out on your next favorite book!

———

Join the Satin Romance mailing list
www.satinromance.com/mail.html

Subscriber Perks Include:

- First peeks at upcoming releases.
- Exclusive giveaways.
- News of book sales and freebies right in your inbox.
- And more!

ABOUT THE AUTHOR

Emma Hartley is an author and artist living in picturesque Maine. She has been writing and making art since childhood and has been insatiably curious and industrious her whole life. Emma was a double major in English and Fine Arts and she received her Masters in Art and Design Education. She is a specialist in ceramics and includes much of this expertise in her novel *The Nature of Entangled Hearts*. Her other interests include playing drums in an indie rock band, making art and exploring every square inch of the Maine coastline. *The Nature of Entangled Hearts* is her first novel.

www.emmahartleyauthor.com
www.facebook.com/emmahartleyauthor

www.ingramcontent.com/pod-product-compliance
Lightning Source LLC
Chambersburg PA
CBHW050511260626
47157CB00004B/1284